How the Dead Live

STORIES BY ALVIN GREENBERG

GRAYWOLF PRESS

SAINT PAUL · MINNESOTA

Publication of this volume is made possible in part by a grant provided by the Minnesota State Arts Board through an appropriation by the Minnesota State Legislature, and by a grant from the National Endowment for the Arts. Significant support has also been provided by Dayton's, Mervyn's, and Target stores through the Dayton Hudson Foundation, the Bush Foundation, the Andrew W. Mellon Foundation, the McKnight Foundation, the General Mills Foundation, the St. Paul Companies, and other generous contributions from foundations, corporations, and individuals. To these organizations and individuals we offer our heartfelt thanks.

Special funding for this title has been provided by the Jerome Foundation.

Published by Graywolf Press
2402 University Avenue, Suite 203
Saint Paul, Minnesota 55114
All rights reserved.

www.graywolfpress.org

Published in the United States of America

ISBN 1-55597-281-0

2 4 6 8 9 7 5 3 1
First Graywolf Printing, 1998

Library of Congress Catalog Card Number: 98-84457

Cover design: Nora Koch

Cover art: Rob Evans, "Evening Ritual," 1988–89, oil on panel, 40″ x 90″

Acknowledgments

Stories in this collection had their first appearance in the following publications:

American Literary Review: "Immersion"
Crosscurrents: "Crimes against Humanity"
Five Points: "Gruber in Traffic"
Great River Review: "FREE-43"
Indiana Review: "A Couple of Dead Men"
Kansas Quarterly/Arkansas Review: "Scholars and Lovers" and
    "Tremors"
North American Review: "No Loose Ends" and "Construction Zone"
Salt Hill, "Found"
Short Story: "The Life of the Mind"
and the anthology *Stiller's Pond*: "Closed Mondays"

In addition to offering my thanks to the editors of the above publications for their support and advice, I would also like to acknowledge the contributions of Macalester College for the writing time made available through its sabbatical leave program; Anne Czarniecki of Graywolf Press for her valuable and always good-spirited editorial assistance; and my wife, Janet Holmes, a fine writer in her own right, who has accompanied me lovingly and generously through the development of these stories and so much more and who has added new depth for me to the last word of this book's title.

Contents

How the Dead Live

Gruber in Traffic

GRUBER, forty-eight years old and in perfect health, a family man even if it was his third marriage, financially secure, well connected in the St. Paul legal community, a specialist in wills and trusts, and altogether a happy man, was puzzled to find himself suddenly obsessed with thoughts of death. No one had died—no one he knew, that is. Both his parents were thriving, and though they lived now in a Sun Belt city he found appalling, they were more active than he'd ever known them to be before their move: walking, bicycling, swimming; great theatergoers and movie mavens and diners-out. They laughed when he called to ask if they'd found a doctor there yet. The kids from his previous marriages were out of college and on promising career tracks with companies that had, he was pleased to know, excellent health plans. The two still at home, like their mother, rarely had more than a sniffle. The last funeral Gruber attended had been his grandmother's, dead a decade ago at the age of ninety-five and a wisecracking sweetheart right up to the last minute. On both sides of his family they regularly lived into their nineties. Even his friends and business associates, men and women alike, were paragons of health: avoiders of fatty foods, moderate drinkers, health-club habitués, lovers of cross-country skiing, weekend canoe trips, and daylong hikes in the North Woods. Why he suddenly found himself turning to the obituaries every morning first thing after reading the sports section, Gruber couldn't for the life of him understand. No one he knew was ever there.

But worse yet, he'd find himself sitting on an orange plastic chair in the tiled hallway of Groveland Park Elementary School, waiting his turn for a conference with Rachel's third-grade teacher—he *liked* doing that sort of thing, he never hesitated to take time off work for school plays or concerts or games—and thinking about death. Or

3

he'd be cutting the lawn, relishing the mixture of smells, the new-mown grass and gasoline fumes that went right to his head, a combination that from the day he'd bought his first gas-propelled mower constituted a heavenly elixir, and actually enjoying the way the whine of the little engine drove all other thoughts from his head and left him wholly concentrated on what he was doing right there and then, but suddenly he'd realize that what he was doing right there and then was thinking about death. Or he could be sitting in his car, like he was doing today, waiting for Arlene to come out of the beauty parlor, listening to the Minnesota-Michigan game on the radio, not even needing to keep the motor running and the heater on, though it was a chilly late-November day, because of the way the sun spilled through the wide windows of the big Pontiac and poured its warmth across his lap, and it would suddenly dawn on him that the only thing that was really on his mind was death.

When he thought of death, as he was doing now during the half-time report, there was nothing particularly grisly about it. No blood, no sternum-splitting operations, no agonizing pain, none of the paraphernalia of the hospital—no IVs, no being wheeled down the hall to radiology, no waiting for the doctor's morning rounds—and no screaming ambulance lights, either, no shattered glass in the middle of an intersection, no bystanders covering their eyes, no weeping and wailing and standing in the rain at graveside. None of that. And there was no Grim Reaper haunting his imagination either, no Angel of Death, no Beckoning Savior, no God of Retribution. There was just . . . death.

"My god," said Arlene, clambering into the front seat, "you look like you've seen a ghost. What happened? The Gophers getting creamed again?"

She was radiant, her hair a deep, rich mahogany, like a precious heirloom side table that had been burnished by experts to bring out the life that lay deep inside the wood, and even the slightly bitter chemical smell that always floated out of the beauty parlor with her gave him pleasure. But he couldn't have said what the score of the game was. The only thing on his mind was death, an abstract, intangible, amorphous, unpicturable, pervasive, and everlasting death.

The shadowy death that was always scratching at the corners of his vision these days, though no matter how quickly he turned his head he never managed to get a clear look at it. The death that somehow, when he wasn't paying attention, when he was just going on with his life the way he always had, driving around with Arlene, playing with the kids, lunching with a client, had quietly taken up residence inside his mind and moved all the rest of the furnishings out and pulled down the blinds and locked the door, so that nothing else could get in and he couldn't get out. The death that seemed to be all he lived with now, though there was nowhere, of course, that he could actually put his hands on it. The death that was all his, though in fact—and he was quick to say this when anyone asked him how he was doing—he'd never felt better.

✳   ✳   ✳

On Monday morning the week before last, in the midst of the first cold snap of the season, Gruber, stopped at a red light on his way to work, his thoughts focused on remembering to get his snow tires mounted before the week was over, had looked around and noticed that the man in the car next to his, in the lane to his right, was staring at him. Like any normal citizen Gruber was moved by this to wonder if there was anything amiss. Had he forgotten to shave? Worn his brown hat with his gray topcoat? Was the car door ajar? But no, the man was staring directly at him. Pretending to adjust the rearview mirror, Gruber surreptitiously checked his face and teeth for remnants of food, even though all he'd had for breakfast was juice and coffee. Still, the man in the next car kept staring. Just an ordinary man, Gruber told himself, why should he be concerned? A man of ordinary size, just like himself, with a worn face and thinning hair. A man in a suit and tie and winter coat, on his way downtown to the office, just like himself. A pale, staring, hatless man, with lips slightly parted, though not as if he were about to speak, who looked neither happy nor sad. Then, just as the light changed and the traffic began to surge ahead, Gruber recognized him. It was the rabbi! Not his own rabbi, of course, Gershon Himmelfarb, a cheery, red-faced golfer who would have smiled and waved, but the other one, the Orthodox rabbi, whom Gruber had seen only a few times in his life, always striding angrily down the street near his synagogue with his thin wife in her dark clothes scrambling anxiously behind him.

But by then the traffic had swept the rabbi, if that's who he was, the staring man, quickly out of sight, the right lane flowing smoothly ahead while Gruber sat stuck in a wintery cloud of exhaust behind a delivery truck waiting to make a left turn. Picking the best lane on these city streets during rush hour was always a challenge, though not one Gruber ordinarily minded. The right lane was for slowpokes, for getting stuck behind the buses at their corner stops, but the left had its own disadvantages, like this. It was a game, the kind Gruber liked best, with minimal risks and small victories and mild disappointments. No one cared if he got to the office five minutes early or fifteen minutes late. It was his own office, after all; what was his secretary going to do, dock his pay? He only wished he'd had a second look, another chance to confirm his identification, before the car beside him had leapt ahead and out of sight, Gruber only at the last second getting enough of a glimpse of its dark green shape to realize it was an XJ12.

But what was the rabbi doing driving a Jag? Gruber wondered. And headed downtown during rush hour on a Monday morning as if he were just another businessperson, an accountant, a store clerk, a lawyer like himself? And if it was the rabbi, where was the wide-brimmed black hat, where were the side curls? And why the stare? There was no way the rabbi could have known who he, Gruber, who only showed up at his own Reform temple on the High Holy Days, was. And what could he have done, anyway, Gruber wondered, to render himself the object of such fixed attention?

Driving home that evening in the early dark Gruber had half a mind to detour by the Orthodox synagogue and check for a racing-green Jaguar in the parking lot, but no, he thought, that's silly, why should I let a meaningless little incident like that bother me? And what if there were no Jaguar there, what would it prove, anyway? That the rabbi had taken it home, that he had returned it to the wealthy member of his congregation who'd lent it to him for the weekend? It

wasn't worth the trouble, he concluded, especially in rush-hour traffic, given how much out of the way the synagogue was. And besides,
Gruber suddenly felt an overwhelming desire to be home with his
wife and kids. So he had taken his usual route, avoiding the freeway,
which he despised—such a world of rush, rush, rush! such rumbling
and roaring! such fury!—easing his way instead from lane to lane
along the crowded city streets, only now and then wondering, as he
sat at a red light, if he would ever again look over and see an ordinary-
looking man in the next car staring at him with such deadly intensity.
But he never did, and within a few days he'd forgotten about the incident entirely, and, until now, it had never entered his mind again.

※   ※   ※

A few weeks earlier Gruber's son, Michael, a fifth-grader, had joined
a Pee Wee League hockey team and in the first period of his first regular game, with his mom and dad and sister sitting in the stands, had
promptly had his mouth bloodied by an errant puck that had somehow dislodged both his mouthpiece and his two top front teeth. It was
a miracle, Coach Sorenson kept saying, gosh, couldn't happen again
in a million shots, who'd ever believe it, whatta guy, huh, folks. They
were sitting in the locker room between periods, swapping dripping
red towels right and left. Gruber, distraught, kept asking where the
teeth were, thinking they should get to the emergency room ASAP; if
they could stitch severed thumbs and penises back on, surely rein-
serting a couple of teeth should be no big deal. He couldn't quite
seem to get a fix on Arlene, who'd already managed to get in a call to
their dentist and was standing right beside him with an open half-pint
of 2 percent milk she'd gotten from a vending machine and into
which, on Dr. Sundeen's orders, she'd already dropped the two
bloody teeth she'd scooped up off the ice.

Seated down almost at rink level, his son swishing up the ice right
in front of him as his teammates charged across the center line,
Gruber had watched as an opposing defenseman took a wild swipe at
the puck and sent it flying head high across the rink right toward his
seat. He'd watched the small flat black rubber disk growing larger and

larger, like an ominous black spaceship intruding at warp speed from some other universe altogether, and then suddenly it had disappeared from view, eclipsed by the green uniform passing between him and the puck. For a moment he'd been relieved, thinking, Jesus, I didn't even duck, what's the matter with me? Then, his wife beside him and his daughter at her side, talking to each other and not paying the least bit of attention to the game, relief gave way to dismay: It could have clobbered either of them, and where was he, just sitting there watching like a total dummy, useless. Some husband, some father! He couldn't have said how long it was before he realized that the kid lying there face down directly in front of their seats, reddening the ice, was his own son.

Later that night, long after a brief moment of rancor with Michael, who'd wanted at first to stay and play but who soon gave in, quietly, as the shock wore off and the pain came flooding in, and let himself be led off to the dentist's office for a midnight reinsertion of the dislodged teeth, Gruber kept seeing the puck, in midair, on a clear trajectory toward his own frozen face, growing larger by the second while his mouth, unguarded, opened wide as if to take it all in. The whole house was asleep by then, Michael by the grace of drugs their dentist had provided after the reinsertion procedure, Rachel out of the simple exhaustion of childhood, Arlene, so far as he could tell, because she'd run out of things to say about men and boys and sports.

Gruber had stayed up a bit to have a drink he'd hoped would help him calm down, but the good bourbon he'd poured smelled like straight grain alcohol and he couldn't bring himself to touch it. He sat in the kitchen for nearly an hour in his bathrobe, with only the small hood light over the range on, and then finally he came to bed, where he lay in the dark like a board, seeing, every time he closed his eyes, that flat black disk sailing his way, growing fatter and wider each second, threatening to occupy the entire sky before it came smack up into his face, and nothing, nothing at all now, between him and it.

His heart went out to his sleeping son, who'd never even seen what was coming his way until his mouth exploded in blood and pain, who was just skating along playing the game until he'd suddenly found himself face down on the ice in a puddle of his own blood, but when he closed his eyes it was still his own face the puck came hurtling at, and behind clenched eyelids all he could do was watch it, helpless, unmoving, his mouth opening wide as if to welcome it in. Here, he understood, was this hard black disk coming at you at high speed and on a trajectory all its own, and it didn't make any difference whether like Michael you never saw it coming or you watched it like he was doing now every second of its flight as it ballooned monstrously in front of your face: It'd get you either way.

*   *   *

When Gruber was not much older than Michael, a kid in the neighborhood where he grew up, a boy Gruber played after-school games with but didn't actually like very much, had died suddenly, a violent and mysterious death. His name was Billy Kutzman, and he had a mean streak that kept Gruber and the others on their toes around him. He was the kind of kid who'd give you an extra hit in a backyard football game after the play was over, who'd elbow you in the ribs just in passing in a basketball game in someone's driveway or whack you hard enough to knock you down in a simple game of tag. They let him play because they were always glad to have the extra guy for making up teams, and besides, he was good: He was faster than any of them, could hit a ball harder or make a basket from farther out than anyone else. He was good in the infield, the outfield, the backfield, the frontcourt, so he was always chosen first when they picked sides, and no one ever challenged him when he said "I'll pitch" or "I'll be quarterback." But no one ever said "Good game" to him when it was over, either, no one walked off the field with him, no one invited him home after the game.

And no one had seen him the day he died. Gruber, arriving a little late himself, his glove hooked through his belt and his bat dragging in the dirt, wasn't particularly surprised not to find him there because Billy went to the Catholic school, which had its own schedule, its own rituals, which he'd never managed to comprehend. But Gilley and O'Faollan, who also went to St. Joe's, were there already, and claimed not to have seen Billy K, as they called him, at school all day, either.

"Fuck 'im," said Gilley. "We'll play without him. It's more fun that way, anyway."

But in the bottom of the sixth, with Gruber at bat, Mr. Kutzman himself showed up, still in his bus driver's uniform, looking for Billy, who'd gone off to school as usual but hadn't been seen since. The school had called, but not till midafternoon, when Kutzman, just finishing his route, found his wife waiting for him at the bus barn. Together, he explained to the boys, they'd driven all over the neighborhood for the past couple of hours; now she'd gone back to the school while he'd continued to search on foot.

He stood right in the middle of the diamond where a line drawn in the dirt with a stick marked the pitcher's mound, right where Billy himself would have been standing, and apologized for interrupting their game. He polished the black bill of his cap on his sleeve and said, "I know you guys don't much like Billy. Truth to tell, he ain't easy. Never been. But I'm worried about him, and that's a fact."

Gruber, perhaps prompted by the fact that he was at bat, perhaps only trying to evade Mr. Kutzman's bald recognition of how little they liked Billy, offered to help search, offered for all of them, in fact. And they did, coming in from the field, dropping their gloves beside the piece of cardboard that served as home plate, and spreading out behind the bus driver as he moved across their weedy playground toward the new development on the other side of the road, where a row of bulldozed lots, basement excavations, and half-finished houses stood abandoned in the late-afternoon sunshine.

But it was Mrs. Kutzman who found her son.

Gruber, who went to the closed-casket funeral wearing the first suit he'd ever owned, one his mother had taken him to buy especially for the occasion, only ever saw Billy K again in his dreams, which were raw and brutal, torn into fragments by the imagined roar of onrushing diesel locomotives and splashed with the gory blacks and reds of rumor. Gruber sat by himself, his own parents unwilling to enter a church, while his buddies all sat with their families, with their weeping moms and the dads who hung their heads and sighed. But Gruber didn't mind being alone because he didn't want to hear any more stories from them about what Billy had looked like when Mrs. Kutzman found him at the bottom of the railroad embankment. "Hamburger," one of the kids had said and laughed, but it wasn't funny, and neither was the absurd-looking priest, a huge man, the largest person Gruber had ever seen, with a bald head and a face as round and pale and pocked as the full moon, in whose gigantic hand the Bible he clutched as if he would strangle it looked no larger than the little note pad in which Gruber kept his friends' phone numbers. The priest pleaded with them not to question the why of poor Billy's death, and Gruber, sitting alone among the congregation in the church that held its midwinter chill even now in late spring, shivered, unnoticed, in his thin blue suit. He understood at once, with an icy certainty that had never occurred to him again until now, that there was no more chance of squeezing the answer to such a question out of that black book that looked so shrunken and pathetic in the priest's enormous hand than there was of finding it among his own penciled lists of names and addresses and phone numbers.

These days, however, death, for Gruber, a middle-sized, middle-aged, and—at least among the legal fraternity he associated with—middle-incomed man, healthy and happy as he expected any man might be at midlife, had taken up a quiet residence in his office, like some senior citizen had filed itself away in the rest-home atmosphere of steel cabinets and computer disks. He did wills and set up trusts on a regular basis, but what he thought about was the living, the beneficiaries of these instruments, the executors and trustees who would manage them, the judges through whose probate courts they would pass, even the clients who sat on the other side of his desk and explained their desires and signed the documents he had prepared. They were alive and animated, these clients, some of them friends, full of desire, no different than his young secretary hovering behind them in her fluffed-out blond hair and iridescent perfume with her stamp pad in hand, waiting to notarize their signatures, all of them thinking, as the living are wont to do, only about the future.

Death was never a participant in any of this; these were bonds made among the living and for the living, and when all was signed and done, when the photocopies were made and parceled out in their sturdy brown envelopes, he and his clients stood and shook hands, pressed their warm, vibrant flesh together, and often, if it was the end of the day, went across the street and had a drink together in the midst of the noisy, after-work crowd at Gallivans: the backslappers from City Hall, the trial lawyers paroled from the courtrooms, the Christmas shoppers with their parcels wedged under their bar stools, all the hurley-burley downtown crowd of strangers and distant acquaintances still in their overcoats because they were only stopping by for a quick one before they headed home, raising their glasses to him as he passed down the long bar looking for a place in the back where he and his client could stand and click their glasses together and partake of all this raucous good cheer that surrounded them.

Now, however, he stood there with his bourbon and water in hand barely hearing what Jackie Brandt, not a client but a friend and fellow lawyer with an office across the hall from his, was saying. He was look-ing back down along the bar, and what he was seeing was not a crowd of cheerful drinkers celebrating the end of another long day, another whole week in fact, chattering about what they'd heard and what they'd done and what they planned, laying bets on the football play-offs and hustling ideas for gifts for their kids and spouses, but a col-lection of shiny white skulls perched on thin columns of cervical vertebrae, a roomful of rattling, bony jaws, of skeletal hands tipping glasses into toothy maws. And from beneath the heavy winter coats he could hear the clatter of bones far more clearly than what Jackie was telling him about his daughter's school play.

"Listen," he interrupted, looking for a place to set his drink down, "I've got to get going, they'll be waiting dinner for me." The ice cubes rattled in his shaking hand.

"Hey," said Jackie, "what's the matter? You look like you've seen a ghost."

Not a ghost, thought Gruber, circling slowly down the exit ramp of the parking garage in a fog of exhaust fumes. Nothing so thin, so flimsy. This was all too solid, like looking in the bathroom mirror one morning and seeing not the stubble on his chin but the empty eye sockets, the protruding frontal bone, then raising his hand—no, stretching the long, articulated bones of his fingers!—to feel how cold and hard it all was.

*   *   *

By the time Gruber reached the one-way street he always took out of downtown it had begun to snow, not badly but enough to slow and thicken the always heavy Friday evening traffic already coagulated by the crush of holiday shoppers. Stuck in midblock through several changes of the lights, surrounded in the six o'clock wintry dark by swirling gray clouds of exhaust from the cars on all sides of him, fat wet flakes drifting down to plaster themselves on the windshield between each swipe of the wipers, going nowhere, he wondered if he shouldn't consult his doctor. But he'd had a complete physical only last spring, at Arlene's urging—it had been five years since his last— and Granger, whom he'd gone to high school with, had given him an A plus, though with a little tickler on the end of it that Gruber couldn't help recalling just now: "for a man your age." In response to which he'd quipped that that was identical with Granger's own age, a remark the doctor had acknowledged with only a smile, the sparkle in his eyes a sly reminder, however, that his own weight and waistline, un- like Gruber's, hadn't changed noticeably since high school. And then on the way out of the office, the receptionist had smiled her toothy smile and handed him a couple of pamphlets on diet and exercise for men in their fifties and above.

"But I'm still in my forties," he'd wanted to protest, only she was already occupied checking in another patient, and besides, as he well knew, neither she nor Granger would be much interested in his quibbles.

Anyway, what could Granger say to him now, except not to worry, it would pass, and if it continued he'd be glad to refer him to a psy- chologist or psychiatrist, it was nothing out of the ordinary for a man his age, a man nearing the half-century mark, to have some feelings about mortality.

There it was again: "a man his age," and—twice now—told he was looking like he'd seen a ghost. What ghost? His own? But according to the actuarial tables, the odds were that he had practically another thirty years to live. Besides, it wasn't his own mortality he was finding himself obsessed with, it was mortality in general, death—no, not just death but Death with a capital D, that huge, amorphous, exhausting fog of the big D that shrouded him wherever he turned, through which he could only dimly make out, these days, the vague shapes of his family and friends and clients passing by him in strange foggy slow motion at some indeterminate distance, not unlike the traffic crawling around him now in the steadily increasing snowfall that shifted perspectives as it swirled through the city streets, vaporizing the tops of office buildings and obliterating the features of pedestrians blown across his line of vision in the crosswalks.

I need to do something to shake this, he told himself, and as he approached the next intersection he flicked on his turn indicator, carefully edged over into the left lane, and then swung over onto the on-ramp to the freeway.

*　　　*　　　*

Things were no better on the freeway. Now, instead of being trapped in three lanes of nearly immobilized traffic, he was enmeshed in five. And it was snowing heavier now, mounding up on the roofs of the cars around him, on his own as well, no doubt, thick and wet. He heard the wail of a siren that seemed to come from somewhere behind him, rising and falling, muffled by the thick snow, an ambulance perhaps, or a fire truck; every winter the city seemed to go up in a conflagration of house fires: faulty furnaces, kerosene lamps knocked over, exploding water heaters, damp wiring, bored kids playing with matches, burglars turned arsonists this year, to cover their tracks, always something. But there was no way to pull over to let an emergency vehicle through; all five lanes were solid bumper-to-bumper traffic. They crept ahead a bit, nose to tail, like cattle in the stockyard pens, and then sat motionless for minutes, but there was no bellowing, no honking of horns, only a patient, white silence over-ridden by the faint, rhythmic wail of the siren.

The freeway was buried in a deep trench here where it passed through the heart of the city, and Gruber couldn't even make out the embankments on either side; in the dark and the snow, the feeling of cold, walled-in dampness, it was as he imagined a mine shaft must be, or the long passage down into the hell he didn't believe in, sur-rounded by masses of indistinguishable, slow-moving souls sound-lessly conveying him along on their inexorable journey. Surely, he thought, if there were a hell, it would sound just like this: the muffled cries of emergency vehicles unable to make their way through to those in need.

He knew, by now, he'd made a major mistake. If he'd stuck to the city streets, to his usual route, no matter how bad it had been, how slow the going, he could have pulled over somewhere, some gas sta-tion or convenience store—he passed countless such places every day on his way to and from work—and phoned Arlene, let her know not to worry. Through the dense curtain of snow that was coming straight down now, filling the spaces between the cars as if they were being wrapped with Styrofoam cushioning before being crated up for ship-ping to some distant, unknown destination, he could just make out the solitary driver in the car to his left holding a phone to his head, and for the first time ever he wished he had such a device himself. Most of his friends had acquired car phones long since, a deductible business expense at that, but he'd convinced himself he didn't spend enough time in the car to justify it, and besides, he liked how the car isolated him from things like phone calls, how it gave him a some-time privacy—ten minutes here, fifteen there—that he rarely had elsewhere, a freedom to think his own thoughts, even if they were, these days, mostly thoughts of death.

It occurred to Gruber that if they were stalled here much longer, perhaps he could ask the driver in the car beside him if he could use his phone for a quick call home, maybe the guy'd even make the call for him, he wouldn't even have to leave his own car and climb across into what he had not observed until now, when he found himself staring at it again, was a big, dark-colored Jaguar, green maybe, it was hard to tell for sure here in the night with only the dull, snow-diffused glow of the city hovering over them. But the guy driving, now that he had hung up the phone that had been blocking his face, there was no doubt about it, even in the darkened car, just in vague silhouette, lit only by the glow from his dashboard lights, it was the rabbi!

For reasons he couldn't explain even to himself, Gruber wanted to slouch down in his seat, to turn up his coat collar and tilt his hat sideways across his face. But he couldn't do any of these things because even as he'd turned away himself, realizing he'd been staring, he'd seen the man turning to look toward him. It'd be too obvious. Just then the traffic in front of him began to move, and Gruber followed, the Pontiac wallowing in the heavy, wet snow as he inched up a car length, two, three, before they came to a stop again, but the lane beside him moved, too. Glancing to that side, without turning his head—he'd always prided himself on having terrific peripheral vision—Gruber could see the snow-splattered hood of the Jag still right beside him.

So what, Gruber told himself, it's just a coincidence. What have I done, anyway? What have I got to hide? I'm a good man. So I think about death now and then—since when is that a crime? And rabbis, aren't they the ones who think about it most of all, visiting the sick and dying, presiding at funerals, saying prayers over open graves, consoling the mourners? Besides, he's not even a real rabbi. He just happens to look like one. Not all that much, either. A businessman, probably, a rush-hour commuter, like myself, only with a fancier car. He's not my rabbi, anyway. You'd never catch Himmelfarb in a car like that. Or staring. Himmelfarb wouldn't stare, he respected a person's privacy. He wouldn't look over your shoulder to see how many strokes you gave yourself on the long, dogleg seventh at the country club and he wouldn't expect you to check his score, either. He had a sense of decency; he left you alone.

*   *   *

It was almost 9:30 when Gruber got home. Rachel, he knew, was sleeping over at a girlfriend's house; Michael was closed in his room, playing, Gruber was disappointed to discover when he peeked in on him, a new computer game he'd just bought himself, the very one Gruber had picked out as one of his Christmas presents. Arlene was in the living room, wrapped in the warm glow of a solitary floor lamp, reading her *New Yorker*, unperturbed. She'd listened to the radio, watched television, she knew all about the road and traffic conditions. His dinner, which he had no appetite for, was in the microwave; all he had to do was set the timer.

From outside he could hear the roar of the snowblowers his neighbors were already at work with, although in his head it was still the siren of the emergency vehicle he kept hearing, the ambulance or fire truck or police car he'd never seen though he'd had to listen to it for an hour or more. Why hadn't they turned it off, he'd wondered; it was never going to reach whomever it had set out to help. The robbers would be long gone, their tracks buried under several inches of fresh snow; the house would be ashes, sizzling under snowmelt; the heart-attack victim would be dead, already cold. What was the use?

His own car sat in the street in front of the house. He hadn't even attempted to pull it up the short, sloping driveway to the garage. It'd be another day at least before they got around to plowing his street; he'd have plenty of time to shovel the sidewalk and driveway tomorrow. He didn't understand those people out there at work on it already, in the dark. Couldn't they see it was still coming down hard, that it looked like it would be coming down all night, for—who knows?—days maybe? Standing in the front window, looking out to the street, Gruber could see the Pontiac, in the glow of the streetlight, gradually turning into a soft white mound. Another car spun around the corner in a swirl of snow, came crawling slowly down the middle of the street past Gruber's house, and he started, thinking it was the green Jaguar—suddenly realizing that that was exactly what he was standing in the window looking for, expecting to see—but it wasn't.

"Are you OK, Sweetie?" Arlene asked, looking up from her magazine.

He turned to look at her, not knowing what to say. He'd shaken the snow from his coat and hat and hung them in the back hallway, had stamped his shoes clean before going upstairs to look in on Michael, but he was still wearing his dark suit, and his paisley tie, which he'd thought about loosening several times on the long drive home, was still knotted tightly about his neck. Every time he'd reached up to loosen it while he was stuck on the freeway, he'd suddenly sensed the rabbi, side by side with him in the next lane, staring at him, and he'd lowered his hand. And once off the freeway, on the narrow, snow-clogged surface streets, with buses and cars and delivery trucks sliding all around him, he'd clung ferociously to the wheel with both hands.

"I'm just tired," he said. "That was a terrible drive. Maybe I could fix myself a drink."

"Why don't you do that?" she said. "It wouldn't kill you."

But instead of going off to the kitchen to get a glass and some ice and the bottle of bourbon from the cabinet, he sat down in the darkness on the other end of the couch and said, "I don't know about that."

She looked up from her reading. He looked down at his hands in his lap, palms up, fingers slightly curled as if still trying to relax from their grip on the steering wheel, and added, almost in a whisper, "There are people dying out there, all over the place, no one can do anything about it."

"Sweetie!" She dropped her magazine on the coffee table and reached over and laid her hands in his. "What's the matter?"

The way the light from the floor lamp behind her shoulder burnished her dark hair, flushed out the vibrant life that lay deep inside it, was, Gruber felt, enough to break his heart. He huddled back in his own darkened corner of the couch, her hands still lying lightly in his, knowing that what he'd clumsily blurted out wasn't right at all, wasn't what he'd wanted to say, not even close. Of course there were people dying out there, there were always people dying. He wasn't stupid about that, he knew what happened, people died, and he read the papers besides, he watched TV. Who could miss the devastation on the freeways, in the cities, on foreign battlegrounds? Not him. Not Arlene either. This wasn't about the dying. You looked at that head-on, sort of, all the time. This was about something else, not the dead and dying but death itself, the death that hung like a shroud at the periphery of his vision, even though when he looked straight ahead what he saw was Arlene, the glow of her dark hair and the light in her blue eyes, and what did death have to do with that?

The last time he'd seen the rabbi—no, damn it, he corrected himself, the "rabbi"—the green Jaguar was still sitting motionless in the middle of the freeway, in the midst of a multitude of other, unidentifiable vehicles, their pale exhaust drifting upward through the thickly falling snow, while he maneuvered slowly up the exit ramp in a long line of cars seeking a way out of the stranglehold of the freeway. Gotcha, he'd thought, smugly satisfied that even though he was barely creeping ahead himself there was no way the green Jag was going to be able to slide across two lanes of traffic to an exit ramp it was already past. But why did he even care? It was just a guy in a car, a classy, expensive car, OK, but probably not the least bit interested in him, surely not even who he'd thought it was, but what if it was that rabbi, so what? It didn't mean anything, it just happened. A car was a car—so what if he'd seen it before?—and the rabbi was the rabbi and the snow was snow. He'd seen snow before, too. This was Minnesota, after all. It happened. All the time. What could you do about it? You put your snow tires on, you drove carefully, you stayed off the goddamned freeways. That's what he told Arlene: no more on the freeways, it was death on the freeways.

"That was my big mistake," he said, but even so he could see, above the little smile she squeezed out, how worry darkened her eyes.

When she tugged at his hands, as if to awaken him from his gloom, and told him everything was OK, not to worry so, everyone was fine, the children were fine and so was she, and he, he was a good man, he began to weep, silently at first, softly. But then as she reached across the couch and took him in her arms, the storm that had been building all these weeks suddenly broke and the tears came in great, heavy gusts, such sobs as he never knew he had inside him until now, great thunderheads of tears emptying themselves all at once, their pent-up floodwaters sweeping down the valley of his life carrying everything before them, houses, cars, children, dogs, friends, clients, and, yes,

shadowy old Death as well, abstract and intangible as always, amorphous and omnipresent as ever, and of course unnoticed by the great
crowd riding the swirling waters with him but—there! and there! and
there again!—glimpsed on the periphery of his vision whichever way
the wild eddies turned him, and not only glimpsed but caught out, for
just that fraction of a second, turning, darkly, to take a sly, sideways
look at him, Gruber. And he saw that there was nothing to do but ride
it out, let himself be borne along the crest of the current, afloat with
all it carried on the turbulent sea of his own emotions but not, he realized, drowning.

A Couple of Dead Men

HE SAT ON THE DECK of his little house watching the dying sun run the colors on the lake through their changes while he sipped the bourbon his doctor had forbidden him and wondered, as he often did these days, whether, if cancer had consciousness, it would know it was cancer. No, he thought, probably it would be just as stupid as we are; it would only know itself as an entity with consciousness. But maybe, if it thought about itself, as anything with consciousness was bound to do, it would see how far it had spread itself over the body of its host, just like the way we've spread ourselves across this earth, and wonder what it was doing there, who had put it there and for what reason. And who knows, he thought, maybe along with the idea of a cancer god it would even develop a cancer ecology. An intelligent parasite knows that it is not in its best interests to kill off its host. In fact, he realized, looking down at the little stream that flowed past his house into the lake, even an unintelligent parasite knows that: The liver fluke that keeps me from dipping my drinking water out of this bay lives in perfect communion with the moose upstream. Or maybe that in itself is a sign of intelligence. In which case we are only a marginally intelligent species ourselves, having come within a year or two of killing off this lake completely.

He took another sip of his drink, found it had become tastelessly watery, and leaned forward in his chair to empty his glass over the side of the deck. In a moment, anyway, the girl in the kitchen would call to tell him that his supper was ready, and then he would hear the screen door opening as she came out to help him in.

"Harry," she said on cue, "supper's about ready."

It had taken him months to get her to call him Harry, a plain, quiet country girl whose parents had obviously had some pretensions for her, naming her Nicole, though there was nothing here in this

beautiful but economically depressed area for anyone to have pretensions about. She had seemed happy enough with the position he'd
advertised in the local weekly, someone to do a little cooking and
cleaning and shopping for him, on a part-time basis. Come winter,
he'd have to find someone to split wood for him, too, and keep the
woodpile full by the stove, and plow the drive.

No, he thought, maybe he wouldn't, either.

"Here," she said, both hands on his upper arm.

"Never mind," he told her. "I can still get out of the goddamned
chair by myself."

And he could. What he had difficulty managing, though, was getting up the two steps from the deck into the house. He could move
his legs along reasonably well on the level, but when it came to going
up or down, his feet just didn't seem to know where they were anymore. Alone, he had learned to pick one leg up, grabbing it just above
the knee and setting it on the next step, then dragging the other one
along after it. It seemed to take forever.

"Cut the son of a bitch out," he'd said to the doctors when they first
told him about the tumor at the base of his spine. But then they explained what the chances were of their being able to get it all, of his
ever being able to walk again.

Now he said, "Thank you, Nickie," when she eased out from under his weight inside the house, just like he said, "Thank you,
Nickie," when she helped him down the steps, onto the deck.

She said, "It's no trouble, Harry," and meant it. She was strong,
solid, probably not much under the hundred and forty or so pounds
he'd dropped to himself. It wasn't a matter of his being too much of a
burden for her. But it seemed to him that his whole life was becoming a series of Thank-you-Nickies: when she changed the bedsheets,
when she came back from the Laundromat or the grocery store, when
she brought an armful of big peonies from her mother's garden, when
he wrote out a check for her at the end of the month. It was beginning
to be too much of a burden for him. It wasn't even a matter of the
thank-yous. He'd been raised a polite child and remained a polite
man all his life, a steady believer in the need for social lubricants, the
pleases and thank-yous and you're-welcomes. But his thank-yous had

always been for acts that graced his life—for the Christmas gift, for the elevator door held open as he rushed toward it, for the unexpected kiss his wife used to bend over to bestow on his bald head as he sat reading—not for deeds he depended on. He had never depended on anyone else.

He ate earlier than he truly liked these days as a favor to Nickie, so she could get the kitchen cleaned up—she wouldn't tolerate the idea of leaving even his small collection of dirty dishes overnight—and be home in time to have her own dinner with her parents and her collection of unmarried older brothers, loggers all, suppliers of his own firewood, in fact. She had just settled him at the trestle table in the large open area that served as his living and dining space and placed a small salad in front of him when they both lifted their heads to the sound of sudden pounding at the kitchen door.

"Wouldn't you know," said Harry, though the one thing they both knew was that he rarely had visitors and never at this hour. That was by his own choice, the price he willingly paid for moving so far from the city, from old friends, from all sorts of people he didn't want to see him as he went through what he was going through. Only his doctor ever came these days, a compulsive fisherman and cross-country skier who was more than happy to spend a couple of days here every month or two, check on him even knowing there was nothing to be done but rewrite a prescription for pain killers. But Doc wasn't due for another couple of weeks. And even those people who distributed the *Watchtower* were too polite to come anywhere around mealtime.

When Nickie returned from the kitchen she looked something between puzzled and frightened.

"He says he's your brother," she reported, "but he sure don't look nothing like you."

By then Harry could see for himself. Ed was standing in the kitchen doorway, filling the doorway, top to bottom and side to side. He was holding what Harry recognized from TV as a semiautomatic weapon in one hand, an Uzi or something like that, but it looked like a toy in his great paw. When Ed saw Harry staring at it, he looked down at it too, as if surprised to find it there.

"Well," he said, "it pisses me off to think of you up here in this goddamned backwoods redneck shithole with no way to defend your-self." He stepped into the room and dropped the weapon on the table with a clatter that sounded like a whole shelf of dishes had fallen.

"Well, Ed."

Ed laid hairy knuckles hugely on the edge of the table and leaned his weight on them. Take a good look, Harry thought. The whole table started to tilt.

"So sit."

Watching Ed lower himself into the other chair, the one where Nickie often sat and talked with him while he ate, made Harry think of the giant red pines her brothers had probably spent the day bring-ing down in the nearby woods.

"You want something to eat, Mr. Krasner?" Nickie was saying to Ed. She was standing in the kitchen doorway now. "There's plenty."

Ed was looking at Harry's salad as if, whatever it was, it didn't fit into the category of "something to eat." Even Harry could see how small it was now, overshadowed by the weapon that lay in the middle of the table. Once out of Ed's enormous hands, the weapon seemed to have grown. It took up most of the space on the table. Ed seemed to have dropped it there quite casually, but Harry couldn't help notic-ing now that the barrel was pointed at him. He noticed that Ed was staring at it, too.

Then Ed looked up at Nickie and said, "Aw, no, honey. I'll just have some booze. Whatever you got. Bourbon, gin . . ." He trailed off. Harry nodded at her, and she was back in a moment with a glass and the bottle of Jack Daniel's. Ed looked at it, leaned back, heard the wooden chair creak—they all did—and sat straight up again.

"Well, shit, Harry," he said.

Harry suddenly became aware that Ed already smelled of booze. Booze and sweat. That the white T-shirt he wore under his wrinkled blue work shirt had a dark ring of dirt around the neck. That his big hands lying on the table were filthy, the fingernails impacted with dirt.

Harry poured an inch or so of bourbon into the glass that Ed was hiding between his two hands: "Take your time, Ed."

"Well, shit, Harry," Ed said again.

Nickie had backed off after putting the bottle and glass on the table and was standing in the kitchen doorway, staring at the weapon.

"Take your time," Harry repeated.

"Well, shit, Harry." Ed couldn't seem to bring himself to actually lift the glass up and drink from it. He just stared into it.

"I'm a dead man," he said.

✳   ✳   ✳

When they were kids, the gap in their ages, nearly a decade, had meant the difference between duty and desperation. Reprimanded by his parents time and again for not demonstrating a proper sense of responsibility in the family, Harry had dragged little Ed along with him to sandlot baseball games, matinee movies, high school pep rallies, even picnics with his girlfriends. When he didn't or wouldn't, he knew he was leaving behind a kid dripping with dismay and rejection, knew he'd be coming home to find his baseball card collection spilled across the floor of the bedroom they shared or his schoolbooks and homework scattered all over the house. Nothing ever destroyed, just messed around with, the way he was sure little Ed felt his whole world had been messed around with by Harry's abandonment of him. And with a couple of parents, long since dead now, who had nothing to say about the great upheavals the world was then going through but plenty of commentary on an older brother's responsibility for smoothing sibling conflict over and cleaning up the mess he was, after all, responsible for. Harry always cleaned it up. Harry loved little Ed. Harry didn't know whether little Ed loved him or not, or whether it was just another case of a hungry parasite clinging to its familiar host. Harry moved out when he left for college and never came back, determined that from then on—though it didn't exactly work out that way—the only messes he was going to clean up were his own.

It seemed like the next time he turned around, Ed had miraculously learned to make the best of his own messes, parlaying a business degree and a job in a junkyard into a multimillion dollar scrap metal business. Ed's hands were still scarred and dirty and his clothes always reminded Harry of a little kid who'd gone outside to play after being all dressed up for a family outing, but Harry, modest in his own aspirations, couldn't help admiring Ed for what he'd made of himself. They were at opposite ends of their fifties now and lived vastly different lives half a continent apart, but were closer now than they'd ever been, talked on the phone every few days, and, perhaps because they both lived alone, told each other things they would never have revealed to anyone else. Harry loved big Ed and had gradually come to accept the fact that big Ed, no longer dependent on anyone except his scrap suppliers, loved him, too.

✻   ✻   ✻

After Nicole had cleaned up and left and the evening had grown dark, Ed announced to Harry that they were going to move out to the deck and watch the stars.

"You know she's got a thing for you," he said, helping Harry out through the doorway.

Harry, concentrating full-time on the doorjamb, on his feet, on the two steps down to the deck, didn't reply. He'd sensed that Ed had been aware of the looks Nickie was giving him from the kitchen, from behind Ed's back, while Ed finally drank his bourbon and he finished his dinner, but he knew they were looks of concern, not passion. Concern for him, Harry. Which was all he figured he was likely to get much of from anyone these days: concern. A little passion wouldn't hurt, though he couldn't imagine where it might come from or, for that matter, what he might or might not be able to do with it.

Settled in his chair again, all he said was: "She's just a kid." Then: "Fetch me that little blanket off the back of the couch, would you, Ed?" Once the sun was down, the evenings cooled off quickly these days, and even as he'd shuffled toward the chair with Ed's helping arm around him, Harry had felt how quickly the chill was entering his own body. He never did this anymore, partly out of deference to Nicole's wish to get home right after dinner, though an after-dinner drink on the deck had once been a regular part of his routine. Routine, he thought: The other part came out of his determination to practice doing without. But the stars, he thought now, looking up into the perfectly clear, moonless, cloudless night sky, how can you do without the stars?

"Some night, huh, kid?" said Ed. Back out again with both the blanket and the Uzi—"Yeah, kid, an Uzi," he'd answered Nicole, who was already turning back into the kitchen almost before she'd asked, "wanna touch it?"—Ed didn't quite seem to know what to do with either. Finally he set the Uzi down on the deck beside Harry's chair, tucked the blanket gently around Harry's shoulders, and dragged the other heavy wooden deck chair across to sit next to Harry.

Harry looked down at the weapon lying between their two chairs and said, "We going out on a snipe hunt, Ed?"

Ed said, "Look at those stars, will you?"

*   *   *

Ed's problems, it turns out, as they sit under the stars and talk, are manifold. Harry, who has had a quiet life as director of personnel for a good-sized manufacturer of medical equipment, has dealt with an endless succession of job-related problems, from petty thefts to layoffs to dope smoking on the assembly line and the family crises of employees. But except for his wife's death, which is still, after a dozen years, something that seems to him to have happened on another plane of existence, only a collection of parking tickets, a few citations for moving violations, and, once, a break-in that cost him a watch and a stereo, have marred a tranquil lifetime. Now he hears things about the scrap business he could never have imagined and Ed could never have risked talking about on the phone. Union toughs. Underworld connections. Payoffs. Price-fixing. Illegal waste disposal. Stop, he wants to tell Ed, this isn't real, this is the stuff of bad crime novels, next thing you know there'll be a body in the car compactor.

Ed tells him about the body in the compactor.

Ed would never have known about the body in the compactor except that it was the end of a long, hot day, no more than a week ago, and he had come out of the office to cool off, to catch the little breeze that was finally coming off the river. Clancy, his yard boss, was running the last few cars for the day through the compactor, with Billy Halftone up in the crane, and Ed was just standing there on the metal grid decking outside his office, looking at the yellow haze that had settled over the city skyline across the river. He watched as a dark blue T-Bird went into the compactor and he watched as it came out, a compact, two-and-a-half-foot-high block of metal. He still got a kick out of watching the compactor in operation, even after all these years. Then, as he watched the crane drop its heavy magnet onto what used to be an expensive, beautiful automobile and swing it away toward the stacks of other compressed car bodies, he saw the dark line of liquid dripping behind it. It was bright red, and he knew right away it was blood.

At the same moment, he became aware of someone standing just behind him, a big man, a man his own size but even wider, even heavier, who was saying, almost with a tone of awe in his voice, "It's a beautiful thing to see, isn't it, the way a machine like that works."

Ed nodded. This was the man who came now and then to tell Ed about certain things that had to be done if certain people were to be satisfied, people whose dissatisfaction would reflect very badly on Ed's success in the scrap metal business.

"What's even more amazing," the big man was saying, "is how dependable a machine like that is."

Amazingly dependable, Ed agreed.

"You never see anything different with it, do you?" said the big man, who by this time was standing right beside Ed, leaning against the metal pipe railing that encircled the deck.

"No," Ed agreed. "You never see anything different."

"I didn't think so," said the big man, turning to go. He was just starting down the steps to the yard from the gridwork platform when he turned back and added, "By the way, how's your brother these days?"

Ed didn't answer right away. He looked down at first, then he bent forward and leaned his forehead against the railing in front of him. It seemed to hold all the heat of the day inside it, but he kept his head there for half a minute all the same. Finally he lifted his head and looked the big man in the eye and said, "He died last month."

"The big C," said the man, almost a question. Ed nodded.

"I'm sorry to hear it," the big man said. Ed nodded again.

"I guess the whole burden's on your shoulders then," said the big man, starting down the stairs.

✳   ✳   ✳

When Ed is finished telling his story they sit for a long time under the brilliantly starry sky, looking up at it from time to time, sipping their bourbon neat, not speaking. The little creek, fairly dry this late in the summer, gurgles quietly along below them. Finally Harry says, very quietly, as if he doesn't want to disturb the light little voice of the water or the heavens sprinkled with all that brightness, "You killed me off."

"Yeah, kid, I killed you off. But I did it for your own good."

Not that I needed any help, Harry thinks. But he does worry about Ed, that they, whoever they are, might have followed him here. At the same time he knows that Ed, who saw a lot of combat during the Vietnam War that he, Harry, missed because of his age, is a wily enough survivor to have taken precautions against that. He doesn't think that the Uzi, in the long run, would be much help, not against the kind of people Ed has been describing, but he can see how having it around might make Ed a little more comfortable. He doesn't say any of this to Ed, however, because he can sense quite clearly that everything that he has been thinking has already been circulating in Ed's mind, too. He doesn't even feel he has to tell Ed that he doesn't mind Ed having killed him off. He already knows that Ed knows this. Talking about it seems superfluous. It almost seems to Harry that saying anything on a night like this, under a sky like this, is superfluous. And Ed must be thinking the same thing, because a lot of time passes without either of them uttering a word, not even to ask for the bottle of Jack, which passes back and forth between them as silently as the stars pass overhead.

Finally, a thought occurs to Harry that he feels he does have to put into words, for Ed's sake: "They wouldn't kill you, you know."

"Ha," says Ed, after a brief silence. "You don't know these people."

"Better than you think," says Harry.

He hears a sort of mumble that could be Ed or could be the bur-
bling of the creek.

"They need you, don't you know? You're their meal ticket. They're
feeding off of you. If they kill you, they go hungry."

"Mmmmm," says Ed.

"Parasites," says Harry. "Fucking parasites."

*   *   *

The first ring of the phone freezes them, each with a hand on the
bottle, Harry so stunned he can't remember whether he was passing
it to Ed or Ed to him. It's as if a lightning bolt has slashed down to the
deck out of the clear night sky above. The second ring seems to shat-
ter everything, the still forest, the trickling creek, the starry silence.
No one calls here except Ed himself, and occasionally Doc, from his
office, never at night. Together they set the bottle down on the deck.
The look they give each other as the phone goes on ringing acknowl-
edges that Harry can't possibly get to the phone in time to answer it
and Ed had better not.

Finally Harry says, "It must be Nickie."

"Nickie?"

"Nicole. You know. Maybe about the firewood."

"It couldn't wait?"

"It's not that late."

After a dozen rings, the phone quits, and they fall silent again, but
it feels to Harry as if even the stars above are crackling with electricity now, as if the creek snaps and sizzles like kindling. He sees that Ed
is now holding the Uzi across his lap.

"She'll worry I didn't answer," says Harry. "She'll come back, or
send one of her brothers."

"Shit," says Ed. "They'll do her, too."

He has one more thing to explain to Harry: that before he left
town, between the morning when he returned the Mercedes to the
leasing agency and the afternoon when he threw some clothes in an
old army duffel bag and climbed in the Jeep Cherokee to start his

the woods, he'd called the police.

"Stupid," says Harry, thinking it was probably just some thug in the trunk of the T-Bird, what difference does it make. But he doesn't really believe that, that it doesn't make any difference. And where did that word pop into his mind from, anyway? *Thug?* He doesn't use words like that. If there was one thing he learned in thirty-plus years in personnel, it was to respect every employee in the company, and to make it show that he did. Someone's dead. Ed called the cops. OK.

"You'd better call her," he tells Ed. "The number's on the wall by the phone."

Ed grunts, gets up, hands Harry the weapon, and goes inside to make the call. In the faint light that leaks out from the house behind him, Harry can barely see the Uzi's harsh, angular shape as it lies across his legs, but it's cold to his touch and smells like old car parts, like the dirty service bay in the old gas station the Chmelski brothers run just down the road from where Nickie's family lives. For Harry, who sat in a folding metal chair there many times in the past, reading the local weekly and drinking a Coke while Fritz or Nathan did an oil change and grease job on his Chevy, it's an unpleasant smell with pleasant associations. He suddenly remembers his mother telling him about that. He remembers being nine and standing beside her watching, smelling the bitter smells, as she changed the baby's messy diaper, and wondering how she could do that, stand that smell day after day, stand getting the stuff on her hands even.

And he recalls her explaining it to him, smiling, saying, "Well, it is what it is and it smells like what it is. But look at this baby, isn't he something? And I did it for you, too. Don't forget that."

Still, when Ed returns from making the phone call, Harry is happy to hand the thing back to him. Ed, holding the Uzi loosely in his left hand, strolls around the deck, looking up from time to time at the sky.

"It's starting to cloud over," he says.

Harry looks up, too. "High clouds," he says, "nothing to worry about," meaning no rain likely, though on second thought he doesn't know why they should care whether it rains or not. And before long the thin screen of clouds that has only barely covered a part of the sky slides away and the sky is just as it was before. Harry watches Ed watching the sky. He hears Ed grunt when it seems he's satisfied that the sky has been returned to its previous state, and he hears the wooden deck chair creak as Ed settles his big body back down into it again, hears the quick click of metal on wood as Ed lays the Uzi down on the deck beside his chair.

There in the dark now, silent together, they can both sense the enormity of the world that surrounds them, a world of deep woods and slowly flowing water and huge, star-bright skies. A month ago, Harry reflects, and they would not have been able to sit out on the deck on a night like this, so thick would the mosquitoes have been. To the best of his knowledge no one has ever died of mosquito bites, but everywhere you turn, he is thinking, there are parasites of varying degrees of intelligence, some uncomfortable, some threatening, others stupidly lethal. Harry knows which kind he has, but he's less sure of what kind Ed has. One way or another, though, he knows that that is one hell of a sky passing over their heads just now. He knows, from the bottle that has sat untouched on the deck between their chairs since Ed returned from the telephone, that they have both had as much bourbon as they want for the night. He knows that even while you are waiting for the worst to happen — no, even after the worst has happened — the sun still goes on setting and rising, the stars slide by overhead and the moon, dark now, shuffles through its phases. He knows the ordinary tiredness that comes at the end of the day. He knows that soon now they will go to bed, he and Ed, and then, in the morning, they will wake up exactly as they were before they went to sleep: a couple of dead men who will sit down at the table and drink coffee together and talk about how they will spend the day.

Tremors

ON SATURDAY MORNINGS, when I was ten and eleven and was taking drawing classes at the art museum, I rode the streetcar, the Eden Park line, through the park to get there. More often than not, that was the best part of the day. Not that I minded the drawing classes; they were enjoyable enough, although I knew even then that, unlike the grandfather who encouraged me in this, I had no genuine talents as an artist, and suspected, as well, that my interest in art, which I managed to sustain for several years after that, was prompted more by a desire to please him than by any aptitude for the work itself. Not, I believe, an ignoble motive, for I loved him dearly and continued to do so even as I grew older and began to perceive the limitations of his own artistry, just as I'm sure his love for me was never shaken by the crudity of the drawings of lions and horses I regularly laid before him. It is not for our achievements, I hope, no matter how much we praise them, that we love each other. And it's surely just as well that I never developed a vocation as an artist, anyway, since in my late thirties a congenital tremor established itself in my hands, controllable enough for day-to-day life with medication but rather a handicap, even so, for the paintbrush — or for the surgeon's knife, which I was, in fact, forced to lay down at that time.

That change, that relinquishing of my life as a surgeon, which was not unlike the change my grandfather himself must have once undergone, did not occasion much resistance or trauma, at least for me, given how far in advance its coming was seen, and how inevitable. There were adjustments to be made, of course, and we made them, my wife and I, my family and I, after our fashion, though I wonder if it wasn't the change that readjusted us, rather than anything we actively did on our own. And even more than that I wonder what adjustments the comparable change brought into my grandparents' lives when my grandfather, in order to take up the financial responsibilities forced upon him by family life, laid down his paints and brushes.

I can't recall what happened when I packed up my own pencils and charcoal at the end of those classes. I suppose that often my father, who tended to go into the office on Saturday mornings, must have picked me up, though in fact that seems very unlike him, and perhaps I went off with friends, went somewhere else, down to Crosley Field perhaps, to use my Knothole card to get into a Reds game for a quarter, or simply made my way home the same way I'd gotten there. That's not important, however: As with so many of our endeavors, it's not the end that matters most but the getting there. And how I got there was on the streetcar.

But I had to earn it, first. Streetcar lines were already becoming increasingly rare in the city by then, most of them having been replaced by the buses that could reach more easily into the expanding suburbs and most of the tracks having been ripped up at the end of the previous decade and sold as scrap metal to Japan, from where, as we were often reminded in those days, they were now returning to us in the shape of bombs and bullets.

But the Eden Park line still ran, though, being a suburban kid, I couldn't just walk out my door and hop on it. No, I had to walk my dozen blocks first, which during the school year—since they were the same blocks I walked on my way to fifth or sixth grade—took a certain dedication on a Saturday morning. Then I had to wait on the corner for the downtown bus, tolerate its long ride through boringly familiar suburban territory into the city proper, and there disembark, paper transfer in hand (good for only an hour beyond the time snipped out on its twenty-four-hour clock by the bus driver), and cross to the concrete island in the center of the street to wait for the trolley to come clattering to a stop there.

I waited for the one that said Eden Park. No doubt there were others still running then, probably even others that paused at that same island, usually quite abandoned on Saturday mornings, but I knew which one I waited for, knew its noises and smells and the rows of rattan seats where, even though I generally had the pick of the place, I always gravitated to the same one at the very back. And I knew the main roads and apartment-lined city streets I still had to put up with, too.

And then, abruptly, we were in the park. I never quite knew how we got there, and I still don't, though in my mind I have a perfectly clear picture of the way the city was laid out then, the park, the main streets, the intersections we must have passed through, and even the way it is now, with much of that territory carved into two by the brutal incision of the interstate. Somewhere, however, without my ever knowing just where or how it happened, we were away from the city streets, no longer riding rough and noisy, caught up in the traffic and bounded by houses and stores and apartment buildings, but suddenly, as if we had passed through a magic doorway into another world, we were running on tracks through a woods, and I remember it as if it were always spring, and the trees were unfurling their leaves even as we swept by, or summer, the forest in full bloom brushing the car itself with the wide-leaved branches of sycamores and even the noise of the trolley muted, as if out of respect for this pastoral world it had entered, and no one there but the silent driver and myself, the quiet car rolling smoothly through the green tunnel of what might as well have been the Brazilian rain forest as a Midwestern city, and then a sudden eruption of brightness as it passed out from under the canopy of trees and onto a narrow trestle over the main road that entered the park, clattering roughly again for a minute above the few cars and fewer pedestrians far below, then flowing on again as if it were the great Amazon itself, gliding back into the smooth silence of its tree-shrouded channel.

Soon, of course, like the noisy, jerky thing it was, it must have come rattling to a stop in front of the museum. I must have climbed down with my pads and pencils and gone around to the side entrance where the classrooms were and put that dreamy journey behind me as I took my place among other young students in front of some simple still life, a squat vase or a few folds of dull, dusty, maroon velvet that had probably been serving the same purpose since my grandfather's days as an art student there.

Although I don't remember that transition into the world of concrete steps and rambunctious children and the authoritative voice of the instructor, I am not the sort of person to be wholly charmed away from it by nostalgia, either. Even then, no doubt, in the way I simply turned to the task at hand, I was manifesting something of the same practical instinct that, as I leafed through the drawing books my parents encouraged me with, pulled me more strongly toward the illustrations of animal anatomy, the diagrams of the skeletons of horses or the musculature of dogs, than toward the smooth, sweeping ovoids out of which I was supposed to learn that heads and torsos, whole figures, could be constructed.

For me the only smooth, sweeping line that took on any real meaning was the curve of the trolley-car track through the woods of Eden Park. Common sense tells me that that lyric segment of the journey must have lasted only a few minutes, five at the very most. And yet that time—as the woods opened up their welcoming tunnel before me and the trees flowed by, brushing the car like painters themselves with their leaf-dipped branches, and the tracks behind were instantly swallowed up by the dense greenery—that brief time was when I came to know how much I loved my grandfather and the world and, most surprisingly, myself.

✻   ✻   ✻

One steamy summer afternoon during those same years, on the way downtown on some long-forgotten errand, perhaps, after I had been picked up at the end of an art class, my father abruptly turned the car off the main street and into a section of town I was only vaguely aware of, one of the several run-down areas surrounding the city's center, this the white slum rather than the black one, which I knew better from the fact that his own business was located there. He turned down one hot, narrow, filthy street after another, craning his head out the window at intersections, obviously looking for something, while I sat silent, puzzled, probably bored beside him, only dimly aware of the packed streets we passed through, full of Appalachian immigrants in flight from rural to urban poverty, the men in stained undershirts, smoking, silent, the women in flowered-print dresses, as gaunt as the men, except, often, for their bellies, and the children everywhere,

barefoot, half-naked, dirty.

Finally he stopped, the car only partially pulled in toward the curb, flipped his cigarette out his window, leaned across me to look out the window on my side, and said, "Yep, that's the place."

The store window we'd come to a stop in front of was so filthy it was impossible to see through it. Peeling lettering on the window, once gold, read: ART SUPPLIES. I had no idea what we were doing there, in front of this shop so obviously in keeping with its surroundings in its dilapidation, looking as closed as the boarded-up hardware store on one side, as decrepit as the filthy, jumbled window of the drugstore on the other, and yet so obviously out of keeping with the neighborhood. No one, surely, painted here. Not even houses, as far as I could see. Nor could I imagine anyone coming here to buy the dried-out paints and inks, the dust-covered brushes and paper that had to be on the dirty shelves, in the stained counters, inside. Even the position of the car, half out in the middle of the street, motor still running, told me we weren't here to shop for supplies.

"That's where your grandfather's brother lives," my father said, settling back behind the wheel.

It was the first time I knew that my grandfather had a brother.

"The artist," my father said as we pulled away.

This object lesson was not lost on me, though I was still naive enough to question, as we drove out of those desperate streets, whether anyone actually lived there.

"Upstairs," I was informed. I was left on my own to picture what life upstairs, in such a place, must be like, though in his taciturn, uninformative way, my father allowed himself to drop other, darker hints: the reasons this man was never seen with the family, the drinking, the woman he lived with, not wife, and, worst of all, the fact that he was, as my father succinctly put it, "a failure."

My grandfather, as I well knew, was not a failure because he was, at that time, the service manager of the largest Ford agency in town. But that object lesson had not been lost on me either. Although the apartment he and my grandmother lived in was hung throughout with his oils, what my father always boasted of were the murals he had once done inside the theaters and the opera house, and the huge outdoor billboards he had once painted before papering them put an end to that craft. Yes, my grandfather still drew, even painted occasionally, though mostly on request from someone in the family who wanted a special piece for the hallway or den of a new house. And he still sculpted small animals from soft wood, like the model of our black-and-white cocker spaniel that sits on my desk even now. But he was no longer an artist. There were better, that is, more important, which is to say, more successful things to do.

*   *   *

Some years later, when I was fifteen and had pretty well given up my artistic pretensions, such as they were, for the chemistry lab and girls, both of which I had recently discovered, the Balkers, friends of the family, asked my parents if I would do a drawing for them. If it was not a commission I could refuse, given the way my mother put it to me, neither, I knew, was it one I could perform with much success. To my parents and their friends, art might still have seemed like something I did; to them I was no doubt still little Arnie the artist, however much I was reshaping myself, in my own mind's eye, into Doctor Arnold Brownstein, battlefield surgeon, much decorated for saving lives under enemy fire. For them, what I had was a talent that could be turned, with no particular effort on my part, to a social favor, but for me it was, now, only something I had once done, a skill I had gained some minimal mastery over, never all that much, however greatly I had enjoyed it. The day my mother dropped me off at the Balkers' home, with only my sketch pad and pencils and the Balkers' black maid for company, I knew I was finally being brought face-to-face not with rumor or family history but, this time, with the thing itself: failure.

The thing I was being asked to sketch was itself a disaster. Perched on, dominating, the mantel over the mirrored fireplace in a living room full of puffy new furniture and deep pile rugs, sat a monstrosity out of eighteenth-century France by way of contemporary Japan, when Japan still meant cheap, not good, though I am sure there was nothing cheap about the price they paid for it in some elegant decorator's shop in New York or San Francisco. It was just that, as I knew even then—a decorator piece and nothing more, quite simply the ugliest thing I had ever seen in anyone's living room and, moreover, well beyond my meager sketching skills: a ceramic carriage with driver up front and groom behind and four prancing horses, all in bright colors that blended one into the other and flowing lines and sagging edges, and somehow managing, in spite of its brilliant glazes and stylized figures and the forward tilt of horses and carriage and men, to look thick and heavy as it sat there, as if it were weighing down the whole mantel.

Sitting there with my sketch pad on my knees, sinking into the overstuffed couch that faced the fireplace, I knew I might just as well be trying to capture the sagging facial lines and frequently drunken slurs of the Balkers themselves.

I did their drawing, of course, after many even faultier attempts, while the maid paused in her chores from time to time to bring me a fresh glass of lemonade and graciously refrained from looking at my latest struggle to reproduce the monstrosity on the mantelpiece. Or was it out of embarrassment? And if so, for me or for that thing I was staring at over there? At any rate, I did it, finally, as one does the things expected by one's parents, joylessly and probably even a little worse than I was capable of—though, I thought, tearing the final version off my pad and laying it on the mantel next to the thing itself for the Balkers to find when they returned home, reasonably appropriate to the subject.

They'll love it, I told myself, as, hearing my mother honk, I gathered up my drawing supplies and thanked the maid for her battlefield ministrations. And they did.

✳   ✳   ✳

When my grandfather died, I was away at medical school and did not come home for the funeral. Even today, when there is a death in the family, as has been happening often, for the years have lately begun to knock on the doors of our parents' generation with some frequency, my wife berates me about this, knowing how much I loved this grandfather.

"You Brownsteins, you never show your feelings," she'll say angrily, pushing things around on her desk, on the kitchen table, wherever we happen to be, showing me that she knows how to show her feelings.

"Sarah," I remind her, "I saw him only the week before. When he was still alive."

And I did, though sitting beside his bed in the nursing home, holding his hand, by no means certain that he had recognized me during the brief moment when his eyes had flickered open, I knew he was already a dead man.

Anyway, what she means, but can't say, is, "In certain ways, as a human being, and as much as I love you, you're a failure."

Translation: "Look at the things you just accept without so much as blinking."

It runs in the family, I think, by way of silent rebuttal.

But the fact is, we have a good life. Between us, Sarah and I bring in an income more than adequate to the family's many needs. The children have had their orthodonture, will have their college educations; we have our house, our vacation home, our travels, our retirement funds. A good life. And what I remember thinking, sitting there in the nursing home, holding my grandfather's frail hand the week before his funeral, watching the head that looked so shrunken on the pillow, the sparse gray hairs, the little quiverings of his lips, was that he, too, had had a good life.

It had been barely a year since my grandmother had died, cancer descending on him in the months right after her death as if it had come directly to him from her, as if this end had grown naturally out of the long life they had shared. They had shared it in apartments, mostly, sometimes in expansive flats full of dark woodwork in elegant older buildings, sometimes in cramped, newer, postwar fourplexes where many of us had to eat on card tables in the living room when the family gathered on holidays. But always, I knew, they shared it with love: love for each other, love for the children and grandchildren, and a love that reflected back to themselves, as well—a thing I never knew better than when I rode that Saturday morning Eden Park trolley car to the art museum — from each and every one of those children and grandchildren. And yet, I also knew, somewhere in that life they shared had come a great disruption. Among the tales of early automobiles, of the Northside home where the children had been born, of trips to long-defunct resorts, of the trials and losses of war and depression, it was never mentioned. But I knew it was there: that tremulous moment when failure had been abandoned for success.

And I wondered, sitting beside his deathbed, just how they had negotiated that transition. It doesn't sound like a tragic move when it's put like that, leaving failure behind for success, especially given the good life they went on to share, but I know, I know, there had to have been a shifting of reality, of the world as known till then. Things were left behind. There was loss. I think of the brushes and rags, the oils and easels and canvases, the knives and palettes and stretchers and watercolors consigned to back rooms and Sunday afternoons, and I want to know how they did it.

I think I am still waiting for some last words from my grandfather.

I think he is still showing me that some things you just have to accept.

*   *   *

Doctor Brownstein was not a heroic battlefield surgeon, nor was he ever called upon to be one. But he was successful at what he did, which was, mainly, removing tumors of the kind that had deprived him of both his paternal grandparents, and on more than one occasion he had happened to hear, or overhear, colleagues speak of his "artistry," a term that gave him no small pleasure. From time to time it occurred to him that the roots of such artistry as he had must have been nourished in the basic anatomy of his childhood drawing manuals, in the equine skeletal structure and the canine musculature that he had once liked to imagine lurking just beneath the surface of his own clumsy drawings of horses and dogs. But he didn't really believe that. He also liked to think that his surgical accomplishments—the successful removal of a large, malignant abdominal tumor, say— were not diminished by the fact that frequently the patient did not long survive, but he didn't believe that, either.

Then, one day, his father sat in his office, waiting to have a small, swollen (and, finally, benign) node on the back of his wrist lanced and drained.

"Kaufman could have done this," said Doctor Brownstein, refer- ring to the old family physician on whom he was happy to know his father still relied.

"For this," his father said, "I wanted to see the best man in his field."

It was a minor office procedure. Doctor Brownstein cleansed the area, applied a light local anesthetic, selected the knife.

"You're shaking," his father pointed out to him.

"It's not every man," replied Doctor Brownstein in his gentlest of- fice manner, "who faces the awesome responsibility of taking a knife to his own father."

By the end of which statement the wound had been swiftly and precisely lanced, the pus ran clear and free, there was a bit of squeez- ing to be done to get it all out, yet another cleansing, the antibiotic ointment to be applied, and a small bandage. It was, in effect, all over.

Except for the shaking.

Which was not, as the neurologist was later to comment in a small attempt to lighten what we both realized was a serious situation, be- cause the father was there, but because, in the beginning, the father had been there.

*   *   *

When the time finally came to say farewell to Doctor Brownstein, it seemed to me that the others around me grieved far more deeply at his demise than I did. My parents could no longer take delight in hav- ing their friends at the country club ask them about their son, the doc- tor, and found themselves instead, as my mother admitted to me, having to accept sympathies that sounded all too much like condolences. My father, when he wasn't using his meager understanding of the concept of congenitality to attack my mother's family, insisted — still insists — that something could be done about it if only I would go to the best man in the field. Not wanting to encourage his persistent dream of resurrecting the dead, I assure him over and over again, and truthfully, that everything possible has been done.

Even my own house, for months, bore all the earmarks of an ongoing wake. There was always an excess of food about, cold cuts and cheeses and rye breads, laid out on silver trays at all hours of the day. From somewhere — a resurrected wedding present? I hesitated to ask, for fear of hearing it was on loan from the funeral parlor — a giant sterling coffee urn began to appear daily on the dining-room buffet, its glowing red light relentlessly announcing its readiness for such occasions. And people appeared too, friends, neighbors, relatives I only saw at weddings and funerals, mostly in the early evenings but sometimes in the afternoons as well. They fixed themselves drinks and sandwiches and, I couldn't help noticing, talked mainly to my wife.

Not that they totally ignored me. In fact, there was always some pointed moment when they approached me directly and fixed me with a deep and serious look as if they were trying to discover whether there might be some sign of life left in me yet. I talked with them on cue, joked with them, urged more food and drink on them, but felt all the time as if they weren't really listening to me, as if that solemn look was all they could bear to attend to me with, as if, in fact, I were indeed the corpse laid out at the wake upon which each guest had to bestow one final, lingering gaze.

In the afternoons, drawn by the quantities of available food, I presume, my children's friends began to accompany them home from school as never before. A friend of my youngest son's approached me one day, sandwich in hand, to tell me how his father, a highly promising pitcher the Reds had made a big trade for only a few seasons back, had suffered such a serious arm injury in his second year with the team that he had had to abandon his pitching career. Now, he said, biting angrily into his sandwich, they were stuck in this crummy town. Now, he said, his father sold insurance and wouldn't even watch baseball on TV. Crumbs scattered around him. I heard his disdain for the baseball-player dad who was no more, for the insurance-salesman dad he was now forced to live with as if he were only a stepfather.

That same evening, after dinner, as we were still sitting at the dining-room table, the evil red eye of the coffee urn glaring at me from the buffet opposite, my older daughter broke the silence by asking me, finally, what I was going to do now.

"Lay down my sword and shield," I told her.

Which prompted Sarah, later that night, as we were getting into bed, to announce that, seeing how I had embarked on a pattern of re-treat from reality in my relations with both family and friends, I was probably in need of therapy.

"They don't treat the dead," I told her, slipping the straps of her nightgown off her shoulders.

"The dead don't do that, either," she said.

"That," I said, looking up from nibbling at her breasts, "is precisely my point. The king is dead—"

"No," she said. "No. No, I don't think so. No."

*   *   *

What some might perceive as retreat, others might see as progress in a different direction. And getting there, as I reminded Sarah that night—and as she agreed, though she was thinking about one thing by then and I was thinking about two—is at least half the fun and maybe what we remember most when the journey is over. The jour-ney adjusts you, readjusts you when you need it, if you'll let it; other-wise you find yourself in constant conflict with it, discomfited by it, always wishing it were over when in fact it will be, soon enough, and what then? We want something more from it, I hope, than merely *souvenirs du voyage*, though they too have their place, and can, for that matter, even be found in unexpected places.

My father comes by for lunch today, as he does once or twice a week now since my mother's death and his own retirement, and is dis-mayed, as always, to find me sitting at the dining-room table, my jour-nal open in front of me—dismayed, I know, to find me home at all,

but of course it's only because I'm home that he's here. The thick,
cream-colored tablecloth is pushed back, and the folds it makes
against the square crystal vase that Sarah, who loves flowers, has filled
this week with pale, delicate alstroemeria, remind me of the still-life
settings from my childhood art classes. For a moment, just before my
father enters, I have the sense that if I look down from staring at the
flowers, the vase, and the bunched-up tablecloth, I will see a sketch
pad in front of me on the table, rather than this notebook.

Then he sits down heavily in the chair across from me and says,
shaking his head slowly, as always, "Such a shame. You had such a career in front of you."

One behind me, one before me, I think, but I've tried that line on
him before. We've been having this conversation for years now. This
time I say simply, "Have."

"Here?" he says, looking around the dining room in a kind of mock
disbelief but also a very real one, for nothing is ever likely to convince
him, the successful businessman who went to his office every working day of his life—which was, until recently, almost every day—that
one can have a real career by working where one lives.

"There," I answer, pointing through the wide archway of the dining room and across the hall to where the open door of my study re-
veals a desk piled high with books and papers and, yes, drawings.
Drawings, yes indeed. And wonderful ones. Not mine, of course, but
I am lucky enough these days to be working with one of the finest
medical illustrators in the entire Midwest, and though she is very
modest about her own work, and persists in saying over and over again
that she is "just an illustrator," she is, in fact, a real artist, whose work
brings out details of nerve and muscle, tendon and vein, that no pho-
tograph can reproduce with half the clarity. We are quite a team, she
and I, rather much in demand in the textbook field these days, and
she has begun to get requests from a number of journals as well, to
provide drawings to accompany certain articles. I would hate to lose
her because her artwork, her ability to know and to depict precisely
what's needed for each particular illustration, is what redeems my
own necessarily prosaic text.

My father, meanwhile, is shaking his great head sadly, slowly, at the clutter of this little home office, the depths to which I have fallen from white tile and stainless steel, from the glitter and glamour of the operating room.

"Come on," I say, getting up from the table, patting his shoulder, "I'll fix us some lunch."

"So now you cook, too?" he says, less a question than an accusation.

"Pop," I remind him, "I've always cooked." It's true. Once, a decade or so ago, I even took a series of gourmet cooking classes, which mostly gave me a few skills, a more inventive culinary imagination, and the confidence to enjoy the kitchen. The little disability that impairs me for some things in no way interferes with my ability to slice onions or mince garlic, and, as I often tell Sarah when we team up in the kitchen for one of our regular extravaganzas, a slight tremor in the hand is perfect for adding seasonings.

"So what do you make?" he asks, rising heavily, my hand still on his shoulder, to accompany me to the many-windowed breakfast room just off the kitchen, where we will sit in the sunshine filtering through the great shagbark hickory in the side yard and eat the barley soup and French bread I made last night and stare, mostly in silence, at the copper bowl filled with apples and pears and bananas that sits in the center of the table between us.

What do I make? At first I'm tempted to say to him, as I follow his slow, unsteady pace toward the kitchen, Everything: pies and cakes, curries and soufflés, you name it, I'll do it, it's not always a great success, but it's fun trying. But then I realize that that isn't what he means at all, that while I have gone happily rolling along on my own little culinary track, he has turned off somewhere else altogether, not somewhere especially surprising—this is my father, after all—just not where I have been en route to myself. So as we cross the kitchen with its drainboard piled up with the lettuce and tomatoes and peppers and onions I intend to make us a little salad with, I give him an answer that I truly hope will satisfy both of us.

"A living," I tell him. "A pretty good living."

Immersion

SPIVAK IS DRIVING HIMSELF to the emergency room in a tidal wave of pain so enormous it has all but washed consciousness totally away. In the first half-dozen blocks he has run two red lights and a stop sign, and only the midafternoon traffic lull has saved him and other citizenry from harm. Not that Spivak would care for himself right now. Each time he's able to rise momentarily above the sea of pain for a quick gasp of sweet air, a new wave submerges him, and once again he is drowning in pain, swept under and held down in its depths while the swift current of pain floods through him, fills up every opening and organ to the point of bursting, owns him. Inasmuch as he is capable of knowing anything just now, he knows he has never known there could be pain like this. Nearly sideswiping a police car angled into the curb in front of a liquor store, he also flashes briefly on the knowledge that he should not be doing this, driving himself to the emergency room, that is, while the whole world is being deep-sixed by a tidal wave that obliterates everything around him: cars, buses, streets, buildings, the very sky.

Believe me, he wouldn't have ever begun this brief journey on his own if he'd been able to think of any other way. A taxi was out of the question; in this town you could rot, the fish could pick your bones clean, before you got a taxi. By the time an ambulance got to him, he'd never be able to tell them what the problem was. His wife, with every reason to believe his medical problems were over and done with for the time being, was somewhere in the thin, pure air, miles above this drowning world, cruising comfortably toward San Francisco. This he knew because he'd seen her off himself not three hours before, following an early lunch with her and two of their friends at their favorite Vietnamese restaurant, after which they'd headed straight for the airport, he and his wife, while Gorman, still gloomy, always gloomy, went off making house-to-house calls selling basement water-proofing, and Schlemowitz, who'd bubbled away all through lunch with the excitement of having just become a first-time grandfather, went . . . well, who ever knew where Schlemowitz went. He didn't have a car, anyway. The whole world that Spivak knew, half an hour ago when he was still capable of knowledge, was off at work in some distant suburb, en route somewhere by car or bus or plane, lost, awash, unavailable, all part of the drowned universe he has suddenly found himself sloshing through the depths of like some bulbous-eyed fish just struggling to make out what's there in the murky light right in front of him.

Poor Spivak! How there could be such pain as this he absolutely does not comprehend, pain that somehow detaches him from every-thing in the world while at the same time making him more physi-cally aware of himself than he has ever been before, pain that makes him the slowly moving center of a world that barely exists around him anymore, pain that *is* him, that swarms up from deep inside like an electrical storm, scatters outward through every nerve, capillary, fin-ger, every strand of hair, then dips and dives razor-edged back into the depths of his guts again, slashing away at nerves and muscle fibers, tendons, and ligaments, wreaking havoc on one internal organ after another. And it's not as if he's been the accidental victim of a drive-by shooting, as if he's been pig-stuck by the neighbor who's made no se-cret of his disgust at seeing him sitting out on the front steps drinking beer in nothing but his running shorts, as if he's been brutalized in a mugging, whacked by the UPS truck cutting the corner at the busy intersection just half a block from his house, struck by a falling mete-orite, waylaid by a banana peel. No, like everything else he's ever suf-fered from in his life — though he never knew there could be suffering like this, gargantuan suffering, biblical suffering, the suffering of all mankind — it's all inside him.

And yet it's not as if he thinks he's going to die from it, no more than he died from all that other suffering, from grief and loneliness and heartbreak. Long ago, his first wife and his father had died within a year of each other, both from cancer, and those paired losses had scraped his young heart raw with the steel wool of grief, reamed out

his blood vessels, and cauterized his nerves. Grief's true pain, he
learned early on, was that you didn't die of it. Nor of the cancer of
loneliness that swelled in your belly like an alien fetus, that weakened
your limbs, blurred your vision, scrambled your hearing, made everything you ate taste like cardboard, everything you touched feel like
glass. And speaking of shattering, what about the heartbreak that
came later, those shards of pain that lingered in your flesh long after
the breakup, that sliced muscle down to the bone every time you rose
up, stretched, twisted and turned, and the tiny fragments, like the bits
of safety glass that you're still finding on the floor of your car years after it was broken into, that rubbed and burned like grit beneath your
tongue, inside your nose, under your eyelids. You could rinse and spit
and blow and rub all you wanted, but it wouldn't go away. And it
wouldn't kill you, either.

So what Spivak had known right away, when knowledge was still
within his grasp, was that he was going to have to deal with it. Without a wife, a friend, a stranger, not even a foe—all by himself, just like
all those other times, and probably just as badly. This he knew standing over the toilet bowl in humiliation (but humiliation doesn't kill
either), naked and dripping right out of the bathtub, which was where
the call to the urologist he'd already spent two hours with that very
morning had sent him, and managing to squeeze only a few bloody
drops out of the tip of his penis. This he knew almost as soon as he settled back in the tub, its warmth only momentarily easing over him before the violent urge to pee was upon him again, driving him right
back out, splashing across the bathroom tiles to stand doubled over
above the porcelain bowl doing . . . nothing.

This is what drove him to the phone again, drove him into sweat-
pants and a sweatshirt without even toweling off, drove him out to the
garage and into his car, out on the streets on his way to the emergency
room where an ER intern whose face Spivak can't even focus on is
soon going to be telling him, even while in the process of threading a
catheter into his penis and up through his urethra, past the tender
bump of his swollen prostate, that, yes indeed, a plugged-up bladder
is one of the most painful things a human being can experience, that
plugging up the bladder is in fact a trick—he actually says "trick," as

if nature or God or the medical profession were playing some cosmic joke on Spivak—often used by torturers. And Spivak, who is ready to confess to anything, can certainly see why.

*   *   *

The world, meanwhile, though it's not the top thing on his mind right now, is cruising its own highways in its own usual reckless fashion. In the Middle East the Israeli religious reactionaries who drive Spivak nuts are once again fanning the flames of Palestinian frustration. In the former Yugoslavia the Serbs are raging at the Croats, or is it the Muslims against the Serbs? Spivak can never keep it straight. Contract murder is all the rage in Moscow. Anarchy reigns in an African country Spivak had never heard of before last week. Colombia is still in the control of the cocaine cartels, who slaughter whom they will where and when they will. Last night's TV news informed him that the IRA had set off a car bomb in a British city whose name he couldn't remember this morning. Many were injured. Fanatics are hard at work doing fanatical things in Japan and India and Sri Lanka. In his own sad country, some vicious new drug of choice has outstripped crack cocaine in the race to destroy the minds and bodies of white- and blue-collar cultures alike. Deregulation, with its pressure to cut costs by sacrificing maintenance and safety, has blasted another fully loaded jetliner out of the sky. No survivors. Radical militias are holed up in odd corners of practically every state in the union, perched atop piles of weaponry that boggle Spivak's semipacifist mind. All across the country, states are granting practically everyone except convicted murderers the right to carry concealed weapons. Congress keeps trying to force more billions on the Pentagon than it even asked for. If the cities of the East aren't burning, it's partly because three months of record-breaking spring rains have soaked their spirits, while a drought of a severity not seen since the thirties is grinding Western topsoil into dust. What's a citizen to do?

Spivak, a professor of humanities, who is finally beginning to float above his personal puddle of pain on a cloud of Demerol jabbed into his backside five minutes ago by someone he never even had a chance to see or the alertness to thank, knows that his own hour of agony is nothing compared to what the world has to offer every single minute, is a mere drop in the world's great ocean of pain, diluted and untraceable in the tides of human suffering that flood the face of the planet every single day. This morning's paper alone, which he knows this little episode of his will never make regardless of the fact that he considers it a violation of the most fundamental of human rights, the right to freedom from pain, was a litany of atrocities that lacked even the demented rationalizations of religion or politics: newborns tossed out with the garbage, men battering their wives and children, children taking guns to their parents, blowing away whole households while they're at it, farmers letting herds of cattle starve to death, drive-by shootings taking out the innocent bystander.

Maybe, he thinks, after the hurried departure of nurse and intern and resident for the next victim of car crash, accidental poisoning, armed robbery gone awry, or domestic violence, left alone for the moment to savor the thick weight of the drug pushing the tide of pain back off the beach of the self, exposing the sea-wrack of old ideas and drowned emotions, scattered like kelp and jellyfish across his soggy mind, maybe there are no innocent bystanders. Wasn't he himself ready to inflict serious damage on the woman behind the emergency room reception desk not fifteen minutes ago? He'd parked his car, illegally, driver's side wheels half up on the yellow curb in the hospital's parking lot, scuttled doubled over around an ambulance parked in front of the emergency entrance, paying no attention whatsoever to the bloody body the attendants were unloading, and gone straight to the desk, only to be told to take a seat and wait till he was called. But he couldn't sit, couldn't stand, couldn't wait, couldn't relieve the excruciating pressure in his bladder, which felt like it'd been taken over by a succubus with a pickax, could barely talk or think, could no more have inflicted harm on the receptionist at that moment than flown, which isn't to say it didn't cross what was left of his mind.

What he managed to blurt out instead was, "I'm going to faint," which was not far from the truth and, anyway, got him the desired result: an instant hustle back into the treatment room where he's now laid out flat on his back on a gurney, sheltered by white curtains, sedated, catheterized, emptied out, abandoned, and only vaguely curious, in his present narcotized state, about what happens next.

*   *   *

Spivak is a month from his sixtieth birthday, five years from his planned retirement, and a long, long way from his ultimate demise, though of course he has no more way of knowing that than anyone else does. He will outlive his good friends Schlemowitz, who at this moment is visiting his daughter in the maternity ward of this same hospital, and Gorman the melancholy, as well as all but the most recently hired members of his university department, by decades. He will outlive the President of the United States plus all the living ex-presidents and vice presidents plus the current leaders of every major nation in the world. In spite of his present setback, which is less serious than he thinks it is and a little more serious than his wife thought it was, or she'd never have left on her business trip, he will outlive three-quarters of the people currently alive on the face of the planet.

Like the good professor of humanities that he is, however, Spivak recognizes life's precariousness right along with its values. The deep, satisfying joy he carries in his heart for his wife, wherever she might be just now on her journey to that distant coast (almost there, but he's in no condition to calculate airline schedules and factor in time-zone differences right now), and for his children from his first marriage, all grown and moved too far away, exists side by side with his conviction that every moment is a blindfolded step off the curb into heavy traffic. Despite his Jewish heritage, he has no god to sustain him in this wilderness of delight and despair he stumbles through, but if there were one, he's long believed, it wouldn't make any difference because the only kind of god he can imagine existing in such a world as this would be just another sightless pedestrian putting one foot after the other into the lethal flow.

Still, like any ordinary god-driven sufferer, he can't help wondering, if only for a passing moment, what he's done to deserve this: this punishment, this torture, this betrayal of the flesh, this . . . he can't help it, it's the—what?—location? of his problem, what he can't do and what others are doing to him, this loss of privacy in the most private of areas, this destruction of modesty, this humiliation. He isn't, as he well knows, Job, but who can blame him for wanting an explanation he knows he'll never get for this arbitrary, unwarranted, and embarrassing torment. Arbitrary and unwarranted are facts, not explanations, nor is the unfolding drama of his genitourinary system, which he rightly imagines his urologist will eventually critique for him, act and scene, the sort of explanation he has in mind, either. Embarrassing he'll just have to get used to.

He's a decent man, after all. He's cheated on neither his spouse nor his taxes, nor has he come down unduly hard on the predictable cheating of his students; he's abused neither his children nor the power of his professorship, such as it is; if he's drunk a little too much on occasion, failed to reread a text he's teaching, given the finger to a maniacal motorist and picked up a couple of moving violation citations of his own, fallen too far into despair at his home team's perennial last-place finishes, succumbed—but only once!—to voting for a Republican, still, flawed as all that may make him, the punishment seems grossly disproportionate.

Like anyone else, all he wants to know is, Why?

And at the same time, not only theoretically in his old professorial and humanistic way but right here and now, in this all-too-pragmatic setting, lying alone and bare-assed under a thin, rough sheet on a hard pad in some back area of the emergency unit while his bladder continues to drain and spasm, screened off from who knows how many fellow sufferers only by the white curtains rustling from their aluminum-tube railings every time some unseen staff member walks by, he knows that that is an entirely, an overwhelmingly, a dismayingly stupid question that is as much out of proportion to his belief system as his pain is to his personality.

What he knows, even in his Demerol dream, is: Things happen.

And what he decides, here with the pain at last beginning to lift from him, with such a strange sense of lifting that he actually feels as if he is being raised right up off the gurney to hover in the thin and antiseptic air just inches above it, is that that is insufficient knowledge.

The world and its insufficiency, reality and its insufficiency, things and their insufficiencies: Are these the irresolvable dichotomies that a lifetime of devotion to the great world of the humanities has led him to?

He needs to talk to his wife.

*   *   *

Time was, Spivak was something of a fighter in his semipacifist fashion: He marched for the civil rights movement and against the war in Vietnam; he got out the vote, chauffeuring the poor and disabled to the polls; he picketed Kennedy at the time of the Cuban missile crisis and Nixon and Reagan any time they came to town; he harangued an ignorant populace about the virtues of fluoridated drinking water and rallied his local caucus in support of Clean Gene; he wrote letters to the editor—good, strong letters that were regularly published—and letters to his senators, even though the form letters they sent him in return rarely addressed the issues he'd raised; and he contributed regularly to the multitude of causes dear to his heart, causes that fought against apartheid and cancer, against the rape of the environment and the mistreatment of animals.

He liked to think he was making a difference.

Mrs. Spivak, as the telephone solicitors insisted on referring to his wife even though she'd kept her own name, Hartman, for professional reasons, stood beside him in all these things, adding her own body to the marching and picketing, her own letters, her own hard-earned dollars, which were, in fact, considerably more plentiful than his. And all the little Spivaks grew up to fight their own quiet battles, some identical to what they learned at home, others divergent, but always—and this was what Spivak took real pride in—with the belief that they were making a difference.

This, too, is what Spivak wants to talk to his wife about. Stabbed in the back, he feels—in the gut, actually—by his own encounter with pain, he wants to know if anything they've ever done has ever made any difference, if it's pushed back the great red tide of pain he feels the world's being drowned in so much as an inch from the fragile beaches of humanity. A millimeter. Pain is the true global warming, he wants her to understand, melting the polar icecaps and flooding our shores. The cities are going under, the low-lying islands and the broad coastal plains, the whole loving littoral of humankind. Has anything they've done helped at all to plug the great hole in the ozone layer of human decency that's responsible for this? Look, he wants to say to her, the waters are up to my own belly now. And we thought we'd moved safely inland, found our high ground, above all that.

When the nurse returns to check on him, Spivak asks if he can make a telephone call. Mumbling his question through the fog of Demerol, he experiences the momentary fear that he's been arrested and half expects the bearded, broad-shouldered nurse to tell him gruffly that he gets one call, and to make it quick. He wonders for a moment what he's been charged with.

But the nurse just says "Sure, man," wheels him out into the hallway, hands him the phone off the wall, tells him to dial nine for outside, and leaves him to make his call. Only he doesn't know the number. He does somehow remember the name of her hotel in San Francisco, and manages to pluck from the Demerol fog surrounding him the area code for the Bay Area so he can dial Information for the number. He knows he'll never remember it, though, and so he tries to explain to Directory Assistance how he's been rushed to the hospital without pen or coin and needs to talk to his wife and here's his US West charge card number, which is somehow stuck up on the front of his brain on a Post-it note forever, and much to his surprise, the guy puts him right through. And the hotel operator does the same, except that after a few rings what he gets is a recording asking him if he'd like to leave a voice-mail message for the guest.

That stops him. What's he going to say? "Hi, honey, I'm in the emergency room"?

The recording is just saying, "Your call is now being transferred to the hotel operator," when Spivak looks up to see Schlemowitz's wide, unshaven face leaning over him. He is dumbfounded by the sudden realization that Schlemowitz, with his scraggly gray hair and one wrinkled suit and scuffed Hush Puppies, Schlemowitz whose own father was calling him an incompetent ne'er-do-well when they were still in high school and who jokes that he's held more jobs in his life than Spivak has classes, Schlemowitz who never moved fast enough to break a sweat or catch a bus, has been, like the speed of light, the one great constant in his entire life.

When the hotel operator comes on, Spivak, fighting his way through the narco-haze that surrounds him, asks her, "Would you please ring that room again?" And this time, with tremendous effort, he lifts the phone toward Schlemowitz. "Liz's machine," he manages to say. "Tell her, call you when she gets in."

Schlemowitz doesn't miss a beat: "Hey, Bits," he says, leaning over into the phone Spivak is still hanging on to. "It's Schlemo. Gimme a jingle. Gotta talk. No big deal, but ASAP, huh?" Then he takes the phone from Spivak's weak grip and slings it back onto its wall hook without taking his gaze off Spivak's face. There are tears in the corners of Spivak's eyes.

"What the fuck," says Schlemowitz, a consoler of the bedridden and master of shortcuts who has long since discovered that the easiest way to the hospital parking lot from most of the patients' rooms, including the maternity ward, where he's just been drooling over his granddaughter, is via the back elevators and corridors leading out through Emergency.

"I couldn't pee," Spivak explains feebly. He doesn't have to explain the morning's tests, the prostate biopsies, that led to this; they've already discussed that unappetizing procedure at lunch. But he does manage to add, just as the big nurse returns to roll him back into his cubicle, "The whole world is going to hell."

"Aw, man," says the nurse, "things aren't that bad. We'll have you out of here in no time at all. The doctor'll be back to see you in a few minutes."

But Schlemowitz isn't buying. "Pay attention, young man," he says while the nurse is straightening out the gurney with geometric precision. "This man knows whereof he speaks. Life is not just a matter of figuring out what to do till the doctor comes."

The nurse—Leon Gurtzl, LPN, Spivak reads on his name tag when he straightens up—looks offended. Towering a full head over Schlemowitz, he demands, "Are you family?"

"Yeah," says Schlemowitz, not backing up an inch. "You bet I am,

Leon. Right now I'm all the family he's got. You got a problem with that?"

When the nurse turns and leaves, Spivak feels as if a smile is breaking out over his whole body, though he has no idea what actually might be showing on his face, which in fact is looking pretty slack and unchanged.

✳   ✳   ✳

Here's what will happen: The emergency room resident, Doctor Ling, will return within a few minutes to check Spivak and his catheter in overnight for observation, at which point Schlemowitz will head home in time to take Spivak's wife's phone call and reassure her that all is now under control and that he, Schlemo, will be back down at the hospital in the evening anyway—"Hey, those two beautiful girls, you know?"—so he'll gladly look in on her hubby, immediately after which Elizabeth Hartman, who hasn't even unpacked, will check quickly out of her hotel and grab a taxi back to the San Francisco airport to catch the night-owl flight home, where she will manage to arrive at the hospital just in time for her husband's urologist's morning rounds, at which time this famous surgeon, Dr. Blenheim, who has operated on the prostates and bladders of presidents and heads of state from around the globe, will quickly—"Take a deep breath"—slip out Spivak's catheter, scrawl a clumsy diagram on the back of a prescription pad to display what's happened, where the bleeding's come from, and how these clots, well, sometimes, they're rare, but it does happen, too bad this had to be one of those cases, but he'll sign the discharge papers and Spivak can go home just as soon as he's peed once—actually, "voided" is what the doctor says—on his own, which within fifteen minutes he does.

Just like that, it's all over.

Spivak, remember, is going to live a long time, outliving everyone else who has been a participant in this twenty-four-hours' worth of events, including that burly young nurse and gentle Doctor Ling and even, though not by much, his own dear Elizabeth, and if not at all times in absolutely perfect health, certainly not in misery, either.

But it's not over for Spivak.

For Spivak it will never be over. Oh, the pain will be over. He'll remember, forever after, for the rest of his long, long life, that he once had a physical pain that was more terrible than he ever knew pain could be. But he won't remember the pain itself, what it was truly like, how elemental it was, both fire and water, simultaneously scorching and drowning him. The organism, he'll acknowledge—as if every woman who's ever given birth hadn't learned this long ago— is quite amazing that way. If it weren't, who would ever step out into the world again? Through the withering away of direct recall of the pain, he understands, we are enabled to go on living, almost as if nothing had happened. On the other hand, he also knows, through the persistence of the memory that there once was such a pain, even if we blessedly can't recall the pain itself, we take those next steps out into the world knowing a little more about the nature of living, well aware that something has indeed happened.

As Spivak has already acknowledged, with intelligence and no satisfaction whatsoever, things happen. And once they happen, even if we go on living almost as if nothing had happened—and Spivak will go on peeing normally, or at least as normally as an aging man does, will return to his home and wife and friends and, yes, to the classroom also, for quite a few years yet, as well as to his lifetime of reading and scholarship, for he's a professor of humanities, remember, and these too are his loves—in fact, nothing will ever be quite the same again.

*　　　*　　　*

One day, on the eve of his retirement, Spivak will be sitting in his office with the warm, late afternoon sun of an early spring pouring its soothing light across his desk. He's moving slowly, for no reason except that he feels no reason to hurry, putting papers in his briefcase in preparation for heading over to the chapel to give the lecture he's been thinking about for some time now. It's his turn to contribute to a long-standing campus tradition of talks by faculty heading into retirement, a series known as "Last Lectures." Some of these, Spivak recalls, have been quite hilarious—a last chance to say anything, and some have done just that—but Spivak doesn't feel hilarious. Hilarity has never been his style, though he can't help smiling as he recalls his former colleague Cooperman's lecture, a "scholarly," according to Coop—"My last chance for respectability, after all"—survey of late-twentieth-century critical theory that used all the latest high-tech terminology in stunning phrases and beautifully constructed sentences that had the whole audience entranced with his linguistic pyrotechnics but made no sense whatsoever. Given Cooperman's reputation as the department comedian, Spivak, like many (but by no means all) of the faculty, presumed it was a great hoax, but they could never get him to admit to it. And Coop, of course, is dead now, felled so soon after retirement by a brain tumor that it seemed as if he'd just stepped off the podium, and that too makes no sense to Spivak whatsoever.

The knock on his door is, he expects, Elizabeth, who's promised to leave work early to attend his lecture, as in fact she's already done, though instead of coming to meet him at his office she's in her practical-minded way headed straight for the chapel to grab herself a front-row seat. Schlemowitz, having taken three buses and a short-cut across campus through the administration building's presidential suite of offices, will already be there, holding a seat for her and another for Gorman, who will be wandering gloomily around a dank suburban basement having totally forgotten about his friend's lecture.

When Spivak opens the door, he finds one of his freshman advisees standing there, a tall and startlingly thin, almost skeletal, young man, Harold something—Spivak can't recall his last name even though it was only last week they'd conferred over next year's schedule—who looks a total fright. Acne eruptions stand out bright red and purple against a searingly white face, dark curls are tangled, uncombed, even his ears seem to stick straight out from his head in alarm; his white oxford shirt is half tucked in, half hanging out, and he has no shoes on, but Spivak knows that on a day like this, the first real warmth of the season, most of the campus is going barefoot.

"Harold!"

"Professor Spivak!"

A terrible thing has happened in Harold's life, right here in the midst of the downward spiral at term's end into final papers and exams, and Spivak, ushering him into a deskside chair as the door swings closed on its own behind them, doesn't at first know what to say. He's like anyone else confronted with the sight of another's great pain: What can he say or do that will make a difference? He wishes his wife were there, with her practical and always helpful wisdom. But she is settling into her seat next to their friend Schlemowitz, who has had his one old suit pressed so he can dress up for the occasion, while the campus crowd sifts slowly into the chapel behind them from sleepy afternoon classrooms and overheated offices and languid Frisbee games on the quadrangle lawn.

Never mind, thinks Spivak, who has a pretty good idea from the clock above his doorway just ticking the hour what must be going on over there right now. Fragmentary recollections of Harold's last name flutter through his mind like scraps of paper drifting to the floor: Watson, Flotsam . . . ah, Pflugman. Never mind. He was going to tell this story this afternoon anyway, as a prelude to what he hoped to explain about the universality of certain experiences, about the things that happen to all of us, whatever they are, if only we live long enough, so he might as well begin with Harold.

Crimes against Humanity

ELAINE HAD ONLY ONE QUESTION, which, for a while, she went around asking everybody. Her question was: "How much bad can a person do in a lifetime?"

"Why do you always have to quantify it?" her father asked. "All your life you've gone around asking, 'How much?' 'How much longer do I have to study my arithmetic?' 'How much is that pair of shoes?' 'How much more nonsense do I have to put up with from Marvin before the divorce comes through?' Why don't you consider the question of quality for a change? Of what value is the study of arithmetic to me? How comfortable will a pair of patent-leather shoes feel? What can a jerk like Marvin really do? What's the difference between the bad a Hitler can do in one day and the bad I can do in my whole life?"

Her mother said, "Be honest with me, Elaine, like a real daughter. Tell me the truth. How much bad do you think I've really done to you?" Then, without waiting for an answer, she dropped the sweater she was embroidering onto the couch and got up and walked out of the room.

Elaine rolled her eyes at her father. "How much longer do I have to go on living in this madhouse?"

"Listen," her father said, "there's no reason for that sort of talk. You're a grown woman. Live where you want. But think about what I was saying." He went back to his newspaper.

"As soon as I get my raise," said Elaine.

He looked at her over the top of his paper. "How much?"

*   *   *

Elaine's boss said, "Just so much. Then she gets fired."

"Have I been that bad?" Elaine said.

"You're the one who asked," said Mrs. Delvecchio. "Now get your ass into the green monster and get those plants downtown to the Radisson lobby before we all get fired. They're tired of looking at dead palms. You can only do so many dead palms in a lifetime, and then you're out of business."

All the way downtown in the green Plant Lady truck, Elaine cried, thinking there was no end to the amount of bad a person could do in a lifetime. What's more, nobody cared. She wasn't having any trouble distinguishing between bad and bad, between evil bad and just-plain-bad bad. There was murder, mass and otherwise. Child molesting. Raping and pillaging. Wife beating. Swindling old people out of their life's savings. Cruelty to animals. Honest to God, she told herself, there has got to be a limit to how much of that sort of thing anybody can do.

But just ordinary bad: What were the limits to that?

To neglect, inattention, carelessness, thoughtlessness. Forgetfulness. Cruel slips of the tongue. Smugness. Pompous little meannesses. Smashed feelings. Sullen responses. Worse yet, faked pleasant responses and all the other petty hypocrisies. Have a nice fucking day yourself. She slammed on the brakes and banged up against the curb in front of the Radisson.

How much of that kind of bad could a person do in a lifetime? One person, hell, how about a family? A whole city? She wasn't at all sure she could live a lifetime as full of bad as one person could do. Just one. She climbed out of the truck, marched around to the back, and opened the door on the forest of ferns and palms all tumbled against one another inside the truck. The doorman came across the sidewalk to her. Look at this, she thought, maybe a person can also offer to do some good.

"Hey, lady, you can't park that truck there."

"The hell I can't," she said. She grabbed the biggest tree off the end of the truck in both arms and marched past him into the lobby. Just as she entered the hotel she spotted a small brass sign fastened to the wall beside the door: All Deliveries in Rear. Up yours, she thought, they probably want me to haul this stuff onto the loading dock, through the subbasement, up the service elevator, and then be invisible while I'm plunking it down in the lobby.

That was half the problem with figuring how much bad a person could do in a lifetime. Most of it was invisible. Even to the person doing it.

*   *   *

She met Marvin for lunch in the lobby restaurant in the midst of her own arrangements of potted plants. The yellowed palms and ferns were inside the truck, which was still sitting on the street in front of the hotel. For five dollars she had made her peace with the doorman. For another five dollars—Marvin's, this time—she was having a bowl of cream soup with asparagus tips floating in it. But aside from the price, it still felt like eating in the workroom at the back of the shop. The long frond of a huge Boston fern on a pedestal behind her kept tickling her neck. Too damned many plants in this place, she thought. Some days she thought there was too much of practically everything. She was never going to be able to finish this whole bowl of soup and the basket of French bread that accompanied it.

Marvin finished off another quarter of his club sandwich and resumed his litany of complaints against the world.

"Why won't your father talk to me?" he wanted to know.

"For one thing," Elaine said, "because you were screwing his little girl."

"Not that often."

"For another, you moved him into some stocks no decent broker would have peddled to his enemies. Then you found him some worse ones."

Marvin held up the last quarter of his sandwich in protest. "Everybody knows what the market's been like. Besides, he was the one who wanted to try some high-risk stuff."

"*My* father? And third, you screwed his daughter."

"I was only following my lawyer's advice. Does that make me a bad man? So we had some problems, you and me, me and him. Look, lots of people get hurt in the stock market, but your father's still a prosperous man. Lots of people get divorced and very few are happy with their settlements. But we're still having lunch, you and me. We're still talking. How bad can it be? It's not like we went berserk and shot people in the streets or kidnapped somebody's little kid and sent them an ear in the mail."

"Maybe you *should* get together with my father," Elaine said. She laid her spoon down. "I don't think I can eat any more of this soup."

"Thank God for your mother," said Marvin. "If it wasn't for her, I think I'd be in the loony bin. You want to order any dessert?"

"That's it, Marvin." Elaine stood up, swatting at the fern behind her so hard she set the pot wobbling on its pedestal. "You're so fucking pleased with yourself for not shooting up the lobby with a submachine gun that it doesn't bother you to sit there and inflict dessert on me."

She wanted to stalk out of the restaurant with her head in the air, to let him see how strongly she felt, but instead, forced to weave her way among tables and potted plants, she had to watch where she was going very carefully. It seemed to take forever to find her way out through the maze she'd helped create, and she thought what a terrible thing it must be for the waitresses. But she also knew that if she hadn't done the plants as ordered, they'd have canceled the contract with her boss, the Plant Lady, and hired someone else to do the job.

Out on the sidewalk the doorman touched his fingers to his cap in a friendly salute, said, "Here you are, Miss," and opened the door of the truck for her. But she wouldn't let herself smile back at him or even look at him as she climbed in. Buying solicitude was bad enough; she sure as hell wasn't about to pretend it was real.

✳   ✳   ✳

Her father thrust the paper at her that evening: "Would you like to see some bad?" Headlines about the drought in Africa. Photographs of bloated children, women with dead infants in their arms, bony cattle, cracked earth.

Elaine sat down in the chair opposite him. "I found an apartment this afternoon."

"Good for you, Elaine," he said. "That's very sensible. So you got your raise, did you?"

"I may have to quit my job," she said.

"What? Because you don't like the flower arrangements?"

She had told them at dinner about the problem for the waitresses, but she had seen immediately that neither of her parents had ever really thought about waitresses and she hadn't wanted to get into an argument about the rights of workers or the Occupational Safety and Health Act, so she had quickly changed the subject and at the same time felt totally disgusted with herself, lost her appetite, and ended up offending her mother anyway by just picking at her food.

Now she said, "Not flowers on tables, plants in the aisles."

"Plants, flowers, what you're talking about, Elaine, is basically a matter of taste. Aesthetics." He folded the newspaper up and laid it down in his lap. He and her mother had bought season tickets to the symphony orchestra for the first time this year, and on Thursday nights they went to an art-appreciation class at the nearby community college.

"I would be the last one to claim that this isn't an important thing," he continued, "but look at it in the long run, Elaine. Tastes change. What one age rejects, the next hangs in its museums. That's the way it always was and always will be, and what harm is done by it, I ask you? Look, your mother and I can't even agree on how to redecorate the bathroom, so I let her have her way and she puts up that crazy wallpaper with the cats and dogs on it, but what's the difference, I can still do what I have to do in there."

Elaine sat, very glum, just looking at him. She was thinking about suggesting to him that they put some little plaster leprechauns around the flower bed by the front door or a family of plastic deer in the shrubbery or a blue reflecting ball on top of a concrete stand in the middle of the yard, but she was half afraid he'd shrug his shoulders and agree or tell her to discuss it with her mother. Soon there could be pink flamingos among the petunias. Things like that had a way of just springing up around you, everywhere. It seemed like there was no limit to it.

Almost as if he had been reading her mind, her father rustled his paper impatiently, making her realize what a long pause there had been in the conversation, and said, "You know what your problem is, Elaine? You take all these things way too seriously. What are you now, nearly thirty? You've got to learn to ride with these things, to take it a little easy. People are going to do what they're going to do."

And that, Elaine was about to say, is exactly the problem, but just then her mother came through the archway from the dining room, paused at the sight of them sitting in the living room almost knee to knee, and said, "Well, what are you two having such a serious talk about?"

"Just art," said her father, at the same time that Elaine said, "Just life."

*   *   *

"You still want to know how much bad a person can do in one lifetime?" Mrs. Delvecchio demanded. "You leave me now and you'll find out, sister. In one act you'll do a whole lifetime's worth of bad. And God knows what I'll do to you. I've got jobs booked through the end of the month. You leave me and I'm dead. Where'm I gonna find someone who can do like you do with the plants? Huh?"

It was after hours, the business was closed, and they were sitting on cardboard boxes of plant food in the corner of the back room that Elaine thought of as her nursery, where she isolated the sick and dying plants that she brought back from the hotels and restaurants and offices they serviced—the wilted ferns and drooping palms and desiccated cacti—and tried to nurse them back to health. It did seem like a bad thing to even think of abandoning them. It also seemed like a bad thing to keep on taking fresh, healthy plants out into the world. Not that she was worried about the plants. She just didn't want to have to face another repeat of this afternoon: one more overworked and underpaid secretary wincing at having the responsibility of caring for an office full of expensive plants loaded on to the collection of

menial chores she already didn't have enough time to do. Elaine had
seen it too many times before. Sometimes when she was carrying the
plants in they glared at her as if it was her fault. Somehow Elaine was
beginning to think that maybe it was.

"A driver," said Mrs. Delvecchio. "Is that what you want? A delivery man? You know I can't afford any more help."

"I wish you wouldn't smoke in here, Mrs. Delvecchio," Elaine
said.

Mrs. Delvecchio stubbed her cigarette out on the concrete floor
under her heel. "Jesus, I wish I could afford a driver when I look at
what you're doing to my truck. It looks as if it's been through a war.
But you always get the plants there in perfect condition, like nobody
I ever had before. Maybe you're a born ambulance driver, Elaine.
Elaine, I need you."

Elaine, staring at the big pots of Swedish ivy she had been trimming back, thought that what *she* needed was a way out of this
dilemma without adding to the sum total of bad she had already
accumulated.

Mrs. Delvecchio tapped another cigarette out of her pack but
didn't light it. "What about *me*?" she said.

"All right, all right," said Elaine, standing up. "It's the weekend.
Let's think about it till Monday, OK?"

"Monday!" Mrs. Delvecchio dropped the cigarette, the pack, her
purse. "Monday we've got Kroger's grand opening!"

"Maybe we'll all be dead by then," said Elaine.

✳   ✳   ✳

Colleen thought that Elaine's problem was religion. They sat in
Colleen's kitchen on Saturday morning drinking coffee, while countless children, many of them Colleen and Harry's, wandered in and
out and Elaine thought of the pathetically empty kitchen in her new
apartment. Marvin, who had never cooked a meal in his life, unless
you call heating up something from a can and eating it right out of
the pot cooking, got everything: pots and pans, china and glassware,
silver, the Cuisinart, her own teapot that she had made in ceramics

class. She vowed that somehow she was going to get in there and re-possess her teapot.

"It's not how much bad a human being can do," Colleen was say-ing, "it's how much forgiveness God has to offer those who seek it." She was no fanatic, no missionary, just a good friend, but she had al-ready told Elaine it was too bad she wasn't Catholic. Then she could have gone to confession every week and been absolved of her sins and not had to live under this cumulative burden she was now struggling with.

"For what I'm talking about they'd laugh me out of the confes-sional," said Elaine. "'Forgive me, Father, for I embarrassed the kid who sweeps out the back of the shop when I found him looking at *Playboy* during his lunch break.' You've got to be kidding."

"Have another cookie," said Colleen. There were three or four left on the cookie sheets the children had been pillaging all morning as fast as Colleen could pull them out of the oven.

"God, Colleen, you're so good. Hot cookies. Do you think you and Harry could consider adopting me?"

"Good?" said Colleen. She dipped her cookie in her coffee—burned ones were all the children had left behind. "What about all the kids I've already got? I've got five kids, Elaine. You think it's a good thing to bring five kids into this world? Look around you." She obvi-ously didn't mean her sparkling bright kitchen, with the white walls and the peach curtains and the copper-bottomed pans hanging over the range. "I tell you, Elaine, sometimes at night after they're all in bed, I . . ." She paused. The cookie she'd been dipping broke off and fell into her coffee.

"I'm such a terrible friend," said Elaine. "I can't even keep all their names straight." She reached across the table and took Colleen's hand, the one with the soggy remains of the cookie still in it.

There was a child's face at the screen door—Elaine wasn't at all sure it was one of Colleen's—asking if there were more cookies. Both women shook their heads. The child's face disappeared and a cry of dismay went up from the backyard.

"It's OK," Colleen said. She was wiping her eyes with her other hand. "You're OK, too, Elaine. Just remember, honey, no one can do everything."

How much, though? Elaine wondered. How much not doing everything could she stand? Who could tell her that?

✳   ✳   ✳

She took advantage of her therapist's unprofessional interest in her to wrangle a Sunday morning meeting with him. When she had called, he offered to meet her Saturday night, since she had said it was so important, but she didn't want him staring at her over some candlelight dinner or holding her hand in a movie. She wanted to talk. As it was, they were having breakfast at Perkins Pancake House, just ahead of the after-the-church crowd. The Jewish Family Services offices were locked up tight on the weekends, she wasn't about to have him come over to her apartment, and, fortunately, he hadn't suggested that she come to wherever it was he lived.

"Look, Elaine," he was telling her, "I'm no professor of philosophy. You seem to want some sort of ethics expert. That's not me."

That much I can see for myself, Elaine thought, or we wouldn't even be here. She wished he could call her Miss Fuller, and she could still call him Dr. Hirschfield, the way it had been when she first began to see him, before he had explained to her that people with Ph.D.'s mostly didn't care to be called Doctor and then, almost without her knowing it, had eased her into calling him John.

"Besides," he continued, "I don't see the point in you and I approaching it on such an abstract level. We're not interested in *people*. What we're interested in here is you. The individual, not the abstraction, right?"

He wiped his chin with his napkin. She had never seen anybody slash their way through a stack of blueberry pancakes with such efficiency. Her own Belgian waffle with fresh strawberries and whipped cream still sat on her plate mostly intact.

She pierced a strawberry with her fork, held it up in front of her, letting the whipped cream drip off, and said, "I've thought it over,

John, and this is the best way for me to do it. Depersonalize it. It's not just my problem, you know. I never saw it that way. It's a problem for everybody. For you. If I can see how it works for everybody, then I think I can see how it works for me."

"My only problem, Elaine, is you." He stared at her, dark brown eyes boring into her, until she popped the strawberry into her mouth, lowered her eyes and her fork, and cut herself a chunk of waffle. But she couldn't bring herself to eat it.

"Please," she said, "there are things I have to know. A lot depends on this, maybe my whole life."

"I know," he said. "Me, too." His voice had become very low and serious. She saw that his hand was shaking when he set his coffee cup down. How much? she wanted to cry out, how much? how much? how much? But you didn't do things like that in a Perkins Pancake House, not even to your therapist. No, what you did was, you went very slowly, because even with all his experience of it, with all he saw and heard day in and day out of how much bad people could do in their lifetimes, looking at it like this, in the abstract, away from the focus on solving a specific problem for a specific individual client, was obviously new territory for him, too. So you didn't cry out, no matter how great the need to know. You whispered.

"How much?" she whispered, leaning across the table. "Tell me. How much?"

"I'm trying," he said. His voice sounded choked.

She waited.

"All right," he said, straightening his shoulders, although his voice remained husky. "I'm married. Three little boys."

"What? What are you talking about? What three little boys? Where?"

"It's OK. They're in Sunday School. Their mother, too. She teaches them. I mean she teaches one of them. Third grade. Look, ever since you've been coming to see me, Elaine, I've felt that, well, then you called me at home yesterday. Sunday mornings are perfect."

"I don't believe this," she said. "You're married. You wanted to meet me last night. You were going to leave your wife home alone on Saturday night to see me."

"It's OK," he said quickly. "I had a good excuse. She never would have known. Don't worry."

"Don't worry!" Well I know, she thought, glaring at him. I know what I wanted to know, I guess. You are a failure at the abstract, John Hirschfield, Ph.D., but you are sure as hell a lesson in the particular, and what's more, so am I, because I'm here too, aren't I? I'm here because I knew how to get you here. Add us up, however, and you do not get one plus one equals two, like you hoped for, Dr. Hirschfield, you get infinity, an infinity of misery, because there is no end to it. That's what the answer is: There is no end to it. There is no end to it, she said to herself again and again until the urge to scream died down.

Then she picked up her knife and fork, smiled across the table at him, and said, "Thank you very much for breakfast, Dr. Hirschfield. It's been a pleasure knowing you. Please don't wait for me. I'm going to sit here and finish my Belgian waffle."

It's the least I can do, she thought. She wondered if cooks in pancake houses were offended when food came back uneaten. Looking up to catch the eye of the waitress for more coffee, she noticed that quite a large crowd was now waiting near the front entrance, under the watchful gaze of the hostess. She knew that someone would be wanting her table soon, so she decided to forgo the coffee and dug into the strawberries and whipped cream and the waffle buried underneath them.

✳   ✳   ✳

On the way home she stopped at the 7-Eleven and bought a Sunday paper and a quart of skim milk, knocking over half a dozen other cartons in the cooler when she pulled hers out. She scowled at the clerk and said yes, of course she wanted a bag. As she got out of her car at the apartment complex, she let all the brightly colored advertising supplements slip out of the center of her paper and then stood there for a minute watching the wind scatter them across the parking lot. The young couple who lived down the hall from her were coming up the walk right behind her as she went into the building, but instead of holding the security door open for them, she let it swing shut behind her and heard its heavy latch click into place. The phone started ringing as she entered her apartment. She dropped her purse on a chair, threw the newspaper on the living-room floor, stuck the carton of milk in the refrigerator, stood in the kitchen for a moment with her hands on her hips, and finally answered it.

She listened to the burst of noise from the other end and then said, "No, Mother, I can't be bothered."

She listened for a little bit more and then, when there was a pause, she said, "Tell them I have a fatal disease," and hung up.

Cousins, cousins, what did she need with all these cousins? Besides, she was highly contagious. Look at Colleen. Look at her God-damn therapist with his wife and three kids. If they knew, they wouldn't want to get anywhere near her, especially with their children. Not that there weren't a few people around she wouldn't like to infect, like Marvin. But they were the ones who seemed to have a natural resistance to it. Even her father, not that she would ever want him to come down with something as bad as this. Not that there was any chance of it, though. He had his own way of immunizing himself. All her life, whatever had happened—whether he was losing a big customer or her mother was having a hysterectomy or she was getting divorced—she had always heard him say, "Things work out for the best."

When Marvin's lousy advice had cost him all that money in the stock market, all he said afterward was, "Look, now I'm out of the market for good. Never again, thank you. So who knows how much money that schmuck Marvin may be saving me in the long run. See how things always work out for the best?"

Still, she remembered, he wouldn't talk to Marvin now, so maybe the prognosis wasn't so good after all. On the other hand, he knew that her mother and Marvin had long telephone conversations regularly, almost daily, in fact, which didn't seem like a good thing to her but didn't seem to bother him at all. She had half a mind to call up Marvin herself, right now, and tell him to knock it off. What kind of creep would divorce her and hang on to her mother? Let him get the hell out of her life altogether. She wanted her mother and her teapot back. And besides, who knew how much resentment her father might be nursing under all that silence, especially when her mother spent an hour or more on the phone with Marvin in the evening after dinner. Maybe he was just afraid to object, the way he'd been afraid to criticize how she'd redecorated the upstairs bathroom. The bad you did yourself by bottling things up inside could be just as bad as the bad you did to others when you let things out, the bad you didn't do just as bad as the bad you did do. It was strictly a no-win situation. A real killer. The silent killer, she added, thinking of how they talked about these diseases during fund-raising campaigns. You either did or didn't do something, it wasn't necessary to say a word, and suddenly you were in its lethal grip. Then it was too late because it was everywhere. A product of neglect, more than anything else. Lack of education on the danger signs. No foundations. No telethons. No poster girls. She thought she'd make the perfect poster girl: dead, to show just what it could do to you.

John Hirschfield didn't think so, the first time she'd tried to discuss it with him, months ago. He said, "No one ever died of hurt feelings."

"I'm not talking about the hurtee," she said to him, "I'm talking about the hurter."

He could see, he told her, that she was a sensitive, thoughtful person. But depressed? Not really, not in any clinical sense of the term. Of course things bothered her, there were things that went on that bothered everybody, but look how well she functioned. Yes, there were even things that bothered him. Oh, she thought now, you sly little bastard, you. He had steered the interview toward her future. Look, he had suggested, there was always room in the helping professions for bright, caring people like herself. And to think that she had been flattered.

"You want to feel better," he said. "Naturally. There are a lot of routes to feeling better. These are things we can explore."

Damn, she said to herself now, kicking at the newspaper on the living room floor, will you listen to that crap! What she had said to him then was, "No, I don't want to feel better. I want to *do* less bad." And what I need to know, she remembered thinking back then, is how much bad a person can do in a lifetime, in order to get an idea of what *less* bad would be.

Well, she'd made a good start on it today. But at this rate, as she could clearly see, it was going to take her her whole lifetime to find out how much bad a person could do in a lifetime. Such a long time to find out such a dreary thing. It sounded exhausting. She sat down on the floor in the midst of the scattered sections of the Sunday paper. Maybe everybody *would* be dead by tomorrow, as she'd said to Mrs. Delvecchio. Then it wouldn't make any difference.

When she thought about everybody being dead, she didn't think about mass murder, the Holocaust, clouds of radiation sweeping across the land, bodies everywhere. She just thought about herself. It accomplished the same thing.

✳   ✳   ✳

Elaine nursed the green Plant Lady truck into the ramshackle garage behind the store, switched off the ignition, and listened as the engine chattered on for a while. She knew the deplorable condition of the green monster wasn't all her fault. She barely had time to change the oil now and then, between deliveries on a dull day, and it needed a lot more than that. It needed new plugs and points. It needed to have the carburetor cleaned out. Hell, it needed a complete tune-up. It needed new hoses to replace the ones she'd wrapped up with duct tape one evening. It needed a new muffler. Probably it needed an alignment, too. It was dying of neglect, none of it her fault. She just drove the thing and left memos on its problems for Mrs. Delvecchio. Well, the exterior, maybe. Even today she'd scraped the side against the concrete base of a giant lamppost in Kroger's parking lot, while trying to squeeze into a spot as close to the grocery store as she could get. But that didn't affect how it drove. What a dumb place for a lamppost. People just didn't think. Right now, she was too exhausted to think herself.

At least there weren't any plants to bring back today. By the time she'd closed and padlocked the flimsy wooden garage door, Mrs. Delvecchio had come through the store from the front, where she'd parked her own car, and opened the alley door for Elaine. They walked together without saying a word through the big storage room toward the office. Elaine didn't even have the energy to look at her little corner of convalescents or to listen to the scurry of tiny feet that fled at their approach. The storeroom had once been a warehouse for a company that sold salted peanuts and other snack foods to bars, and Elaine was still waging a slow war against the rodent population that remained from those days.

The office, at the front of the building, had been a shoe-repair shop and still smelled vaguely and pleasantly of leather and rubber, but Elaine was too tired even to take note of that now. The Plant Lady, Inc., didn't do any retail business and so didn't need a showroom; and the condition of the office showed it was not a place where customers were ever expected to appear. Mrs. Delvecchio called on the customers herself.

Elaine, clearing off a wooden chair so that she could sit down, felt like she did everything else. Bills, memos, torn envelopes, a clipboard, a box of green business cards, even a white sweat sock: She held them all in the air for a moment, then dumped them on an already loaded desk behind her and flopped into the chair, her back aching.

Mrs. Delvecchio was doing the same thing with the only other chair in the office. It was barely noon. They had both agreed on their way out of Kroger's that they were done for the day.

"Maybe we should have stopped for lunch on the way back to the shop," Mrs. Delvecchio said.

"I don't think I could lift my fork," said Elaine. "I never saw so many orange trees in my life. Who invented those pots? They must weigh a ton apiece."

"You made what," said Mrs. Delvecchio, slumping in her chair, "four trips? Five?"

"I couldn't have done it without you, Mrs. D. I'd still be dragging pots."

"*I* couldn't have done it without *you*, sister. Remember that."

Well, I just may remember that, thought Elaine, if I ever get around to asking for that raise. She knew this should be a good time to do it, in fact, but she was so tired she couldn't figure out how to phrase such a request. Amazing, she thought, the things the body does to the mind. To say nothing of what a potted orange tree does to the body. A hundred potted orange trees. Two hundred. In the heaviest pots ever invented. A criminal conspiracy against her back. And such orange trees! For a grocery store, and the oranges on them weren't even edible. Try and explain that one to your customers, Mr. Kroger. A crime against humanity, if you asked her.

"Well," said Mrs. Delvecchio, after a little time had passed in exhausted silence, "what can I say, Elaine?"

Elaine thought about it for a bit. Then she said, "A simple thank-you will do just fine."

"Thank you," said Mrs. Delvecchio. She seemed to slump down even farther into her chair. "But what about tomorrow?"

"Please," said Elaine. "No difficult questions. Not now."

They sat quietly a little longer, the only sound the rumble of trucks from the street.

Then Mrs. Delvecchio said, "The fact is, though maybe I shouldn't bring it up, I don't even understand about today."

"Neither do I," said Elaine. "Neither do I."

✳   ✳   ✳

That evening after she left work she stopped by her parents' house and let her mother talk her into staying for dinner. When she and her father sat down at the dining-room table, while her mother was still in the kitchen dishing things up, she said, "Well, Dad, you'll be glad to hear I've decided not to kill myself."

Her father smiled. "See how I told you things always work out for the best."

Her mother, just walking into the dining room with a bowl of green beans in one hand and a bowl of mashed potatoes in the other, let out a small, stifled scream.

"Never mind, missus," her father said. "You should know your daughter by now. It's just her way of expressing herself."

Don't push it, Elaine thought, reaching up to take the serving bowls from her mother: Unlike the other way, it's not an irrevocable decision. Her mother turned her head away and marched stiffly back into the kitchen. When she returned with the platter of roast beef and the gravy boat, she seemed to have regained her composure. Sitting down opposite Elaine, she made a brief, abortive gesture with her right hand, as if to reach across the table and touch her daughter's hair.

"Such a pretty girl," she said. "I don't see why you have to talk like that."

How the Dead Live

"Very good, white man," said the voice from above the knife, "very, very good."

It was a thin voice, sounding to Feidelman like there was a bit of a laugh in it, almost a laugh, something like a laugh, something, he might have said, not exactly amused maybe, but not not amused, either. But he couldn't be sure, no more than he could be sure of the look on the face, which he also couldn't make out, because he couldn't take his eyes off the knife, a short, broad blade, held down belly-low where reflections from the streetlight bounced off it as it angled this way and that in the gloved hand. He'd always heard that was the way knife fighters came at you, the blade held low, cutting edge up, the other forearm wrapped in a jacket, defensively. This guy's other arm, Feidelman could see, the right one, was bare and bent up and back. He was scratching the back of his head, under his wool cap, as if unaware of the weapon he held in his left hand.

And he was repeating himself. "Good. Good, man. Very, very good. Maybe the best I ever hear."

This time he added, "But that shit ain't gonna do shit for you, man, no shit."

Feidelman didn't really think it would, but he had meant what he said when he said it, even if it was the only thing he could think of to say at the time. It was true as well. There was no way out except talk, and the best talk he'd ever known was true talk. And what did he have to lose? The attacker, who had Feidelman backed all the way into a deep, unlit doorway, where the door behind him, which he could feel more than see, was boarded up, nailed shut, didn't seem interested in doing anything but taking that knife to him, in its own sweet time. He didn't want Feidelman's Rolex or his wallet.

"Time don't mean shit to me," he'd said when Feidelman started to unbuckle it from his wrist. "Not to you neither, man, not no more."

"Tell me about it," Feidelman said, wondering if he'd seen this guy somewhere before, or would be able to recognize him again. He didn't seem to mind being stared at. Even in the dark his skin had a pale, unhealthy look to it. The black T-shirt hung limp, too large, over a narrow chest, its sleeves flapping around thin, hairless arms. All his strength seemed to be in the grip he had on the knife that Feidelman's eyes kept dropping to. He looked down at it, too.

"My buddy," he said.

"My wallet's in my back pocket," Feidelman told him.

"I don't want that paper shit. I don't want that plastic shit, neither."

Feidelman shrugged. The guy didn't want what Feidelman had, that only left Feidelman himself, and the more that knife nicked his eye with its reflected gleam the more Feidelman understood that he and it wanted him for the same thing. That was when Feidelman looked back up from it for a moment and said to him, eye to eye, "Don't mess with me, buddy. Never mess with a dead man. Dead men don't have anything to lose."

"Very good, white man," he started saying then, though Feidelman wondered who this guy thought he was to be calling him "white man."

When he stopped telling him how good it was, Feidelman told him it wasn't a matter of good, it was a matter of true.

"I've got nothing to live for," Feidelman told him.

"What nothin'?" the guy said. "You got the big C or what?"

"No big C," Feidelman explained. "No AIDS, no emphysema, no MS. I'm pig-healthy. It's a lot simpler than that. I'm as good as a dead man because I don't care whether I live or die, it doesn't make any difference to me because I don't have anything to live for, but it may make a difference to you because you don't want to mess with someone who doesn't care whether he lives or dies. Trust me."

Feidelman knew it sounded like a bluff, but he meant it. He also knew the argument that said that if he didn't care whether he lived or died, he might just as well let this pale, skinny creep, who looked like he didn't have the strength to slice a ham, stick it to him and get it

over with. But he knew, too, that it didn't work like that. There was
the matter of pain.

Listen, he could have said to the guy, if it weren't for the pain . . .

And the guy himself, Feidelman could see, was . . . what? nervous?
not too bright? drugged up? But he got it. His eyes, moist and white
as the hot, humid sky Feidelman had kept his own eyes averted from
all summer long, kept climbing up and down the ladder, from his
knife to Feidelman's face and back again, like he was trying to figure
out if there was some connection between the two. Maybe he was just
trying to figure out which was the more dangerous weapon. Maybe
he was as scared of sharp things as Feidelman was.

Finally he said, "I done this before. It ain't no big deal. All pigs
squeal at the end."

"Not to a dead man you didn't," Feidelman shot back at him.

"You think that makes a difference to me? I don't give a shit
whether you're dead or alive, man. I'm as dead as any man alive."

"I believe it," Feidelman told him.

"Don't mess with no dead man," he said.

"I wouldn't think of it," Feidelman said, and then edged around
the guy and out onto the sidewalk, the man and the knife both rotat-
ing slowly with Feidelman's movement like they were on some sort of
spindle, like there was some cogwheel connecting the two of them to
him, so that when Feidelman turned they turned with him. But then
Feidelman broke the connection and walked away, on up the empty
street, and never looked back. He knew what they said about looking
back.

All along, even with that knife stabbing its shards of light into his
eye and him knowing exactly what was coming—and this is the part
Feidelman hated to admit—he was hoping the guy would ask him
what made him say he was a dead man, why he didn't think he had
anything to live for.

"If you're such a dead man," Feidelman wanted him to say, "who
kilt you?"

"Probably the same people who kilt you," Feidelman would have
said back to him. His attacker was the one who looked the corpse
part, after all: the long, dirty nails sticking out where the fingertips

had been hacked off of the fake leather gloves, the thin, sweaty blond hair strung down under the knit cap, upper arms all tendon and bone, the T-shirt looking like it was about to rot right off his rib cage. Enough to make a person look around for the grave robber's clay-clotted shovel tilted up against the plywood-covered store window. Feidelman was the one in the beige raw silk sport coat, the cream-colored linen trousers and tassel loafers, the blow-dried haircut and spicy cologne. Feidelman smelled like he'd just flown in from Sri Lanka. Nobody was going to mistake him for a dead man. It was one thing to be one, but another to let the world know you were one. You had to be careful who you let in on something like that. People didn't like to do business with zombies.

Meanwhile, Feidelman was already up the street and around the corner, beeping open the remote door locks on the Lexus as soon as he had it in sight, still parked right where he'd left it, right where he'd stepped out into the waiting knife, right across the street from the only all-night drugstore in town. A main street, too, but half the lights were out, the way they were all over this depressed town, which was why Feidelman hadn't seen the guy waiting for him, hadn't gotten a real look at him the whole time the guy was backing him around the corner and into that doorway with the tip of his blade. It was only when the dome light came on inside the car that Feidelman saw the rent down the front of his jacket. Raw silk, what can you do? It was a total loss. For just a moment Feidelman thought of getting out of the car and going back around the corner and showing the guy what he'd done.

"Just because I'm a dead man," he'd tell him, "you think I don't care about anything? Look at this!"

Then Feidelman thought about getting back out of the car and go-ing across the street to the drugstore, like he'd originally come here to do. Dead men need to brush their teeth, too. Dead men like to keep a supply of condoms handy. Dead men need their pain killers. But he'd lost his zest for midnight shopping trips just now, though usually they were the only kind he could stand.

*   *   *

Even though he was out flitting around alone in good clothes and an expensive black car in the middle of the night, Feidelman was no vampire. He believed as much as any rational human being that the dead stayed dead, and he would never have thought of biting anyone, except perhaps in self-defense. And much as he hated to see the sun come up every morning, shaking the sleep out of its shaggy blond locks in the unbreathable muck that passed for air above his polluted town, he wasn't afraid of it, he wasn't tempted to pull the covers over his head like a coffin lid. He just didn't sleep anymore, and he didn't appreciate its daily reminder that he'd spent another miserable night trying to.

But Feidelman went home to make the effort, anyway, being still as much a creature of habit as when he was alive. He shucked his ripped jacket the minute he stepped through the back door, not even bothering to turn on a light what with the hazy last-quarter moon angling in from the backyard, and stood there in the kitchen awhile giving some thought to what to do with it. Finally he opened the door to the basement and tossed it down toward a box he keep on the landing for things to take to the Goodwill. It sailed down the shadowy staircase, landed with a swoosh on top of the pile already filling the box, and folded itself neatly over as if that was where it had been meant to be all along. As if it had known from the moment Feidelman first tried it on that it, too, was just a dead thing, and all it was waiting for was a chance to fold itself up in its grave, along with the shirts and pants and suits and shoes that Feidelman shoveled in there week after week. But, he reminded himself, sport coats don't know anything. Here he was, after all, about to give it new life. The more Feidelman looked at things from this perspective, from beyond the grave, the more he could see that no one, nothing, knew anything.

At the sink Feidelman turned on the tap and waited till the water ran cold, then poured himself a tall glass, drank it down, then another, then refilled the glass and set it on the counter while he stood in the dark kitchen considering how he might someday meet that sport coat in its new life, walking a downtown sidewalk toward him, the sewn-up rip on its front panel a visible scar, like a face slashed down one side from hairline to jawline and badly stitched up by some young intern in the ER. Was he doing the right thing, Feidelman wondered, giving too much thought to the fate of things? But it was things we lived with, mostly, wasn't it, so didn't it matter what we did with them, how we took care of them, what fates we assigned them to? Didn't the way we took care of things say something about who we ourselves were?

"If you're gonna have nice things," his father had told him regularly, back when the old man had finally gotten both the cash and the confidence to buy the Caddy he'd always wanted and then spent every weekend washing and waxing it, "you gotta take good care of them."

So Feidelman took another sip of water, then kicked off his loafers, picked them up in one hand, walked back to the top of the basement steps, and tossed them down. They landed softly on top of the coat. No socks. Feidelman unbuttoned his Egyptian cotton shirt, slipped out of it, and sent it whispering after. Took out his wallet and keys, tossed them on the counter, then unbuckled his pants, stepped out of them as they dropped around his ankles, and drop-kicked them down the stairs. Pulled off his Jockey briefs, hesitated, then turned and stuffed them into the flip-top wastebasket that stood by one end of the counter. Stood alone in his own dark kitchen, running his fingers through his thick hair, his skin as pale as the white cabinets and countertops in the thin blade of moonlight slicing in from over the roof of the garage, as naked as . . . he didn't know what to say. As naked as the day he was born? as Adam? as a corpse laid out for embalming?

Feidelman went through a lot of clothes like that and kept ending up in the same undefinable place.

*   *   *

When Feidelman was a young boy, his father, a salesman of many things—wholesale automotive supplies one year, office furniture the next, bass boats, Feidelman thought he recalled, at this particular time—told him what a wonderful head of hair he had. Feidelman remembered the occasion in great detail: the glossy catalogs spread out

on the chrome-edged Formica kitchen table, his mother at the sink
cleaning up after dinner, himself kneeling on the padded, red-plastic-
covered seat of one of the chrome kitchen chairs, his father seated opposite, leaning forward over the table, head bent down over the
catalogs, shimmering photographs of green boats with fishermen
poised in raised chairs, their lines whipping out of blue water with sil-
very fish arcing at their tips. Then Feidelman's father raised his head
and looked across at him. Or, no, maybe that was the yard and garden
year, the year of catalogs filled with gleaming green photos of brightly
umbrellaed tables, plastic-webbed chaise lounges, birdbaths, fauns
and elves and naked-little-boy statues. Anyway, Feidelman remembered his mother's head outlined against the darkened window over
the sink, gusts of snow lashing silently against it.

Then his father lifted his head and said, "That's a wonderful head
of hair you got there, kid."

It was, in fact, identical to his father's: thick and dark and wavy.
Feidelman remembered lifting his then-pudgy hand off the Formica
and running it through his hair with something like amazement, as if
he'd only just then discovered that he had hair.

"You're a lucky kid, kid," his father continued. "You coulda got her
hair instead."

He didn't turn to look or even gesture at Feidelman's mother, behind him, but Feidelman did. He couldn't tell if she was looking out
at the snow or down at the sink full of dirty dishes, but he could see
the bronze highlights that the overhead light struck in her brown hair
and felt strangely warmed by that.

"What you got," his father told him, "is good as gold. Better. You
got salesman's hair."

Feidelman—what could he have been then, six, seven years old?—
looked blankly across the table at his father.

"You ever see a bald salesman?" his father asked, staring right at
him.

Feidelman didn't know what to say. The only salesman he was
aware of ever having seen was this thick-haired father, who after a
brief pause answered for him: "You never seen a bald salesman."

The boy slowly nodded.

respectfully backed off and then stared at him with barely concealed amazement, as if they were seeing a ghost, while the VPs and division managers spoke to him in the hushed tones usually reserved for the funeral parlor.

Only Feidelman himself remained unchanged. Same thick salt-and-pepper hair, same trim sturdy figure, same good health and solitary life. He still lived in the same house he'd raised his son in, a large but unpretentious twenties-era, Tudor style in an older urban neighborhood, once predominantly Jewish, now a melting-pot mix of races. Not that he hadn't redecorated, repainted, in all these years of prosperity, but who could tell? Outside, inside, walls, carpeting, furniture—it was always the same mix of beiges and browns. Always a big black car in the two-car detached garage. The same cleaning service, every Wednesday; the same window washers; the same lawn and garden people. The same red and yellow tulips lining the front walk every spring, the same lush bed of pink impatiens in the shade beneath the big oak tree, and the same chrysanthemums bordering the hedges in front of the house every fall. But he didn't look at them much; he knew what it meant when you found yourself surrounded by flowers.

There had been, occasionally, women in Feidelman's life, but they never seemed to stick around very long. Not that anything overt ever erupted to cause them to depart; they just seemed to gradually fade away, and often Feidelman was surprised to discover that this Jean or that Nancy was no longer around. It was as if they had only been there on brief visits of consolation and had found him so barely present that they hadn't even bothered to say good-bye when they left.

Only once had anything resembling a confrontation ever brought one of his affairs to an end. He had been going out with a bright, beautiful anthropology professor from the university, a woman exactly his own age and height, sociable, charming, and, he thought, happy in their six-month-long relationship, until one winter evening, as they returned to his house after dining out, she turned on him. She had tossed her long purple coat across the back of the couch and was standing dead center in the living room, while he was barely inside the house yet, switching on lights, still wearing his tan London Fog.

"Look at you!" she cried out, turning around and around in circles and pointing at everything around her—at the walls, the couch and loveseat and chairs, at the coffee table, at the carpets, even at him—"You're brown! Everything is brown! This is a brown world!"

Feidelman, unsure of what she was getting at, took off his coat, ready to hang it and hers in the hall closet, but then suddenly, uncomfortably, he noticed that he was wearing a dark brown suit, a favorite of his. Brown-and-white striped tie. Brown shoes, of course.

"It's like living in the earth," she said.

"Underground," she added.

She stopped spinning and stared, pointing, right at him: "It makes me feel like I'm being buried alive."

Feidelman, caught totally off guard—hadn't they just had a lovely meal together, talked, laughed, drunk a fine chardonnay?—hadn't the slightest idea how to respond to such an attack and so simply stood there in the doorway of his living room, tan coat draped over his arm, while she snatched her purple one off the couch, threw it over her shoulders, and brushed quickly by him as she stalked out, failing to close the door behind her. Feidelman watched through the half-open doorway as she climbed into her green Saab and sped away in a swirl of snow, and that was the last he ever saw of her.

But that was whom he was thinking of when he woke up, five years later, the morning after the knife attack, sweating under his enormous goose-down comforter, bronze, the same color as the nightstand lamp shades, the drapes, the silk pajamas hanging over the chair in the corner. He was still naked; the last glass of water he'd poured himself sat untouched on the nightstand. He'd slept the sleep of the innocent or the dead, not waking once in the night. This never happened; he was always up at odd hours, most of the night it seemed, peeing, guzzling water, wandering the unlit house, watching the sun come up. He hadn't even dreamed, unless this recall of that final evening with—what was her name? Eileen!—that final evening with Eileen, was some sort of half-waking dream. And lying there—it was a Thursday, 6 A.M., he could hear the birds going nuts outside his bedroom window, as if the big oak tree out there were some small-town coffee shop where everyone gathered for breakfast and gossip—he still couldn't figure out how he should have responded to her charge. What was the matter with brown? If brown was such a terrible thing, would they sell brown suits, brown carpeting, brown paint? Would people panel their offices with wood? Would they pack your groceries in brown paper bags? Would they spend millions advertising khaki pants?

But of course she was an anthropologist, and anthropologists studied how people lived, didn't they, and came to conclusions about the nature of their lives, how they worshiped their gods and raised their children and buried their dead. But weren't anthropologists supposed to be nonjudgmental? Even when it came to things like eating insects or dogs or other people? Wasn't it their job to understand, not to condemn? And why, he wanted to know, did this still bother him, five years after the fact? What did she mean, "buried alive"? What about all those lively brown creatures out there in the woods: squirrels and bears and beavers and moose? Maybe what he should do—it was a Thursday, after all—was go into the office this morning and arrange to have her hired as a consultant, Eileen Elliott, Ph.D., to do a study of their corporate culture. She wouldn't have to know he was behind it. No, never mind, she knew perfectly well it was his company, she'd never forget a thing like that. But so what, she had the credentials, why shouldn't he recommend her? She could be a real service to the company, and he could have plenty of opportunity to run into her there. They could talk, nothing romantic this time, just, maybe, a kind of throwaway line at coffee some midmorning: "What was that business about brown all about?"

And that was the moment, getting slowly out from under his fat comforter, sitting on the edge of the king-sized bed, his toes practically out of sight in the thick wool carpet—what had they called this color, anyway? mocha?—when he suddenly realized that that was the occasion, still standing there on the gleaming parquet floor of the entrance hall, still peering out the half-open door as her taillights winked away around the corner at the end of his street, his tan London Fog still draped over his arm, when it first began to dawn on him that he was a dead man.

So what could he have said to her?

What can a dead man ever say?

Except what he had said last night: "Never mess with a dead man. Dead men don't have anything to lose."

She, Eileen, had messed with him, of course, with his head at least, but that was different. He hadn't yet understood that he was a dead man. He didn't know yet that he didn't have anything to lose. These were things he had only just begun to learn. Maybe he owed her for that.

*   *   *

But what does a dead man—even a dead man who had recently been informed that time didn't mean shit to him—do with his time, especially on a Thursday, a workday, and when he's up with the sun? Isn't night the time for the dead to walk? Feidelman, dressing, remembered last night: how soft the air had felt when he stepped out of his car across the street from the drugstore; the lingering smell of asphalt that had been warmed by the sun all day; the spark of light off the knife blade, like a newborn star flaring up in a dark corner of the sky. Even a sudden, accompanying, metallic, almost gritty, taste in his mouth, not fear, exactly, just—what?—the unfamiliar, the unexpected. And then that ragged whisper driving him around the corner into a deeper darkness yet: "Move it, man."

Feidelman moved it. He let the lightweight wool slacks he'd been pulling on—a rust color he suddenly realized he'd never liked—drop to the floor, rummaged around in the back of his closet till he found a pair of blue jeans, noticed they still had streaks of dried roofing tar on them but put them on anyway, found a clean white polo shirt in his dresser, wasn't there that double-breasted blue blazer in here somewhere? Yeah, still in the plastic dry cleaner's bag. Shoes, shoes. OK, the black loafers would have to do. For a dead man, he was surprisingly animated. And feeling rested, too, after that first straight-through night's sleep in who knew how long. Where did that come from?

Maybe, it occurred to him, from finally acknowledging it last night, saying it right out, even to a stranger, or maybe especially to a stranger, announcing in public, more or less, that he was a dead man. Once you faced up to something like that, you could rest easy.

But at the moment, good night's sleep and all, he wasn't easy, he was ready, dressed and shod, combed and brushed, primed to be up and out, without either a cup of coffee or a sense of destination, impelled by a question he knew he had to get a move on answering now: How does a dead man live?

Not all that badly, he had to admit, pulling the door of the Lexus shut with a heavy, gold-trimmed *thunk*. It must have rained during the night; the car, which he'd uncharacteristically left out in the driveway, glistened in the morning sun with the last drops still clinging to its hood. The whole neighborhood, for that matter, looked freshly polished: the neatly mowed and edged lawns, the trimmed hedges, the flower beds lining the front walks with blue and yellow, the new maroon shingles on the Capellis' house across the street and the glossy green trim around the Guptas' clean white stucco two houses down. His own house as well: the dark, exposed beams, the two redbrick chimneys, windows giving back the brilliance of the early sun. A lot of people who were actually alive weren't doing anywhere near as well as he was. Backing out of the driveway into the empty street, he wondered if that was something he should feel guilty about. Every year he contributed heavily to organizations devoted to improving the lives of the living, to keeping them alive, to giving them things to value in their lives, and he made sure the company kept up its annual contributions, too; his will included major bequests to most of these same causes. But who, including himself, was doing anything for his own life?

Pausing as he backed into the middle of the street—Goldberg, the judge, came up behind him in his silver Jag, tapped his horn, and whipped on around, waving—a saying Feidelman had heard ages ago—how long? where? he couldn't recall, in family conversation maybe when he was a kid? in a book?—and had never understood suddenly popped into his head: Let the dead bury the dead.

He shifted into drive, pondering this new responsibility.

*   *   *

This time, not even knowing it was where he'd been headed, he parked in the lot alongside the drugstore. He did his shopping efficiently, the only customer in the entire store this early so far as he could see, dropping all the items he'd started out for last night into the little red basket he'd picked up as he entered, including a second giant-sized bottle of generic ibuprofen, just in case. He paid with his bank card, carried his plastic bag of mostly bathroom-cabinet-replenishment items out to the car, just like any ordinary citizen habituated to keeping the larder well stocked, and dropped it into the trunk. He shucked his blue blazer, tossed that in the trunk too, and slammed the lid. Then he crossed the street in the middle of the block, waving at the passing pickup that honked at him in annoyance, walked past the spot where he'd parked last night, and turned the corner.

I am, he told himself very deliberately, almost as if he were spelling out the words one by one, in large block letters, I am revisiting the scene of the crime.

If the street he'd just turned off hummed like the neon lights inside the drugstore with morning activity—the flow of early traffic, cars pulling in and out of the SuperAmerica a block back and the string of fast-food restaurants stretching out along the next quarter mile or so, the city crew arriving to patch potholes in front of McDonald's, the red bus wheezing away from its corner stop—this little side street he'd entered, still deep in early morning shadows—it wasn't eight o'clock yet—was like a graveyard. The boarded-up storefront he'd mostly recognized by feel when he'd been backed into its doorway last night was, he now saw, only one of many. The whole block looked like there'd been a monster sale on plywood. Above street level, there was hardly a window intact; the window frames themselves were rusted or rotting, the brickwork blackened. At the far corner there was an abandoned gas station; pumps gone, windows smashed out, it looked, from where he stood, as if it had burned. And on the corner across the next street from it, spotlighted by the broad beam of sunlight slashing down from the cross street, there was just a concrete slab, with twisted hunks of metal jutting up from it. Feidelman couldn't imagine what might have once been there. There was no traffic, and he could see why: Another half block away the street ended in a mass of weeds, windblown newspapers, plastic bags, other junk Feidelman couldn't make out, and three or four sets of railroad tracks, rusted, he was sure, unused in who knew how many years.

In the doorway where he stood—last night's doorway—Feidelman couldn't even hear the traffic back on the main street. It was like being in another world, the world of the dead, where no one moved, where the light was dim and no sounds penetrated—not from the outside, anyway; he could hear the crunch of broken glass underfoot as he shuffled around in the doorway. A world where nothing happened. Well, yes, things decayed, crumbled, disintegrated, even disappeared, like whatever had once sat on that cracked slab down at the corner, like the trains that had once rumbled by on those overgrown tracks. But (well, yes, he had to admit those weeds down there sprouting greenly every spring, the cockroaches and rodents and bats and pigeons raising their young in the abandoned rooms above him, but that was another matter altogether, wasn't it? Wasn't it?) nothing new.

Unless you count someone holding a knife to your gut. Feidelman could still see him, those bony, tendon-strung arms. He could even smell him, that musty wool cap and sweat and . . . something else, moldy, earthy, as if the guy spent his days sleeping in some deep forest, among mushrooms and rotting leaves. And he could hear: the two of them, their ghostly voices whispering out of the night air still lingering in this side street the sun hadn't yet found its way into: "Never mess with a dead man"; "I'm as dead as any man alive." Remembering, now, how he'd walked, well, sidled maybe, away, slipping out from under what he'd found himself in—almost, if you wanted to put it like this, tiptoeing off, as probably the other guy had also done a minute or two after—he added, to that absent attacker whom he felt sure would agree with him, to that Eileen whom he probably didn't need another consultation with after all, to the empty street and the crowd just now pushing through the front doors of his corporate headquarters, to his long-gone parents, ex-wife, ex-in-laws, to his busy kid with his own life and everyone else who hadn't even bothered to stay around for the wake, to, finally, most of all, himself: "You never know what a dead man might do."

Scholars and Lovers

TO WATCH A HUMAN BEING bursting the mind's sleep before your very eyes, to watch the life and excitement of the intellect suddenly blossoming, is a sexually stimulating thing. And when the human being in whom you are watching these not wholly unexpected but still surprising developments is neither child nor adolescent nor one of the flocks of late adolescents who populate our universities, but someone rather closer to your own age, then the experience is a little like falling in love. My male colleagues may lust after the young women who so willingly spread open their minds before them, but I, I am a sucker for what we call here the Adult Scholar: for the housewife who's come back to complete her own education now that her children have gone off to college, for the out-of-work clerk or mechanic determined to use the empty time to develop the mind or the weary businessman trying to rediscover his, for the over-the-hill and past-their-prime crowd who have suddenly, somehow come to the realization that life has got to be more than *this*, and who come here to find what more it can be. These are my people, the objects of my desire. For them I sing. For them I ache, the way my colleagues ache for their sad illusions of fading nymphets. For them my heart leaps. For Martin Weinstein, for example. Not literally, of course.

For one thing he's a man and I am a devoted, married, and monogamous heterosexual. For another—another couple—he is one of the uglier human beings I have ever known, and one of the strangest. Never, when he comes to class, does he take off his hat, coat, or gloves. Yes, I know that those are mere physical details and that I have said it was the minds of these adult scholars that turned me on, but I have also confessed, remember, that there is something sexually stimulating about it. Other students, of course, also keep their coats on in class; they are too lazy to remove them, or they know they have to go out in the cold to a class in a different building as soon as the one they have with me is over, or perhaps they didn't have time to put on a shirt in the morning, I wouldn't know. Sometimes they also leave on their heads a baseball cap or a homburg they got from the Goodwill, which I think may be a little more in the way of a hint at confrontation, though wholly futile, for I am long past such petty challenges as that. But none of them is consistent the way Weinstein is. Eventually the heat gets to them, if nothing else does, either the early spring sun or this overheated room itself, and off comes the coat, the hat, often the sweater as well. But not Weinstein. And who else wears gloves indoors? That, I had to admit, I really wondered about. Gloves, all the time: in class, in the halls, in my office. Why? What was it? Did he have some horribly disfiguring disease?

Once, when he came to my office to confer with me about a paper on which he was puzzled to have received a less than perfect grade, I took advantage of the privacy of the visit to ask him about the gloves, though I didn't think it proper to admit that I was provoked into this intrusion only by my own curiosity, my own secret lust.

"Some of the other students were wondering, Mr. Weinstein," I said, "why it is that you never remove your gloves in class."

He looked down at them, where they were holding his essay in his lap, as if he himself didn't consider them of any particular interest, and then he said, "Well, you see, it's the touch. It is too painful."

"Oh," I said.

Of course I didn't see; I didn't feel that had cleared up anything at all. Maybe there was some kind of disease there after all, the awful aftermath of some terrible occupational hazard he'd worked with all his life, not even knowing it was eating away at his body, like the mercury used in felt making that once drove hatters mad, like coal dust and asbestos fibers and formaldehyde fumes. Like Agent Orange. They owe you for this, Weinstein, I wanted to tell him — see how protective I was! I told you it was like love — is this what you spent a lifetime of labor for, to live out your last decades in pain? But I didn't say anything more; as I have long since learned in my marriage, it is also the duty of love to be a respecter of boundaries.

The next time I was over in Old Main I happened to run into Rasmussen, who's the administrator for a number of special programs, including the Adult Scholars, so I took advantage of the opportunity, while we were standing in the hall exchanging pleasantries, to mention that I had Weinstein in my humanities class.

"Ah ha," he chuckled, "old hat-and-gloves."

"Listen, Gary," I said, "you don't happen to know what he did for a living, do you?"

He thought about it for a moment, couldn't recall that he did, then took me around the corner to his office, scooted behind his secretary's empty desk and rummaged around in a file cabinet for a few minutes, and finally came up with a folder.

"I'm not sure about this, George," he said, holding the folder closed. "There are some pretty strict privacy laws these days. Maybe you'd better just—"

"Gary! His job. What the man spent his life doing. I'm not asking you about his sexual preferences. Well, forget it," I said.

"All right, all right," he said. He cracked the folder open and peered into it. "Realtor. That's all it says. I wouldn't know if that's what he spent his whole life doing, but that's what he's put under Occupation. Why?"

I wondered myself. Was the real estate business so hard on the hands? I would never have thought it a profession subject to many occupational hazards, but I suppose that from the outside you never can tell. Maybe it was having to be out showing properties in all kinds of terrible weather or taking clients through unfinished buildings where you were always picking up splinters from studs or contracting metal poisoning from stepping on stray nails. Maybe he came to real estate from one of the building trades, I thought, after a lifetime of labor there had destroyed his hands, made it impossible for him to continue: cement work, maybe, that was a killer, or sheet-rocking, that was the very worst. I had done it once myself, when we refinished an attic room for one of our sons, and I knew how the lime in the plaster dried out your skin, left your hands hard and cracked and, if you kept at it long enough, even bleeding. Weinstein, I thought, you poor bastard. My heart went out to him even more than before, and I could have wept when he raised his gloved hand in class and then, when I nodded in his direction, stood up straight beside his desk.

Yes, stood! Who stands to speak in a college classroom? No one, of course. Only Weinstein. He stands beside his desk with his arms straight down at his sides the way I have not seen anyone do since I was made to do it myself in grade school.

"Professor Zupperman," he begins slowly, messing up my name once again because he always says a *z* for an initial *s*, but I don't care because he is about to ask a question that will go well above the heads of most of the rest of the students, and I don't care about that, either, because he is Martin Weinstein and he is one of mine. My heart leaps when he climbs slowly out of his desk in my classroom and rises bulkily to his feet, fur hat, black woolen coat, leather gloves, and all, and I will go to the wall for him.

"Professor Zupperman," he continues, unimpeded by my adoration, "conzerning existentialism . . ."

✳   ✳   ✳

On a Thursday afternoon in March, just prior to the week of spring break, Weinstein stands in my doorway at the beginning of my office hours and apologizes for disturbing me.

"Come in, come in," I tell him, assuring him that visits such as his are precisely what office hours are for. "Sit down."

I am sure that he has come to discuss the paper assignment I gave the class on Monday that is due immediately after break. Short deadline, but also a short paper, which is the way I prefer to work them. Give them a month of lead time and half the class will still wait till the night before it's due to get to work on it. Tough topic this time, though: an existential theme in a work by a modern artist. Take your pick: painter, poet, novelist, dramatist, someone we've already discussed in class (for the weaker students; you also have to make room for them), or another work by one of those we've studied, or a different artist altogether, someone you've always been itching to get at. Three-page limit: that gets them right to it (and challenges the bright ones, who have to make the most of that tight space for all their complex imaginings).

What, still belaboring existentialism, after all these weeks? Well, not exactly. It has its place in the course, which was not when Weinstein disrupted the syllabus by raising his gloved hand in class to bring it up several weeks ahead of its proper time. Well, that happens occasionally: A knowledgeable student jumps the gun, brings up a topic that the rest of the class just isn't ready for—sometimes even a topic that has nothing whatsoever to do with the course, say U.S. policy in Latin America—and you hate to discourage such enthusiasm, but after all, you've got the whole course and the whole class to think of, to say nothing of your own carefully thought-out plans: the introductory lecture on nineteenth-century backgrounds; the beginnings of modernism; selected readings in Sartre and Camus; brief exemplary looks at this painter, that poet; maybe the guest lecturer from the philosophy department.

Try and explain that to Weinstein. In front of the class, yet.

Still standing, his gloved hands at his sides, he said, "I do not zee how you can discuss Mr. Eliot's memorable poem without taking into account existentialism."

It was, obviously, not a question. It accomplished nothing to explain that as a class we were not yet prepared to take the existentialist approach. Mr. Weinstein simply repeated his statement, prefacing it with a "But" this time. Mr. Weinstein, I could zee, was already taking the existentialist approach. And I? I was getting the feeling that we were like a pair of lovers having our first quarrel, testing our relationship in public. It often happens that way, as I have seen at many an academic party. It is a situation in which there are no winners.

"Well," I finally said, "I guess we will just have to manage."

Mr. Weinstein sat at last, and the hour crept sullenly to its close, the wasteland of its final fifteen minutes unredeemed by so much as a single drop of conciliatory rain.

But now we are in a virtual monsoon of existentialism, in which some are paddling their way to new discoveries and others are, well, simply adrift. Mr. Weinstein has had his day in class, several of them, in fact. We have revisited Mr. Eliot's memorable poem from our newly informed existentialist perspective. Also Mr. Mann, Mr. Kafka, and Mr. Hemingway, among others. Mr. Weinstein, seated across from me in my office in, of course, his hat and coat and gloves, though as we can see through my window it is almost threatening to become a decent spring afternoon—almost—undoubtedly has an intriguing existentialist thesis already defined, which he wants to test out on me before setting pen to paper. Go ahead, my dear Mr. Weinstein, speak.

"Professor Zupperman," he says slowly, "if I may speak frankly . . ."

Speak, Weinstein, speak, have we not made up our petty differences long since?

". . . it being the halfway point in our zemester . . ."

Well, not till tomorrow, actually, Weinstein, but why should people like us quibble?

". . . my evaluation is that you stink."

✳   ✳   ✳

Was I twiddling a ballpoint pen in my hands, as I have tended to do in meetings of all sorts ever since I gave up smoking, when Weinstein dropped his bomb in my lap? Was I thinking only about the best when, as always—I *am* a professor of humanities, after all—I should have been preparing for the worst? Did the one eye I was keeping on the blue skies outside my window prevent me from seeing the dark clouds gathering within? Was I somehow deluding myself into imagining that with people like us, which is to say, adults who have come together for a common purpose, nothing could possibly go wrong? Have I, in fact, learned nothing from all the years I have spent in education?

These and other rhetorical questions that no doubt flashed through my crumbling mind at that moment were blown to the far corners of academe by the megatonnage of Weinstein's blast. Let me admit at once that what I felt was not in the least professional. Did I say, Well, Mr. Weinstein, what is it precisely that leads you to feel there are some deficiencies in my teaching? Did I say, It appears, Mr. Weinstein, that we have some pedagogical differences? Did I say, Could you possibly

be a bit more specific, Mr. Weinstein? Did I even say, with a little
more bite to it, Who is teaching this course, Weinstein, you or I?

Obviously not: Who could ask rational questions when he is feeling like a teenager who has just been devastated by his true love's suddenly announcing that she never wanted to see him again?

What is there to say when you have just felt the world come to
an end?

      ✳   ✳   ✳

The fur hat, woolen overcoat, and leather gloves of Weinstein, Martin,
did not reappear in my classroom after spring break, but the spirit of
Weinstein seemed to remain all the same, infecting the class with a
certain edginess, a certain quarrelsomeness. Often, when I lectured,
though they dutifully—and probably inaccurately—jotted down what
I was saying in their notebooks, they would pause in their scribbling to
look up at me with a certain querulous glint in their eyes, as if they
couldn't believe I'd actually said something as stupid as whatever I'd
just said. Day after day they even took to picking fights with each
other, quiet little Arlene Sample, who hadn't said a word in class all semester, rising up—not literally beside her desk, like Weinstein—to
challenge the acknowledged intellectual bully of the department,
even the smiling Peterson brothers getting into such a wrangle over the
metaphor of the two thieves on the cross in *Godot* that they left class
not speaking to each other. Which will be saved, I wondered, watch
ing each of them sidle through the doorway as if the other didn't even
exist, and which damned?

I personally couldn't wait for the term to end.

Meanwhile, I kept expecting to run into Weinstein in the halls, between classes, in the john maybe, in the student union when I went
over to pick up a sandwich at the basement grill. I'm getting a reputation among my colleagues because I'm so busy looking for Weinstein
when I'm walking across campus that I don't even see them anymore.
Karp, the chair of my department, stops me on the path in front of
Old Main one noon to ask if there is anything wrong. No, I tell her,
I was just preoccupied. The cliché of the absentminded professor

suffices. Perhaps in my case it isn't all that wrong; the evidence suggests that I am not all there. There were some things I thought of to say to Weinstein as soon as he left my office that afternoon, which he did as soon as he'd made his statement and observed that after several minutes had passed I was still sitting there speechless. And even if I no longer remembered those particular things after a week or so had gone by, I was sure I'd come up with something when we met. Nothing so whiny, I hoped, as, How could you? With any luck, maybe something as strong as, Take off your coat, Weinstein, and let me see what sort of hard heart you're hiding under there.

After midterm it's too late for students to drop and add classes, so I didn't expect to see Weinstein walking hatted and gloved out of a different humanities course, chatting earnestly with one of my colleagues, though the mere idea of it was enough to make me squirm with jealousy. Our Adult Scholars are required to take two courses per term, however, so I knew he had to be around the campus somewhere, sometime, unless his experience with me had so embittered him about higher education that he'd decided to drop out altogether. But what, exactly, had I done? Held out on existentialism for a couple of weeks? Was that such a terrible thing? Existentialism wasn't about to disappear in the interim. You'd think a man of his years would have learned a little patience, at the very least. All right, so he didn't get the grade he thought he deserved on the first paper. How many in the class did? Couldn't he survive a little setback? What did he come here for, if not to learn, to improve? Who was this Weinstein, to think he should get it all right away?

When I couldn't stand it any longer, I called Rasmussen, told him I was worried about Weinstein because he hadn't turned in his paper and hadn't shown up in class for several weeks, found out what other course he was enrolled in — Cooperman's Modern Ethics — and started hanging around the Faculty Lounge in the basement of Old Main in my free hours, knowing that I'd soon run into Coop, who was notorious for all the time he spent down there, and meanwhile making good use of the opportunity to mend some fences with the colleagues who'd felt I was snubbing them on my walks across campus.

I'd done a fair amount of mending before Coop, who been down with the flu, showed up the next Monday morning.

"Coffee," he said, practically falling into one of the beat-up old chairs, hand-me-downs from the president's outer office that were all we ever got for furniture. "I'm too sick to teach."

"Jesus, Coop," said Lambert, from geology, who was just leaving to meet his first class of the day, "you look terrible. Why didn't you stay home another day or two?"

"I'm too sick to stay home with my wife," Cooperman said. His bald, bony head gave him a skeletal look on the best of days; now, emaciated by the flu, his forehead glistening, his eyes dark and sunken, he looked like a veritable death's-head.

I brought him his cup of black coffee — like many faculty members who were regulars in the lounge, he kept his own private cup there, a white ceramic mug emblazoned, in red, with "HANDS OFF!" — chatted with him for a bit, and finally brought up Weinstein's name, mentioning him casually as a student I knew we shared.

He brightened up when he heard the name and said, "That old son of a bitch is the only possible reason I could feel guilty for sitting down here instead of being up there meeting my class. Only I don't think I could make the climb to the third floor."

"A good one, huh?"

"You don't half know what you're saying, George. Why, one like that is worth the entire rest of the pea-brained class. Why . . . ," he gasped, but then paused, running out of what little energy he had, sipped his coffee, waved a hand in my direction and said, "but you know that as well as I do."

"To tell you the truth, Coop," I confessed, "I haven't seen much of him in class lately."

"What! Why, that's the most backassward thing I've ever heard." He suddenly seemed to have all his energy back. "Why, with one like that, you and I might just as well be the ones to skip class and let *him* teach it."

I have to admit the idea had occurred to me, and perhaps to Weinstein as well, but unlike Cooperman, who gave every student the grade of his or her choice—as, he claimed, an object lesson in personal ethics—Weinstein, as I knew all too well, would prove a pretty tough grader. Few, I think, would risk an otherwise terrific GPA in the hands of Weinstein's fierce evaluations. Not by choice, anyway. With Weinstein, it would have to be a required course.

*   *   *

Meanwhile the semester is slogging toward its end through an unusual spring heatwave. The temperature climbs into the upper eighties by midafternoon, ninety is threatened by the end of the week, and no one wears coats to class anymore, not even the faculty, who loosen their ties, those few who wear them, and leave their sweaty jackets hanging over the backs of their desk chairs. The students are down to shorts and T-shirts and, some of them, bare feet and no shirts at all. No Weinstein, either.

In spite of the heat, my other classes are going well, but humanities—what a mess!

It feels as if Weinstein, in his departure, has left us something to remember him by: that enormous black woolen coat of his, which it seems we are every day more and more tightly buttoned up in. Such a weight! I never knew what a heavy thing it was. In the very same classroom where we were freezing at the beginning of the semester as the winds out of the northwest slashed their way in through the poorly fitted window frames, we are all gasping for breath now as the afternoon sun reaches in through the open windows to wrap us in the heavy garment of its heat. It is an effort for me to talk—sometimes even to remember what it is I am supposed to be talking about—and as for the students, they no longer even make the effort. Trying to talk is like breathing through many layers of wool, the urgent desire to gasp and cry out instantly undone by the lack of energy to make even the slightest sound and the knowledge that only by remaining quiet and breathing gently can this lack of oxygen be survived. And what would I cry out if I could cry out through all these woolen layers of heat?

"Suffocation," I would cry out, "thy name is Weinstein!"

The semester is devoted to the study of something called the modern world, but we are in the grip of an age-old heat. We are desert people. Or we are merely the last survivors of desert people. The sun we know. The heat. Not much else. No one even brings books to class anymore.

"Too heavy, man," says Ollie O'Day, one of my football players.

One day I asked them, in as much of a comic mood as I could muster, if they thought this would be a good time for us to reread *The Stranger.*

Kieffer, the intellect, my sole hope for succor here, looked me in the eye and said, "It doesn't make any difference."

Sample, whose active warfare with him had been reduced by the heat to sporadic guerrilla maneuvers—a look here, a grunt there—rose up from the slouch into which the whole class had fallen just long enough to say, "Your motha."

Then she slouched down into her chair again, and no one responded. I was beginning to understand desert warfare, I thought: the long battle of attrition, nature itself the primary enemy, not even nature but the whole weight of the universe, something impossible to come to grips with, there but not there. It could go on forever like that, and the best you could hope for was just to survive, gasping for air. There were no winners, really. No one even took notes. We showed up for the days and hours assigned, and that in itself seemed more than should be expected of us. I said a few things, when I could manage. The Peterson brothers sat side by side again, because neither could muster the energy to move to the other side of the room. This was The Modern World.

Yesterday I said, "Has anyone seen Weinstein lately?"

Somehow—what else was there?—I had decided that it was Weinstein who was my one remaining hope. What we needed was for Weinstein to come back and put on his woolen coat again, freeing us from its impossible burden. Weinstein standing by his desk with his gloved hand raised returning us to the real modern world. Weinstein an oasis of difficult questions around which we could gather to be humanized once again. Weinstein the Adult Scholar, learner, awakener, symbol of all that could happen yet, even in this end-of-the-century desert where, as I had noticed on the thermometer in my office, the last two digits of the year were identical to the midafternoon temperature. Weinstein, my darling, where are you when I need you?

I repeated my question, to which no one in the class had responded with even the slightest gesture. Again, nothing. It was as if the sun blazing through the tall windows had melted my words even as I spoke them.

Finally, O'Day said, "I don't think that was on the syllabus."

*　　　*　　　*

Nobody made me stop at O'Leary's for a beer on my way home from school Friday afternoon. Being the only bar within a good many blocks of campus, it was the traditional student hangout, and therefore a place I generally made it my business to avoid. As a firm believer in keeping at least a few boundaries intact between one's personal and one's professional life, I thought it was sufficient to work with my students—and most of my colleagues, too, for that matter—during the day without having to socialize with them in the evenings. O'Leary's, however, was also the only decent bar between the college and my home, and it was, I knew, cool and dark, and since it was still only late afternoon, hardly even the cocktail hour—not a custom I believe is generally observed by college students, anyway—I thought I might pause there with immunity from student intrusion for the span of a mug or two of O'Leary's tap Guinness. I had decided that this was to be the evening when I confessed to my wife, Helena, the cause of my persistent grouchiness of the past few weeks, a small unpleasantness, to be sure, but one that, in the absence of any other explanations, she was beginning to take personally. Just yesterday, at dinner, when I snapped that she didn't have to say it three times after she had said three times, without getting a response, that there was a movie she was interested in going to, she came right out and asked if there were, as she put it, "someone else." I needed just a little hiatus between school and home to figure out how to tell her that, in a way, there was.

The bartender is an attractive young woman, with long brown hair

and a pleasant smile, who might well be a student herself, working
her way through college. The man standing at the bar in front of her
holds a shot glass delicately between a gloved thumb and a gloved
forefinger. Weinstein downs his drink in one swallow and sets his glass
on the bar.

"Will you join me in an Irish whiskey, Professor?" he says, turning
toward me. "It zpeaks to every zense of the peat bogs of old Ireland."

"Feel that boggy old damp right through your gloves, do you, Mr.
Weinstein?" I say. Here, the student-professor boundaries are clearly
down, a good reason for my usual avoidance of the place. "No thanks,
I'll have a Guinness."

Ignoring my barb, he says to me, "I want you to meet Annie, Professor. Annie, meet Professor Zupperman, a professor of humanities."

The pretty bartender refills Weinstein's shot glass, sets my brim-
ming mug of stout on a green paper coaster in front of me, then goes
on about her duties behind the bar. Weinstein, meanwhile, is continuing to talk away at me as if we are the best and oldest of friends.

"Have you lately noticed, Professor," he says, lifting his shot glass
with one hand and gesturing in the direction of the busy young bartender with the other, "how the running of the world is being taken
over by its young men and women? Surely you remember—how long
ago can it have been?—when all the doctors were touched with gray,
their faces lined and zerious? Now it is you with the graying hair and
deepening lines, while the doctors, though ztill zerious, of course,
look young and ztrong, like your own children perhaps. And the polite pharmacist I am sure you will also recall, to whom you were always so careful to zay 'Zir.' Now he hands you the prescription for
your heart medicine and zays—very respectfully, to be sure—'Thank
you, zir.' Even the politicians already promoting themselves for the
congressional election in my district this fall look young, young. Far
too young, they look, to be entrusted with the running of the country."

"They want to run the country," I tell him, "let them run the
country."

"Professor Zupperman," he says, then pauses long enough to toss
his shot of Irish whiskey down before continuing, "you miss the point.
They *are* going to run the country, with or without your approval.

The question is: What will be going on in their heads while they're running it? This is what I want to know. You know, Professor, before, I never had time to think about that. Like anyone else I just went about my business, passionate about some things, yes, but ignorant of the rest. But then things happened that gave me reason to think about that. I came to want to know what was in the heads of the people who ran countries. Yes, and how it got there, too. That is what I came to your college to find out."

"So how are you doing?" I ask him.

"Thanks to you, Professor, not especially well."

"Well," I say, with a little more vehemence than I really intend, "my opinion of you is not especially high either, Mr. Weinstein, as it never is of quitters." Why did you get involved with me in the first place, I want to ask him, if you were just going to dump me as soon as the going got tough? But he answers my unspoken question anyway.

"I am getting to be an old man, Professor, and I no longer have a lot of time to waste. Here and there, Professor, you find out what you find out. The mind says 'Aha!' and then what? As my fellow students like to say, I want to be where the action is."

"Listen," I demand, "what makes you think it comes that easy? You want too much, Weinstein."

"Me?" he says. "*I* want too much? What about you, Professor Zupperman? What do you want, tell me?"

The fact is, I wasn't aware we were talking about me; I thought the subject of the hour was Weinstein's interest in the intellectual predilections of the future managers of the nation's health and welfare. The subject that interests me is, of course, Weinstein, Martin, the intellectual awakening of. But now that I see how he rambles, how he attempts to slide out from under the burden of his own mind's growth, I have to wonder, as every lover must at some point, what it is that accounts, in spite of great difficulties, for this continuing infatuation. Why does he treat me like this?

"Another Guinness, Professor?" asks Annie.

"Yes, thank you," I say, "and an Irish for Mr. Weinstein, please."

"It doesn't come that easy, Professor," he says, though he does not

reach out a gloved hand to prevent Annie from refilling his glass. The
hand he raises he lays, instead, on top of my own hand, which lies on
the bar. The leather glove feels cold, moist, alien, not a thing I prefer
to have resting its weight on my own flesh. What surprises me most is
how heavy it feels, almost as if there is something more than just hand
in it. Just a little more pressure, I sense, and we would be in the realm
of pain. But do I want to risk offense just now by asking him to remove his hand or attempting to slide my own out from under it? Just
when, perhaps, we are finally getting somewhere, or what does this
sudden reaching out signify?

"In a way," he says, ignoring his drink but keeping his glove
clasped firmly onto my hand like some sleek, dark rodent, "you may
be correct. Probably I do want too much. Zo maybe does everybody,
no? But the question is, what is this too much that everybody wants?
What do you want, Annie?"

She is standing just down the bar from us, filling a trio of mugs
from the tap. "Right now," she says, "I just want the semester to be
over."

"For now, enough," he says, then turns to me again. "And you,
Zupperman, I repeat myself: What do you want?"

I look at his heavy, gloved hand where it bears down like a chunk
of molten iron on my own. Without a word he lifts it, turns it over,
stares hard at the leather palm, as if somehow he can see right
through it.

"Like I have already informed you," he says, "too much pain."
Then, moving his hand as swiftly as if it weighs nothing at all, he lifts
his shot glass and tips it into his open mouth, sets it lightly back down
on the bar, waves a quick farewell to Annie, and departs.

Annie, coming down behind the bar, picks up his glass and the
change he has left her, wipes up his place with a bar rag, smiles at me,
and says, "Interesting guy, isn't he, Professor? He could be a teacher
himself."

Well, I think, using my recently freed right hand to lift my mug of
Guinness to my mouth, as a teacher I am not altogether sure I would
adore him, not with what passes for pedagogical style there. Too

opaque, too grating, too . . . what? Unresolved? They wouldn't stand for it. Just wait till he got *his* first course evaluations. On the other hand, as Annie says, he's an interesting guy, which she could only know from his being around here on a regular basis. An interesting guy, indeed! Weinstein, I think, we have got to stop meeting like this. I tilt the mug and take a great, long drink. The Guinness goes down cool and heavy, an alien fist laying in my guts its sudden weight and dark flavor.

The Life of the Mind

WHEN HE REALIZED how impossible it was to shave without looking in the mirror, he let his beard grow out. But then he couldn't get comfortable with how ragged it felt, so he started going to the barbershop weekly to have it trimmed. The barber was a skinny old guy who'd been cutting hair all his life, just a neighborhood barber in a one-, sometimes two-, chair shop, not a stylist, not a hair designer. He was already keeping Bill's thick black curls cropped close on a monthly basis, so Bill never had to pick up a comb and stand in front of a mirror but only had to towel his head dry when he got out of the shower and then run his fingers through that dense mop. Now he came in every Tuesday afternoon, and the old man never asked him what he wanted, he just cut. He trimmed the dark beard close, the mustache, too, and then once a month he also cut the hair. Bill closed his eyes as he sat down in the chair and felt the cloth being pinned around his neck. It was a wonderful half hour, very relaxing. He knew he would emerge looking just fine for the rest of the world—he had no desire to offend anyone—and relieved of the necessity of looking at himself. Not even the customary mirror when the cloth was whipped away and the chair spun around at the end of the cut. That had been settled long ago.

"No," he'd said, holding up his hand and waving the mirror away when the old barber started to hold it up in front of him, angling it so he could see the back of his head as well as the front. "If it looks good to you, it looks good to me."

Looking at the front of his head was terrible enough, but looking at the back gave him vertigo. It always looked like somebody else's head. Even when he'd been able to look at his face, the back of his head, when it was forced on him in a barber shop, looked like an odd, unfamiliar thing. A thing, not him. A thing like that could just as

111

easily belong to anyone, and he always thought how bizarre it was that he should be expected to examine it in this intimate way when he felt no connection with it whatsoever. And since, being roundish, it was shaped like a container, he tried especially hard not to think about what was in it. If he had to think about what its contents were, as well as the fact that it belonged to him—*was,* in some way, him—he became queasy. There had been times, in the past, before the old man had learned not to present the mirror to him, when he'd had to close his eyes and sit in the chair for a few minutes after the cutting was finished, for fear that he'd be too dizzy to stand.

Not anymore. Now he could stand up easy, relaxed, and pay for the trim or the cut and trim, and hand the old man a nice tip as well, and pick his coat off the coatrack and say, as he always did, "I'm outta here."

Although he didn't wear hats himself, because they always felt heavy or constricting or sweaty, because one way or another they always reminded him that his head was there, he thought other men ought to. He didn't like seeing the bare backs of their heads when he came up behind them in the street. If the back of his own head could look like a strange head to him, then any one of these strange heads could look like his. The faces of other people he could deal with just fine, because a face was a face, at least as long as it wasn't his own, and you could look at a face, talk to a face, without thinking of the head it was attached to, and what was in it. But coming up on an uncovered head from behind, especially one as close-cropped as his own, or, worse yet, a bald one, was, for him, what looking down into bottomless depths from a great height was for others. He understood how people who climbed to the observation towers of tall buildings were grateful for the barricades they found there, even though they spoiled the view. Rather than this all-too-frequent incitement to vertigo, he would gladly, at the cost of whatever personal discomfort it resulted in, have supported a law that required men to wear hats at all times in public places. In the streets, he often felt like a desperate man, and at times like that he thanked God that he lived in a cold climate, where, for the most part, for most of the year, men did keep their heads covered.

Women were less of a problem. They generally had more hair, or it was fuller, or they did things with it that disguised the shape of a head. And they truly liked hats. One glimpse of a woman in a straw hat in the summertime—the dreaded summertime, when most of the world went bareheaded—and he was in love.

*　　　*　　　*

When Brenda, just back from a business trip to New York and over to see him that same evening, came out of the bathroom, she grabbed his arm, splashing his icy drink onto his hand.

"Why didn't you call me?" she asked.

"Hey," he said, "that's cold."

"I know I was in meetings all day, and dinners and conferences in the evening, but you could have left a message. They take messages. I'd have got right back to you. Who was it?" she said. "Your mother?"

"No," he said, perplexed. "I haven't seen her all week."

"Well, who was it then?" Brenda demanded. "Who died?"

"Died?" He had a sudden vision of a body in the bathtub, doubled over, covered with a bloody shower curtain. But there hadn't been anybody but him in the apartment since Brenda left town. As far as he knew.

"The mirror," she said, still holding onto his arm, grabbing his shoulder with her other hand. "No one covers mirrors unless there's a death in the family."

Then she let go of him, turned away, and hurried down the hall. He followed her, watching how her hair bounced on her shoulders as she turned into the bedroom, silver streaks flashing among the browns, the auburns, a world of distractions there. She was standing in front of his dresser, looking at the sheet that covered the mirror that hung over it.

"Listen," he said, "no one died." He put his hand on the back of her neck, but she walked out from under it, strode across the bedroom, and flung open the closet door. Nothing but screw holes top and bottom.

"I took it down," he said. "It's downstairs in the storage room. You want it?"

She sat down on the edge of the bed: "What I want to know is, what's going on here?"

He sat down beside her. "Nobody died. Honest."

"I'm glad," she said, then paused. "Are you sure? Something sure smells rotten around here to me."

He reached over and took her hand, but she shook him loose and said, "No, first I want to know what's going on here. Honest, Billy, sometimes . . ." She didn't seem to know how to go on from there.

He folded his hands in his lap. "Nothing, really. I just didn't want to look at myself anymore."

She stood up, walked over to the open closet door, stared at its blank pine surface, then closed it. She crossed back over to the dresser. Leaning on it, she stared at the white sheet that covered the mirror.

He said, "Please."

"Well, I just don't get it," she said, turning away from the covered mirror and leaning back against the dresser. "I just don't get it. Forty fucking years of looking at yourself in mirrors and suddenly you decide you won't do it anymore?"

"Not won't," he said. "Can't."

She walked out of the bedroom and left him sitting there staring at the mirror over the dresser, or rather at the sheet that hid it. It was a large, expensive mirror, with an ornate wooden frame, very heavy. He was wondering if he could take it down himself, and what tools he would need. Maybe the landlord's son could help him. Finally he got up and walked into the living room, where Brenda was sitting on the couch, turning his drink glass around and around on the cocktail table in front of her. She didn't look up at him.

"I liked it when you grew your beard," she said. "And the way you walked around the bathroom in the morning with your eyes closed, brushing your teeth with your eyes closed, because you said the mornings were too bright. I thought it was funny."

He didn't say anything.

"It wasn't funny," she said.

"No," he said, "it isn't funny."

"I thought somebody died," she said.

"No," he said, "nobody died."

*   *   *

His therapist wanted to know what mirrors meant to him, his mother wanted to know what she'd done wrong, and his father thought that perhaps he was onto something. A squat, heavyset, cigar-chewing man whose round face and full head of thick curly hair, still dark in his late sixties, made him look like a parody of his only son, he had long thought that vanity was the curse of the human race. And now here was his own son acting out his own most heartfelt principles! There was hope for humanity yet.

"Maybe you'll start something," he told his son.

"But you're such a good-looking boy," his mother said.

"I wonder," said Dr. Sheffield. "Is it therapy itself that you're rejecting?"

Bill picked at his fingernails, thinking that summer would soon be over and people would put away their terrible mirrored sunglasses and don hats again, and the world would be a more decent place, and told Dr. Sheffield that he didn't think so, really, he wasn't particularly concerned with therapy itself, whatever that was. He wasn't rejecting therapy itself, he wasn't rejecting Dr. Sheffield—"Look," he said. "I'm here, aren't I?"—and he wasn't even rejecting himself.

"I just stopped looking in mirrors," he said. "Nobody died."

To his mother he said, "Thanks, Ma."

His father was a more difficult problem. Although he finally did manage to tell him that he wasn't in the least bit interested in starting anything, he felt like he was letting his father down, and as a result piled up so many apologies around that simple statement that he wasn't sure it got through clearly at all. It was the truth, though, that he wasn't interested in starting anything. Especially with his father. As far as he was concerned the rest of the world could devote all its waking hours to staring at itself in mirrors.

"Wonderful," his father said. "Wonderful."

But because the constant soggy cigars his father chewed his words around rendered all tones one, Bill couldn't tell whether his father had missed what he'd been trying to say and still thought that his not looking in mirrors was wonderful or whether he thought that all those elaborate apologies were wonderful or whether what he, father, was giving him, Bill, was just plain and simple irony.

Irony was what Bill would have preferred.

*   *   *

When he was in the fourth grade and read, in a book of Greek myths his parents had given him on his birthday, the story of Narcissus, he went outside at once in search of a pond to study his own features in. Not that there weren't plenty of mirrors in the house: the twin vanities in the bathroom he shared with his sisters, hand mirrors on his mother's dresser, the guest bathroom downstairs; even the fireplace was mirrored, and there was a mirror over the little table in the front hall, which he knew people used to check themselves over before they left the house. But a pond was different. It wasn't a thing in people's houses, it was a thing in the world, and maybe it could show you something about yourself that only the world could show you. But the problem was it was mid-August. Even then he preferred winter, at least to the extent of wishing his birthday was in the winter, so he could get ice skates; nobody gave you ice skates for a summer birthday no matter how badly you needed them. Now there were no shimmering icy sidewalks he could see his face in. This was the hot, dry center of August. There were no puddles in the gutters in this flat, suburban neighborhood where it hadn't rained for weeks. Water from sprinklers evaporated in the air, soaked instantly into parched lawns, dried off the sidewalks as soon as it splashed down. He walked and walked through the fiery streets. Finally, beyond the suburbs, he came to the edge of a wide, rolling field. He ducked under a barbed-wire fence and started across the field. The grass, or whatever was in the field, was burned and dry. He ducked under another fence, crossed another field, came to a narrow road, crossed that, entered another field, and then another. Then in a field that dropped sharply

down, away from him, he saw a small herd of brown-and-white cows
standing in the shade of some tall trees at the bottom of the slope and
decided that there must be water for them down there. Keeping his
distance from the cows, he descended the hill. There was indeed a
stream there, reduced to little more than a trickle by the long summer. But in one small spot, below where the cows stood, blocked by
a large fallen branch, the stream pooled, quiet and motionless. He
crept carefully to the edge, not wanting to ripple the still water, but
what with the dense shade of the overhanging cottonwoods and the
mud the cows had stirred into it from their drinking, he couldn't see
a thing. It was then that he realized he was lost. He had circled
around at some distance to avoid the cows and then had crossed the
stream several times to get to this little pool, and now he couldn't remember which way he had come from. At first he felt like crying, but
that didn't last long, and he sat down on the dry bank of the stream
and waited. Time passed and the sun began to go down and the cows
started to drift away in a single file. He followed them. When they got
to the farm, the farmer's wife phoned his parents. He listened to her
giving them directions, while her many children, who all seemed to
be about his own age, sat around the kitchen table and giggled.

*   *   *

He sat in his office scheduling production runs for the next month.
This was the part of his job he liked best. It took less time than it used
to, now that the office had been computerized and he had developed
an effective program for handling his data, but it was delicate, important work and, most of all, totally absorbing. He saw this task as the
fulcrum on which the entire business balanced. Too much production and the overrun would have to be disposed of at a loss. Under-
production and the customers would be screaming for their orders,
looking for other suppliers. Try to make up for that later on by extra
runs and you're into overtime and the bosses are having a fit about in-
creased costs. Cut things back and the plant foreman is making temporary layoffs and the union steward is pounding his fist on your desk
demanding to know why. It was the job for which you had to know

everything: inventory projections for the end of the current month, sales estimates for the coming months with precise breakdowns on every item in the company's whole line of products, efficiency levels on the various production lines, projected downtime for maintenance and repair, absenteeism rates, even the credit ratings that might have you canceling or delaying a customer's shipment, giving you an inventory buildup you had no space for or maybe letting you divert those goods to someone else's rush order, even weather predictions, because a fleet of snowbound trucks out on the interstates wasn't going to keep things moving out on schedule and where were they going to put the excess production? Yes, even the top management's plans, their dreams of expansion, their marketing strategies: Add a new item to the line or subtract an old one and everything changed, alterations meant shutting down the lines to make adjustments, give him a little more warehouse space, let the shipping department add another semi or two, extend their routes, what if interest rates fall, a new flu bug decimates the work force, OSHA comes in with a new set of guidelines, the Pollution Control Agency says you can't do this or that anymore, there's a power outage, a supplier goes bankrupt, the foreman has a heart attack, some competitor suddenly starts cutting prices like mad, a new foreign market opens up . . . He loved it.

At his desk he was a happy man, the fulcrum of a little universe. Information flowed in to him from all directions, and what he lacked he sent for. He had the latest industry publications within easy reach, the *Wall Street Journal*, government forecasts. He had a little radio on the shelf above his desk that gave him continuous weather updates, and a flick of his finger brought the stock market to his computer screen. He could look out his office window into the busy factory itself. Twice during the morning the plant foreman came in to consult with him. He was an old man and had been with the company since its inception. They set up a meeting with the head of the personnel department and the big boss himself to discuss his impending retirement, the transfer of power. That would be an important moment for the company; things could change. Twice the sales manager called with some slightly revised estimates. Everything went into the computer, but the computer wasn't everything: There were still judgments to be made, conflicting demands to be balanced, long-term considerations that couldn't be factored into the program. Once the big boss himself stuck his head in to say hello. He, too, was an old man now and didn't come in every day, but he liked to know what was going on and knew where to find out. The company was a great organism, reaching out to pull in supplies, labor, power, orders, reaching out to deliver its products, submit its bills, track its sales, but here, right here, at the center of everything, was its mind.

As the morning went by, however, Bill found himself less and less able to keep his mind on his work and more and more distracted by his upcoming lunch with Brenda.

Brenda, he told himself, who has not wanted to see me since the night of the mirrors, or rather the nonmirrors, now wants to have lunch with me, in spite of the fact that I have turned down her first two suggestions of places to meet, one because of its enormous long back-of-the-bar mirror and the other because the tables themselves are mirrored. I should be wondering what Brenda is thinking now, after two weeks of brooding on the subject, but what I am really thinking, he told himself, is, What am I thinking about all of this? And that, he told himself, is a bad business; in fact, that is not business at all: A little more of this and the whole place—and I do not mean what I can see through my office window—will shut down, and what then? This, he told himself, is not a problem I was having before. Before, I was doing fine, I was not looking in mirrors and going about my daily business and everything was just dandy, I wasn't thinking about not looking in mirrors—what's to think about it?—I just wasn't doing it. Even, he told himself, my barber didn't care, a man whose very life is constructed around mirrors.

More and more he had begun to perceive his barber as a truly remarkable human being: Working with heads all his life, he had learned not to be concerned with what was inside them; they could be anything as far as he was concerned, coconuts, hairy pots or bowls; and the faces, too, into whose eyes he had no cause to look, between whose eyes and his, most of them at least, he could readily interject a handheld mirror, turning them away from his, back upon themselves. A thought that made Bill, elbows on his desk, momentarily queasy, but nonetheless he overcame it and continued to admire his barber's achievements: a supreme objectivity, a benign detachment from one of the most appalling facets of the world, an ability to survive in the midst of the worst the world had to offer, no, not just to survive, to be pleasant in the midst of it, chatty, a comfort to those who came his way, a god at his daily chores, like a surgeon who can wallow in blood and guts all day long and then go home and sit down with his family to a dinner of liver and onions.

Brenda, he told himself, wants to sit down at lunch and talk about what goes on in the operating room.

Dr. Sheffield, he told himself, wants to look at the scraps on the operating room floor.

My mother, he told himself, is just happy she has a son who's a doctor, and God only knows what my father thinks.

And me, he told himself, me, mirrors or not, I do not think I am going to be able to eat any lunch.

❊ ❊ ❊

Not to be able to look at oneself in a mirror is one thing.

> *Those twin orifices.*
> *Windows on the soul.*
> *Et cetera.*
> *What he if were to begin to ponder the entryways?*
> *The great dark cave of the mouth.*
> *Nasal passages.*
> *The canals of the ear.*
> *What of the structure?*
> *The loose hinge of the jaw.*
> *Eye sockets.*
> *The shifting, manipulable plates of the skull.*
> *To say nothing of its contents.*
> *The liquids sloshing around in there.*
> *Gray matter.*
> *The fine flicker of electrical currents.*
> *He hung a sheet over it.*
> *Something died.*

❊ ❊ ❊

Yes, it was Brenda at his door, the wide angle of the peephole lens distorting her face grotesquely. An amazing thing, the human face, looked at this way and that: The more he stared at her through the little hole, the less he was sure he knew who was there. Those lips. That nose.

"Hello," she called. "It's me, Brenda. Anybody home?"

"I suppose so," he said, unhooking the chain and opening the door.

She looked the same as always, olive skin and dark eyes, straight nose, hair shot through with silver, and he was truly glad to see her. But she was a mess. Her blouse was misbuttoned so that the collar stood way up on one side. Her neck was dirty, her lipstick wandered off in strange directions, and her bangs were crooked.

"Well," she said, "what do you think?"

He said, "I think you need a good barber."

He opened the bottle of wine he'd put in the fridge to chill when she called to say she was coming over, picked up a couple of glasses, and they went into the living room and sat on the couch, side by side, very close, touching shoulders, hips, thighs, clinking their glasses together like a pair of conspirators, while she told him what it had been like all day, doing this. He told her he had a lot of respect for that, for the whole principle, in fact: You can't know a man until you've walked a mile in his shoes and so on. But at the same time he felt like she was reducing his whole life to a bad joke. She should only see herself! Well, of course he understood that that was precisely what she was trying not to do. Still . . .

"But how do you do it?" she asked him, a matter of genuine concern at this point, like a novice chef who's just curdled the sauce.

"When you've spent a quarter of a century tying ties," he explained, "you don't have to be a genius to do it with your eyes shut. You just look down when you're done to make sure the ends came out right. You can do it all by feel."

"You think today's the first day I ever tried to put lipstick on?"

What could he say? You could see on the basketball court how some players always had the talent for knowing precisely where the hoop was. Even if they had their back to it and three other guys were towering over them, they could move right to it, never a hesitation, never even using the glass. No, stay away from the glass especially. One hesitation to look at what you're doing—OK, I'm ducking under this guy's arm, moving around that one, driving for the baseline—and it's all over: A quick steal, everybody's suddenly at the far end of the court, slam! Wait a minute, that's not the way I saw it. No, but that's what you get for looking, and the score, the whole flow of the game, shifts, the competition is taking over, the inventory's piling up, the salesmen are screaming their customers are getting the wrong orders—why don't you watch what you're doing!

"That's it," he said. "You've got to watch what you're doing."

"But that's exactly what I was trying not to do."

A legitimate complaint. Maybe he wasn't making himself clear. OK, forget the basketball players, forget the paisley ties and the tubes of pink coral lipstick, but he couldn't get it out of his head how all the ball games had their common roots in the primitive sport, if you could call it that, of kicking a human head around a field after the battle, the fleshy head of a just-decapitated enemy, with its eyeballs bulging and hair standing out all around, the mouth gaping and the neck pouring blood, stuff oozing out from the cracks in the scalp, till all that kicking around, bouncing across the hard ground, thumping against rocks, sticks smashing at it, finally stripped it clean and left just the bare white skull, laced with cracks, jawbone unhinged, empty eyesockets, hollow as a basketball, lying at last alone in a clump of weeds, not even of any interest to the scavengers, while the players trundle off to the locker room, which in this case is the nearest riverbank or pool of rainwater, where for just a second before plunging their hands in to splash water on their sweaty, bloody chests and faces they pause to see that, yes, they are the lucky ones, their own heads are still attached to their bodies, heads that could just as easily be bouncing around rock-strewn fields, rapidly emptying, heads that tomorrow . . .

Brenda took his wineglass from his hand and set it down on the cocktail table in front of them. "Billy, what are you thinking?"

"This is no game," he said. "This is a matter of life and death."

✳   ✳   ✳

Dr. Sheffield, who did not believe in the past, set his patients the task of doing certain mental exercises in the course of their sessions. Thought-experiments he called them, in the Einsteinian tradition, designed to stretch the boundaries of the imagination, to expand the self's options.

"William," he said, "you're a young man, you have an entire lifetime before you. All the choices are open to you. What do you want to be?"

"When I grow up?" said Bill.

"Well, if you want to put it that way, yes."

"I want to be a vampire."

"An interesting choice," said Dr. Sheffield, a little hesitantly. "Well, shall we explore this choice, then? What it means. To be a vampire."

"Easy," said Bill.

"So," said Dr. Sheffield, who liked to participate actively with his patients in working out these exercises, "what is it, then? The appeal of constant resurrection? The power to shape others to your own mode of being? A dismal view of the nature of human interdependence? Sexual fantasy? A desire to change shape, to fly—?"

"No," said Bill.

Dr. Sheffield was out of ideas. "Well, then?"

"It's easy," said Bill.

Dr. Sheffield waited, eyes bright in his round white face.

"When you look in a mirror," said Bill, "there's nobody there."

*   *   *

Hi there. You probably wonder where I've been lately. I know the feeling. Well, it's not an easy thing to explain, but to you, of all people, I suppose I do owe an explanation, only I'm not sure I have one. It's not like I've really been anywhere. Where would I go, after all, without you? Absence, yes. Don't start with the accusations. This is hard enough as it is. Months, I know, months. All right, then, I'll try to be honest with you, though this isn't any easier for me than it is for you. Confrontation has never been my way, but I don't need to tell you that. That's the heart of the problem, you could say. But you don't need to. Hey, it's not your way either, don't I know that? But we've got to do it, right? So OK, here it is: You bore me. Well, no, that's not exactly it, either. It's more complicated than that. Like: You distract me from doing what I want to do while adding nothing of value to the quality of my life. No, that's too formal. It sounds a little harsh like that. And besides, that's not quite right, either. The fact is, you repulse me. There it is. I look at you and I get sick to my stomach. I'm sorry, but the truth's the truth. Nausea. Vertigo. Whoa, I've got to sit down, close my eyes, wait for the world to stop spinning, or . . . And why? You're just . . . You didn't . . . You're not . . . But look what you do to my life. And there's no getting away from you. Oh yeah, I can hide, that's easy enough. But look what everyone thinks of me then. And meanwhile, I still know you're there, no matter I don't actually catch a glimpse of you from one month to the next. Well, maybe a glimpse, passing a store window, out of the corner of my eye. Ugh. But I keep on along my way, doing what I'm doing. Damned if I'm going to let you spoil it. And yet I know you're there all the time, trying, trying. I used to wonder what it was you really wanted. What it was you thought you were doing to me. I tried to empathize. To understand how desperate you must be to be acting like this. But where did that ever get me? Nothing changed. You didn't stop. I felt as miserable as ever. You did what you did. What you had to do, I guess. Always there, damn you, always there! Yes, and I know you're still at it, too. But I've had it with you. Had it. Just had it. That's what I'm here to tell you now. I'm through, finished, kaput. It's all over, between me and you. We're done, got that? You're outta here, and I don't care how you do it, though frankly I think the best way is, well, you know, I don't like to say it straight out. But what's the point? If there's no place for you here, there's no place for you anywhere. Got that? I don't know how you're gonna do it and I honestly don't care, just, well, do us both a favor and get on with it. OK? Listen, I'm glad we understand each other now. This was hard stuff, but it had to be said. No hard feelings, you understand. I did my part and now, well, now it's your turn to do yours. Listen, I've got to be going. I know how it is, but I don't want to be late for work. There's nothing more to say, anyway. I'd like to say it's been nice knowing you, but . . . Oh hell, what difference does it make? It's been a pleasure. You've been a buddy. There you are then, OK? Gotta go. Good-bye. I'll be . . . no, no, I won't, either.

✻   ✻   ✻

Soon after, on the evening of his mother's birthday, he arrived at his parents' house for supper. There had been some wrangling about the evening because he had wanted to take them out for supper, but his mother had insisted that she wanted to cook something special, and his father had finally persuaded him to let her have her way. After all, it was her birthday. Why shouldn't she be able to do what she wanted? But now, when she answered the door, he could see that she was all dressed up for an evening out. She was pulling on her dark cloth coat and his father, behind her, was also taking a coat from the hall closet. He didn't know what to say.

"But it's warm, Ma," he protested. "It's still like summer out, you don't need a coat."

A little woman, she reached up toward him and patted his thick beard with her hand.

"So pretty," she said. "I don't know why you should want to cover up such a pretty face with all that hair."

"So," his father said, "where's Brenda?"

"But you didn't invite her," he protested. "You said we were just going to—"

"What invite?" his mother said. "She's like family already. What does she need an invitation for?"

"OK, then, I'll give her a call. She can meet us."

He tried to step around the two of them in the hall to get to the telephone, but his father had his arms stretched out pulling his trenchcoat on and his mother grabbed him by the wrist.

"Not now," she said. "You know how your father is once he's made up his mind it's time to eat."

No, Bill wanted to protest, he didn't know any such thing. He'd been in restaurants with his father hundreds of times probably, and the old man had always seemed to him to eat like a normal human being. And he wanted to protest that it would only take a minute to call Brenda anyway, and that given how she operated she'd probably be at the restaurant before they got there and have a table reserved for them besides. He was sure his parents hadn't made reservations. But then it occurred to him that his entire conversation, since the moment he'd rung the doorbell, had consisted of protestations, that somehow he hadn't really managed to say anything at all, only to protest one thing or another, and he could suddenly see how, if this whole scene they had just enacted were to be written out, nowhere would it say of him that "he said" anything but only that, again and again, "he protested." And here he was, wanting to protest more, about his father's eating habits, about the failure to invite Brenda, and now he wanted to protest even more strongly about how his whole presence here had been reduced to a series of protestations, but he didn't know how to do that or where to turn. He couldn't understand how it had happened. It felt like there was something missing, but when he turned around and around in the little hallway, he couldn't see anything there. It was so narrow, the front hall in this little house his parents had moved into after he and his sisters had grown up and moved away, that there wasn't room in it for the little table and mirror they'd kept in the front hall when he was a boy.

His father had finally gotten his coat on, though the belt was dragging on the floor, and squashed an unlit cigar into his mouth. "Hokay, folks," he said, with a sweeping flourish of his arm toward the door, "let's make an evening of it."

But his mother was already outside on the front walk, tapping her heel impatiently.

Bill wanted to protest that this was not an auspicious beginning for the evening. He wanted to protest. No, he wanted to "protest."

*   *   *

Late one afternoon, not long before closing time, the old man himself came into Bill's office, pulled up a chair close to Bill's desk, and, keeping his voice low so that Bill's secretary couldn't hear, said he was sorry to have heard from some of the people in the main office that

Bill hadn't been quite himself lately. For an answer, Bill had his secretary, Patsy, bring over a copy of the quarterly efficiency report they'd just run off that morning. Then she went back to her computer-entry tasks and Bill to double-checking and initialing work orders while the old man read over the report. Bill knew perfectly well what he'd find there: not a minute of overtime, not a single order delayed or misshipped, no inventory buildup with its attendant financing charges, no maintenance costs outside budgeted limits, no layoffs—for the old man really did care about his employees—and all this in spite of a brief truckers' strike, uncertain market conditions, a major promotional fiasco that the whole company was still in a state of turmoil about, and, of course, the turnover in the crucial position of plant manager.

When the old man finished reading the report, he reached over and punched Bill lightly on the shoulder and said, "I knew those folks in there were full of crap."

"You're looking good yourself, sir," said Bill.

"You know what I call this place?" said the old man, indicating Bill's whole compact, tidy office with an easy sweep of his arm. "I call this place my CNS. The central nervous system of the whole company. This is where it really happens."

"And you," he added, reaching over again to tap Bill's shoulder with his knuckles, "you, boy, are it."

Bill felt like he'd just been drafted into a game of tag. While the old man was smiling and getting up and waving good-bye, Bill looked over at Patsy, who was also getting ready to leave for the day, shutting down the computer, putting things away in desk drawers, gathering up her personal stuff, taking her coat off the rack. She was in her late twenties, small and slender and fair-haired, recently out of both a bad marriage and a mediocre secretarial school. She didn't seem particularly bright to Bill, had admitted to him, at lunch one day, that she never read books and wasn't much interested in doing so—he'd just mentioned a couple of new things he'd been reading—and only picked up the occasional women's magazine for a look at fashions or makeup tips. But she'd learned her job quickly enough, did it well, was completely dependable, and liked being there. In fact, in what seemed to Bill a kind of brainless way, she seemed to like everything and to delight in saying so: the view onto the factory floor, the retarded boy who brought them coffee, the layout of her computer keyboard, the row of fast-food restaurants across the street, the old suit Bill'd worn to work today, the new plant manager she'd hardly gotten on a first-name basis with yet, and even the sour-faced bitch from internal auditing, who always invaded the office several times a year and had just finished settling in for several days right at Patsy's side, demanding that Patsy go over each stage of their operations time and again, questioning in her harsh, nasal voice every detail that Patsy brought up for her, every fact and figure, waiting at the door for her every morning and keeping her late every evening while the important work of the office piled up all around her.

Bill's own sense of relief at watching the auditor finally pack up and leave, however, had been tempered by his realization that as soon as the door closed behind her, Patsy would turn to him and say, "What a nice lady."

Bill's sense of almost everything was tempered by his realization that right now, after little over a year with the company, Patsy could probably do his job every bit as well as he could. For exactly one-third of his salary. And with absolutely as much pleasure as he took in it. He wondered what this said about the nature of the CNS.

Meanwhile, Patsy, on her way out the door, paused to say good night.

He looked up from his desk, winked, and said, "You're it."

She looked puzzled for just an instant, then smiled, said good night again, and closed the door behind her.

Bill knew that she was thinking, What a nice man.

What a nice man, he said to himself, what a nice man, what a nice man, what a nice man. He couldn't imagine whom he was talking about.

*　　　　*　　　　*

He stood in his living room with his coat still on, took down from a shelf the Funk and Wagnalls dictionary his parents had given him many years ago, and read, "It has the functions of coordinating, controlling, and regulating responses to stimuli, directing behavior, and, in man, conditioning the phenomena of consciousness." For a moment it gave him a certain sense of power. Then the nausea took over. The room started to spin about him, the dictionary fell from his hands, landed on the carpet, and flipped open to a page of vomit-yellow illustrations, and he had to sit down on the couch, still with his coat on, and hold his head in his hands. When at last the phrase "phenomena of consciousness" had spun about in his head so many times that it ceased to have any meaning, the world began to settle down again and finally stopped moving, and he looked at the dictionary that had fallen open between his feet and saw that the illustrations were of various kinds of rock. Marble, shale, slate, granite. He stared at them for a long time, bent over, the book still on the floor. Limestone, basalt, gneiss. The colors were almost indistinguishable, all shades of yellow and gray; and though he knew this was no doubt the result of the inexpensive color process that Funk and Wagnalls had employed rather than nature's coloring processes, he liked it all the same. Limestone, he thought, watching the innumerable shells of tiny dead crustaceans drift slowly down to pile up at the bottom of his mind. Granite, he thought, watching the dark weight of the molten mass as it flowed sluggishly over everything. Gneiss, he thought, feeling the enormous pressures of the earth bear down on it all. Yes, especially gneiss, he thought. Gneiss, gneiss, how very, very gneiss.

*   *   *

"So," said Dr. Sheffield, "you insist on telling me this dumb story in order, I can see, to prove to me what a smart kid you were. Do you think I care?"

Bill shrugged.

"Follow the cows. A dog could have done it."

Bill shrugged again and mumbled, "I suppose so."

"But even if that was a smart kid," said Dr. Sheffield, "which I'm by no means convinced of, do you know what I would say to that?" He didn't wait for a reply. "What I would say to that is, So what?"

Bill sat across the little table from him in stony silence.

"You want to think that was a smart kid," Dr. Sheffield continued, "go ahead, be my guest, think that was a smart kid. The world's full of smart kids, what's one more? But this one, we couldn't test his IQ now even if we wanted to. Not that that should stop you from thinking he was a smart kid, if you need to. After all, IQ isn't everything. But we couldn't even ask him to count to three, to put the round peg in the round hole. Not this one. No, with this one, we couldn't even ask him," and here he hesitated for a moment, "if he recognized his own face in a mirror."

In the chair opposite, Bill felt like his body was a solid mass, as if he weighed a ton. Tons. He couldn't understand how the little padded chair, with its spindly legs, could support his weight. He held his breath, waiting for it to collapse underneath him.

"So," said Dr. Sheffield, "for the little boy that was, dumb, smart, whatever, what should I care? Not this." He leaned across the table and snapped his fingers under Bill's nose.

"Ghosts," said Dr. Sheffield. "I don't treat ghosts.

"But for the little boy sitting across from me trying to hold his breath until he turns blue," said Dr. Sheffield, leaning back in his chair, "well, now, that's another matter altogether."

At first Bill didn't realize who he was talking about; then, even when he did realize whom Dr. Sheffield was referring to, he couldn't, for a little while, put that awareness together with the fact that it was he himself who was holding his breath; and even then it took him a bit to figure out what, exactly, he was supposed to do about this situation. Finally he exhaled, felt things begin to shift, slowly, somewhere deep in the interior, inhaled, exhaled . . .

"So," said Dr. Sheffield. He reached behind himself, pulled some papers out of the stack on his desk, then turned to Bill again. "So. Meanwhile, these test results. Your inner ear is all fucked up. It's a miracle you haven't been falling on your face since you first started to walk. And sense of direction? Forget it. Take my advice and never go anywhere without a map. A compass, take a compass, too. And a guide, if you can find one."

Bill was having trouble understanding him. Go anywhere? The

whole idea seemed preposterous, impossible. He wanted to laugh but was afraid to; he couldn't imagine what might happen: fissures open up in the earth, cliffs crumble into the sea, landslides bury whole villages? Mudslides, tidal waves, rivers abruptly changing their courses, sending walls of water racing through densely populated cities. The cost in human lives was inconceivable. Laugh? No, this was no laughing matter. This, he thought, must be what they call thinking the unthinkable.

"Never mind," said Bill.

"Right," said Dr. Sheffield. "Good for you. This you can live with. OK." He tossed the test results over his shoulder, the sheets scattering across his desktop. "Now we can get down to the serious stuff."

What's the rush, Bill thought. He wasn't going anywhere, so why couldn't the rest of the world just relax and wait it out with him? Storms, winds, seasons, the moon's tug, the tide's gouging. Eventually the surfaces would wear away, under the fine blasting of windblown sand, the tumbling streams and rivers, and they would get down to the serious stuff, whatever that was. Meanwhile, the freezing and thawing, the great plates shifting, the tedious scraping of the glacial creep. Yes, he thought, the long, slow millennia of erosion. What could you do about it, anyway? Natural forces. Weren't they the best kind? Turning mountains into rubble, rubble to sand, sand to soil, washing down turbulent rivers, churning into the sea, great chemical broths stewing in the bubbling oceans, violent thunderstorms electrifying the warm seas and all that formless life swirling within them, small organisms flowing with the nutrient currents, taking root in muddy estuaries, edging, at last, ashore, eons and eras practically flashing by now because he knew where it was heading, all this grinding down and building up. You didn't have to move to see what was happening. You didn't have to spend your centuries spinning around in circles to get dizzy. All you had to do was to stay in one place and the world would come spinning around you and around you and around you, if you could bear to look at it, spinning and spinning until you couldn't distinguish it from you, you from it. Yes, this was the serious stuff all right, and it came at you faster than you could imagine, the speed of whirling planets, the expansion of galaxies, the first wild seconds after the big bang, and you knew suddenly that you were totally filled with it, stuffed, packed tight, that you couldn't take in anymore. One more glimpse of that sloppy, whorling, whirling, evolving, gray mass and you were done for. You had to look away, you had to make it so you couldn't look back again even if you wanted to, you had to say,

"No."

"No?" said Dr. Sheffield.

"You've got it," Bill said. "No."

They sat there a long time like that, their two small padded chairs remaining firm underneath them, the small table blank between them, the room gradually darkening, the sound of the heating system switching on and off eroding, from time to time, the silence.

Occasionally one or the other of them said, "No."

It satisfied Bill somewhat to realize that more often than not, as the day passed, he didn't know which one of them had said it.

*   *   *

The questions have actually gotten a lot easier.

His barber says, "What'll it be, same as last time?" and Bill, settling back in the chair, eyes closed, feeling the sheet wrapping around him, tightening about his neck, says, "You got it," though that's not been a hard one to answer for some time now.

His father looks up at him over his dripping, unlit, chewed-up cigar and says, as if it were a real question, "So, still not looking in mirrors?" This is an easy one for Bill to answer because he simply doesn't understand it. "No," he says. "I suppose not."

His mother asks him when he's going to get rid of that dreadful beard so she can see his pretty face again. This is one of his favorite questions. She asks it all the time. It has a sense of solidity. He says, "Sure, Ma, sure."

Dr. Sheffield stares at him from across the empty little table they meet over and says, "No?" "No," says Bill. It has an agreeable feel to it.

Brenda just asks him how he's feeling, and he has no trouble at all saying, "Fine, fine." Sometimes he also asks her how she's feeling and she says, more hesitantly, "Well, OK, I guess, considering," to which he then says, "Fine, just fine," which is the same thing he says about their wedding plans.

Patsy, who's begun to read, summarizes an article for him from this morning's paper, about the overthrow of a distant government, and says, "Isn't that nice?" Bill agrees, agrees, agrees.

From time to time the big boss himself sticks his head in and says, "How's the old CNS? Everything under control?"

"You bet," Bill says.

Everyone else says, "That Bill, he's a rock."

Oedipus at Columbus

IMAGINE! Seventy-two years an orphan and suddenly, in the autumn of my life—that's a joke, you understand; it just so happens it's October when the moment of discovery arrives—I have a father! Well, a dead father to be exact, but who am I to be picky at this stage of my life? If he were alive he'd be in his late nineties, a shriveled-up old wisp of a guy, built something like me, frail, broke, probably cancerous, maybe with Alzheimer's. Dead, of course, he's also in his late nineties, which is where he'll be forever. Like a character in a story— I've gotten into reading these days, imagine that—he'll never grow older than he is on the last page. So it's probably better this way. What would I be doing with the old guy? Visiting him in some nursing home where half the residents are younger than I am? No, thanks. And of course I still don't have a mother. Is that something to complain about? Before, I didn't have either parent; now I've got one, that's a start. With luck I could have a mother, too, before I'm finished, grandparents as well, I suppose, maternal and paternal both, who knows, aunts, uncles, cousins, maybe even siblings. Agh, already I'm feeling strangled by all this family, I'm not accustomed to it, so many of them, such a suffocating lot, I never imagined. This is nothing I was looking for, this father thing, believe me.

How it happened, you truly wouldn't believe. Not how I was orphaned, that's another story and one that even I haven't heard yet, but how I got a father. It wasn't like I was looking for one, believe me. You live as long as I do without parents and you get used to it, you don't wake up every morning wondering what happened to them, you have a life to get on with, and besides, you hear stories from your friends about *their* parents and, well, sometimes you consider yourself lucky. Of course by now all my friends are orphans, too. Molly Kirschman's mother was the last to go, just this past year, and a relief at that. She'd suffered for years, doped up, incontinent, memory gone. Every time I ran into Molly she'd be in tears over her mother's suffering, weeping onto the already soggy lettuce in the A & P, holding her head in her hands between frames on our bowling nights. I was at the funeral, of course.

"Well, Molly," I said afterward, when I'd finished with the usual condolences, "now you're one of us."

"'Now'?" she said. "Carl, we've been friends for years."

"But now," I explained, "we're all orphans together now: you, me, Bernie, Mary Beth, Goblinsky, all of us."

The tears started again, and she turned her back on me. Hey, I wanted to tell her, grow up, join the human race, it's no disgrace to be an orphan, it's everyone's condition. Think of all the animals that kick their young out of the nest as soon as they can. A few quick flying lessons and out you go. Don't let us see you around here again, you're on your own now. Like any orphan.

Seems like I've been on my own forever, I was thinking, when Goblinsky came over with a fat corned-beef sandwich in his hand, dripping mustard on the carpet—well, it was his house, he and his wife had agreed to host the postfuneral feast, we do this sort of thing for our friends when we get older, you know—and wanting to know what I'd said to poor Molly.

"'Poor Molly?'" I said. "She should be kicking up her heels," though that was hard to imagine. "The old lady's out of her pain now, and when was the last time she even recognized Molly?"

"You're a hard one, Rubin," he grumbled through a mouthful of sandwich. "Why, the old lady's not even cold in her grave yet."

"I'm a realist," I told him, thinking that's what a lifetime of orphanhood makes you. But I chose not to get into all that with Goblinsky, who had turned their sun porch into a nursery for wounded animals, everything from a neighborhood squirrel that'd gotten a paw smashed in someone's driveway to huge, sharp-beaked creatures, owls and hawks and eagles he brought home from the vet school for weeks of rehabilitation. I marched off to the buffet instead, which seemed the realistic thing to do at the moment, leaving Goblinsky to dust the crumbs from his hands and put his arm around Molly's droopy shoulders.

And now I'm waxing sentimental over this family thing! Over a dead dad! Who'd believe it? Listen, I've been taking care of myself since I was old enough to change my own diapers. Honest, it's one of my first memories, being told they'd never seen a kid toilet train himself so fast, which seems like something of a joke now—give me another ten years and I'll probably be pissing my pants like Molly's mother. But I did OK. I may not look like much right now—scrawny, a little hunched over, my hands as gnarled as my head is smooth— but I'm telling you, I did OK. I've got a nice retirement fund, plus I still own a quarter of the business, which is doing very well, thank you. I'm in good health, you could check with my doctor. I take good care of myself. I live well, I go where I want, do what I want. I'd do a lot more if I could figure out what it was I wanted to do. I don't need parents, dead or alive. At my age? Get real. Don't need any inheritance, either, not that there is one. But I don't seem to be able to think about hardly anything else these days, even in the midst of some hot National League play-offs, except that now, suddenly, I've got a father. Sort of.

And on top of that I find my name isn't even my own. Ignorant me, I've been a Junior most of my life. It's taken me all these years to come into my own, and I didn't even know it. Here's how it happened.

*　　　*　　　*

My ex-wife calls me, the first time I've heard from her in who knows how many years. Ours was an abbreviated middle-age marriage— what Bernie likes to refer to as my midlife crisis—that ended with our mutual realization that sleeping together couldn't possibly solve all our problems.

"My God, Carl," she says, the second I answer the phone. "You're alive!"

Seems she saw my obituary. She lives in Philadelphia now, runs a clipping service, has a bunch of small colleges among her clients. They're always looking to find out if any of their alums have died, hoping for a bequest, I suppose, though maybe they just want to list their names in the alumni magazine, the In Memoriam column, you know. Who reads those things? Anyway, she scans the obits in all the major papers, for her it's just a job, and then she sees one that says Carl Rubin, in my local paper, the *Dispatch*, which of course I never read, not the obituaries anyway, mostly just the furniture ads. I still like to see who's pushing what. And it has none of the usual information, this obituary, no relatives to be sadly missed by, no interment at, no sitting shiva, none of that, and she thinks, "Holy shit, that's him," meaning me.

But that comes later. First thing I say to her is, "If you think I'm dead, how come you're calling me?"

"I didn't know what else to do," she says, with the kind of logic I never was able to follow. "But if it's not you, then who is it?"

"No 'buts,' Margie," I tell her. "No 'ifs.' It's not me. Who knows, maybe it's my father."

Now I have no idea why I said such a thing. Freud—OK, I haven't read him, but who doesn't know Freud in this day and age, he's in the air, like pollution—says there are no accidents. Is that what this is all about? Anyway, Rubin's not such an unusual name. There are over a dozen in the phone book. I know, I've looked. I'm the only Carl. It goes from Aaron to Solomon, no Carls in between except me. OK, Carl Jr., it should have been, but the way I understand it, once the Senior is deceased, there's no more Junior. That's a relief. Just think, I could have grown up being called Junior. People would still be calling me Junior. I mean, after all these years of calling me Junior, they wouldn't suddenly start calling me Carl, would they? Or maybe the old man would have been one of those pretentious types, like those competitors of mine who call their salespeople design consultants; maybe he'd have put a II after my name if he'd had the chance, the choice. Well, I don't know that he didn't have the chance. I'm just grateful that I didn't have to be Carl Rubin the Second.

Thanks, Dad.

A septuagenarian offering up thanks to his dead dad—do you see what kind of position this puts me in?

✵   ✵   ✵

So I went down to County Hospital, which according to what turned out to be faulty information in the notice Margie read me was where he passed away. Their term. For me, he'd passed way out of my life long ago, back at the very beginning, he and my mother both, it was hard to imagine him going any farther. Fatal stroke. It said that, too. On October 12. Columbus Day, and there went my father, sailing away into the great beyond, only the discovery was all mine: Carl Rubin *Senior,* which Margie hadn't even spotted in the notice. No funeral home given, though, which was why I found myself walking up to the information desk at County.

I'd shrugged off Margie's condolences, verbally that is—"Big deal," I told her—and I did more or less the same in the administrative office to which I was directed at the hospital, a literal shrug of my thin shoulders this time, maybe not even visible under the wool sport coat I was wearing. I chill easily, especially during that time of year, the change of seasons.

Then this plump, smiling woman with a tight-fitting helmet of blond hair went on to point out, "Of course, there's nothing here, under Next of Kin."

It was no surprise, I told her, we weren't a very close family. She was scrolling down her computer screen, but I couldn't read it from my side of her desk. I asked her if she could give me an age, give me any details, for that matter. I only wanted, I said, to be sure it was him.

The number she decided to give me was astounding: the bill. "Could it," I asked her, "really cost so much to die?"

"You'd be surprised," she said. Then she gave me the rest of the details: one hundred and twenty-eight pounds, five feet seven, male, Caucasian, full upper dental plate, no distinguishing scars, of well-advanced age, no next of kin, no insurance.

"'Well advanced'?" I repeated.

"It's all approximate," she told me. "He was DOA."

Meanwhile she had printed out the bill and I was scanning the charges, amazed at how many there were and how fast they added up.

"Emergency room?" I queried. "Were they trying to bring him back to life?"

"They always bring them to ER," she explained. "The rescue

squad can't take a chance. What if someone were to come out of a coma in the morgue? The liability?"

"Of course," I nodded. "The liability."

"Then you'll accept responsibility for this obligation," she said, reaching over to me with a pen and pointing to the line at the bottom of the bill where it said "Other Responsible Party." She'd already scratched a blue X at the head of the line.

"No," I said, getting up out of my chair, all five feet seven, one hundred and twenty-eight pounds of me. "I don't think I have any obligation here."

Out in the hall I discovered I was still clutching the bill in my hand, three whole pages of it. I dropped it in the first waste receptacle I saw, not realizing till the plastic door flipped shut on it that the container was marked for recycling. CLEAR GLASS ONLY, it said. I shivered slightly—there must have been a draft in the hall—just as a pretty young nurse came by, the smile on her round black face bright enough to warm the whole floor.

"Are you all right, sir?" she paused to ask.

I managed a little smile myself, a nod. I was wondering, as she went on down the hall, if I was obligated to retrieve the paper from the glass bin.

*   *   *

It was a cop, a nice Jewish boy named Leibowitz, who helped me with the rest of it. He was the one who'd shown up after the manager of the rooming house, actually an old hotel down near the river, had found Carl Rubin—Carl Rubin Senior, that is—on the third-floor landing, already stone cold. That's what it said in Officer Leibowitz's report, what he'd taken down verbatim from the manager: "stone cold." I shivered myself when he said it, though it was a beautiful fall day and we were seated in a small interview room at police headquarters with the sun pouring warmth through the high windows and Leibowitz across from me wearing a short-sleeved uniform shirt. He was slender, swarthy, not much taller than me, could have passed for my grandson except for his head full of thick, curly, black hair, which

I never did have, even when young. I kept wanting to ask him if he knew who his father was, but at the same time I could imagine him answering, very sweetly, to be sure, "Of course, doesn't everyone?"

And I could hear that Dr. Freud in my head tch-tching. "Not everyone, my boy, not everyone. Not even everyone who thinks he does."

Meanwhile, like the gumshoe is on the other foot, I'm actually grilling Leibowitz about what I can't help thinking of, under the circumstances, as the crime scene. But all I'm getting is a coming-apart-at-the-seams vinyl wallet with a Social Security card so old you can hardly read the numbers, a couple of equally thin two-dollar bills, and last month's fresh, carefully folded, uncashed Social Security check, which I suppose I'm going to be stuck returning to sender.

All right, Leibowitz, I want to say to him, give. Withholding evidence is gonna get you in deep shit. Don't mess with me, Leibowitz.

Imagine, me playing the tough-guy private eye, and that Freud in my head saying, "What did I tell you about this search-for-the-father business? Next thing, you'll be moving in on your mother." And meanwhile the suspect, Leibowitz, cooperative as can be—maybe I've found a new calling—is even handing over to me a copy of his report, the whole half-page of it, OK, so there isn't much to say. An inventory of the possessions found in the room of the deceased, attached, lists some items of clothing, a portable radio, a few books, by title even: Ross McDonald, *The Drowning Pool*; Peters, *The Seven Habits of Highly Effective People*; Kirkegaard, *Either/Or*. My father, the literary man, imagine.

"You've been very helpful, Officer Leibowitz," I say to him outside the interview room, shaking his hand and thanking him. "How'd a nice Jewish boy like you get into police work?"

"My father was a cop," he tells me.

What can you say?

*　　*　　*

Like a dutiful son and responsible citizen, which for all I know may be one and the same, I returned the uncashed check to the Social

Security Administration. It had been addressed to him at the ex-hotel where he'd been found, the Riverside, "A" — and I quote — "Residence for Gentlemen." As I learned from the manager for a small, discreet fee — see how quickly I'm catching on to the tricks of this PI trade? — Mr. Rubin had been a gentleman in residence there for considerably longer than any of the other gentlemen residing there, well over a decade, since long before this Mr. Hermann, a beady-eyed, weasely looking fellow if I ever saw one, took over as manager. He was an ideal guest, this Rubin, clean, quiet, always paid on time, never any trouble. Till the end, of course. In the end, it's always trouble.

"These old guys," said Hermann from behind his counter in the lobby. "You never know." He adjusted his oily hairpiece and winked at me.

It was a weasely sort of wisdom, but wisdom of a sort all the same. You never know. Right. I walked outside into an afternoon that had suddenly clouded over, turned chilly, feeling a little oily myself, wondering if I had crossed over yet into becoming one of "these old guys." And if so, was it recognizable? At least Hermann the Weasel, top of the list in my new career extracting information from low-life characters, hadn't mistaken me for that other old guy, Carl Rubin Senior.

✶   ✶   ✶

Bernie Katz and I eat lunch together at the same deli every Wednesday, exactly at noon. He's like me, old, bald, and alone in the world, but as round as they come: round head, round face, round eyes, round nose, round body. Whenever I think of Bernie, I think round; I think in another life he could be a basketball. He is my best friend in the world, he's known me longer than anyone, we went to the Vo-Tech together and never, either of us, used anything we learned there. Instead, we went straight into the army together, where they totally ignored his mechanical skills and my tailoring ones and made us learn other things that we also never made any use of because in the end all they did was stick rifles in our arms and ship us across the ocean to take the place of the dead or wounded and try not to become dead or wounded ourselves.

Now, over our chopped-liver sandwiches, when Bernie asks me how I am, I tell him, "Like a new man. I have a new life," I tell him. "I have a family. I have a career."

"Carlos, you're an orphan," he reminds me. "A divorced orphan, at that. And you're retired. Remember? You couldn't wait."

Just then the waitress comes by and I ask her if she could ask Gussie, the manager, who's known us almost forever—where do you get regulars like us anymore?—if she could turn up the heat just a bit.

"You're a funny guy, Carlos," Bernie says when she's gone, taking off his tweedy tent of a sport coat that is maybe a forty-eight short. "All your life it's this orphan thing. I remember in the army, the hassle about the no next of kin to be notified, like you were proud of it even. You were The Orphan, Carlito, it was like a second profession for you. Your calling. It *was* you. Whatever else you were doing, even when you were married, you were always The Orphan. You were there to welcome us all into your society of orphanhood, one by one, Goblinsky, Mary Beth, Molly, me, who else? I remember when Mom and Pop went, not that it was a tragedy at their age, but it was like you and I started our friendship all over again then. Orphans together! Now you tell me you've got a family?"

I told him about my father.

"And a career?"

I told him about the PI racket.

"And now you want to play detective?"

Bernie, who learned how to take apart and reassemble automobile engines but never got his hands greasy, who learned how to be a field medic but never tied the first tourniquet, who walked halfway across Europe with a weapon he knew how to use but never fired, who came back home safe and sound, went to school on the GI Bill, got his Ph.D. in English, and taught right here at OSU till his retirement, said, "Perhaps you've forgotten Oedipus."

"I don't think I ever knew him."

He told me about Oedipus.

*   *   *

It's taken me awhile to figure out what he meant. Dear old Bernie, always the teacher, giving his students their reading assignments and then sending them off to do the hard thinking on their own. Well, it's winter now, I don't go out much at this time of year, I'm happier in my own condo where I can crank the heat up to where I like it, and the fact is, I've always liked to read, I've just never managed to get around to doing much of it, a life in the furniture business just gives you so much time for other things. But that's another story, though not an unrelated one. I always hated to see the couch and loveseat go off and leave the matching chair behind. Anyway, while the other *alter cockers* have gone off to Florida for the season, which would be like living in exile to me, I've read *Oedipus Rex*, sitting right here by my big living-room window watching our usual winter weather wiggle back and forth between rain and snow. Like one of Bernie's regular students, hard working but not too bright, I've read it twice now. I suppose I should have read it long ago, that and a lot of other things, but I wasn't as smart as Bernie about taking advantage of the GI Bill. My education hasn't been all it could have been, not that that's ever held me back, but like they say, it's never too late to learn.

And I was impressed, which I suppose is no surprise, since Bernie tells me people have been impressed by it for a couple thousand years now. I didn't much like the way the chorus nagged at everybody, but the basic plot, that's a different matter. It's a hell of a detective story, if you ask me, the worst kind, where the guy follows the trail of blood until he finds it leads right to his own bedroom door, and meanwhile you're plugging right along with him, like that old blind guy, knowing it all the time and wanting to tell him to stop, stop, for Christ's sake, let it go.

But that's half the point, isn't it? Who can ever let these things go?

Shortly after that lunch with Bernie, I called Margie and asked her if I'd been a pain in the ass with my orphaning.

She said, "It was your most endearing quality."

I asked her why Bernie always called me Carlos.

She told me it was his most endearing quality.

I asked her what she thought I should do about my father.

"Let the dead bury the dead," she said.

I thought about that, but I couldn't make head or tail of it, it seemed like another classic Margie kind of thing. Finally I said, "What the hell is that supposed to mean?"

"It's an old saying," she explained, as if that explained everything.

The only thing I could think of to say at the time was, "I never heard that one."

But I've given it some thought since, and though I don't believe I could actually explain it—I'm not Bernie—in some odd way, I sort of get it now. At least enough to say I'm willing to let the old man go, him and whatever goes with him, which if you look at it is actually quite a lot. Not that I could ever have gotten my hands on the real him anyway. He was ashes before I knew he was flesh and blood, basically my own flesh and blood, and I didn't choose to pursue the matter of their disposal. But he was also a doorknob, if you see what I mean, and I did have my hand on it, and I was in the process of turning it, curious as you or anyone else would be about what could be lying in that dark closet behind it. And I know it's a big thing these days: the adopted, which I never was, seeking out their birth families and all that. Maybe it was the "all that" that kept me from turning the knob, which had a keyhole in it into which his Social Security number fit, which might have unlocked "all that"—or at least some of it. But at the last moment—and I was just about ready to go plunging into the county records office with that worn old card of his in my hand—what I thought was, What would I do with all that?

Maybe it's the gap, gaps, in my education, though I don't think it's an exaggeration to say that I've become, over all these years, sufficiently wise in the ways of the world; maybe it's like Bernie says, that I've become a professional orphan and don't need another career at this point in my life. Who knows, maybe it really is my most endearing quality, and if so, why should I give it up? What would I be without it? So in the end I didn't slip the card, a skeleton key if there ever was one, into the keyhole, I didn't turn the paternal knob and open the closet full of family ghosts.

You may think I'll go on wondering till my dying day what I might have found there, who would have come fluttering forth—dear old Mom, dusty old Gram and Gramps, all those wispy aunts and uncles—but I'll tell you—and you, too, Dr. Freud—who needs it? I am what I am, as the sailor man used to say, and from my point of view, at least, that's not half-bad. For seventy-two-plus years I've been nobody's son, free to be myself, which I haven't done too bad a job of, if I do say so myself. Call me an orphan—as you must know by now, it's what I've always urged people to do—but it's a role in which I've prospered. For better or worse, it was a good fit. Now, it appears I may be somebody's son after all, that there is, perhaps, well, there was then, very likely, this father. And if a father, then a mother, and if a mother, then . . . But what difference can that possibly make for me after all these years. If I find out who I am, will I suddenly become someone else? If so, who? Would it be someone I liked, someone with any endearing qualities whatsoever, someone I could stand to live with? Or would I be stuck spending my old age with a stranger? And besides, at my age, what's really likely to change? For what do I need this dead dad and his ghostly entourage? Let the dead . . . let the dead . . . well, let the dead do what the dead do. Who can stop them?

What I do wonder sometimes, though, is this: What if once upon a time, when I was a young man, a freshly discharged vet, alone in the world and feeling it owed him something, hurrying to make his fortune, full of vim and vigor, as we used to say in those days, I had bumped into him down at the corner of Fifth and Scioto, and he, caught up in the onrush of his own life, had nudged me off the sidewalk and into a gutter rancid with trash and rainwater? It could have been worse, much worse.

No Loose Ends

HENRY HENRY, the world's most amazing bachelor, is so perfectly ordered in everything he does that even his first and last names are the same, a problem for some people when they first meet him because they can't figure out whether to call him Henry or Mr. Henry, but ultimately a solution for all because they're right either way and, like a lot else in Henry Henry's life, it doesn't make any difference. He has just been off meeting a lot of new people, too, all of whom soon ended up calling him by his first name whether they intended to or not. Back home now from a three-day business trip to the West Coast, late Wednesday night, actually Thursday morning already because his plane didn't land in Minneapolis until after midnight, Henry, with a meeting set up with his boss at eight in the morning to review the results of his trip, is doing laundry.

The washing machine is picking up speed on its entry into the final spin cycle, load two, all white. The dryer is already bouncing and fluffing the colors. On the ironing board nearby, which always stands at the ready, the iron is warming up toward the cotton setting for the three or four items Henry knows will need to be touched up. Anyone watching Henry would think how proud his mother would be to see him now, but Henry knows the truth: Either she would be finding him perfectly ridiculous for staying up at 2 A.M. doing the laundry or she would be checking to see how much detergent he used and re-ironing the sleeve of his blue shirt.

Henry, liberated from his ancestry by ignorance of his family's remote relationship to famous and long-dead Patrick, isn't thinking of either of his parents, though; he is watching the two vibrating white cubes that sit side by side in his immaculate basement and visualizing how in a few minutes he will move the clothes from the dryer to the folding table, the clothes from the washer to the dryer. He is sipping from a glass of instant iced tea, the only dirty—if that is the word—piece of kitchenware in the house. When he left for the airport Monday morning, the dishwasher was running; tonight, while the first load of clothes churned away in the basement, Henry was just above it in the kitchen, emptying the dishwasher, putting everything away in its drawer or cabinet. Even the spoon with which he stirred his iced tea has been rinsed, dried, and returned to the silverware drawer. Now, while the second load of wash dries, a small load that will take little time, Henry folds the first, irons the few items that have emerged a bit wrinkled, and carries them upstairs to hang them up in the bedroom closet or lay them neatly in his dresser drawers. Soon he will go back down for the load of whites, which will be finished drying by then. He will fold them and carry them up. On his way back up he will stop in the kitchen, rinse out his iced tea glass, set it in the dishwasher, wipe up any spots he has left on the kitchen counter, then finish his trip to the bedroom to put away the carefully folded whites. Finally, he will take himself to the bathroom. He will shower and then put himself away in his bed, between crisp, clean sheets, for the few remaining hours of the night.

So how do you like Henry, Mr. Henry, so far? People—especially people like his college roommates and Vito Pappenheimer, with whom he shared an apartment for a couple of years and Vito's off-and-on girlfriend, Crinoline, who stayed there frequently, and the coworkers who admire the broad, empty expanse of his desktop—have often remarked that he would make someone a good wife someday. But that was before the days of sexual equality, of course, and besides, as his ex-wife could tell you, it was wrong.

By coincidence, though she didn't just get back from anywhere and doesn't have to be anywhere especially early in the morning, she is also awake at this hour. Her name is Malvina Knott, and she is a distant relative of the people of Knott's Berry Farm fame, though she has never been there and her own solitary attempt at jam making ended in a boiled-over disaster. She is not washing clothes, either; what she took off to go to sleep lies scattered around the floor of the living room—yes, she does have a bedroom, whose floor is also littered with clothing, but she often prefers to sleep on her big couch—and now

all she is wearing is a torn gray sweatshirt that says University of
Massachusetts, which is no place where she or anyone she knows ever
went to school. Propped up on a pile of multicolored throw pillows
and covered by an old purple afghan, she was reading just a moment
ago, but now her book — *The Fabulous Philippines* — lies face down
against her breasts, and she is thinking about the son of a bitch she
used to be married to.

That was not pleasure reading Malvina was doing, by the way, but
homework. She owns a small travel agency located in a classy suburban Minneapolis shopping mall, and specializes in finding off-the-
beaten-path vacation spots for her well-to-do and much-traveled
clients. Thanks to her profession, she has even had the opportunity to
do a fair amount of traveling herself. She has had a lot of very interesting trips and a few adventurous ones and even some highly educa-
tional ones, but the marital journey she took with old Henry, she is
thinking, was none of those.

She is even thinking about calling him up. The telephone,
stretched to the limit of its long cord, is on the floor next to the couch,
buried under her skirt, sweater, somewhere. Yeah, maybe she'll call
him up. In spite of the late hour, she can see him standing there in
his bedroom holding up a freshly ironed shirt on a hanger and turning it this way and that to check if he's missed anything.

"Hey, Mr. Clean," she'd say to him, "how's your wrinkle-free life
these days?"

Actually, Henry has already hung up all three of his perfectly
ironed shirts and is standing in the bathroom, staring into the toilet
bowl. Just above the waterline faint rust stains mar the white porcelain. The urge to sleep — it's past three now and the long business day
and long flight are finally beginning to catch up with him — and the
urge to clean are doing battle in him, and he just can't manage to say,
"Screw it, I'll do it tomorrow."

The reason he can't do that is simply this: He fears that one little
bit of putting it off, one small chore postponed, one tiny corner left
unwashed, one weak moment of deciding to "do it tomorrow," and
the next thing you know, probably by the time tomorrow arrives, the
day after at the very latest, he will be living in Malvina's world, with

rust stains laminating the whole inside of the toilet bowl, old socks hanging over the backs of kitchen chairs, the vacuum-cleaner motor burned out from being run with the bag full, three glasses and a handful of silverware sitting in the cold, greasy water in the sink, an open carton of spoiled milk in the refrigerator, in the garage a dirty car low on oil that should have been changed months ago and with an almost empty gas tank, in the yard overgrown shrubbery and the only untrimmed lawn in the neighborhood, and back upstairs in the bedroom closet a wrinkled shirt that will have to be ironed first thing in the morning so he'll have something to wear to work.

That's living? he thinks.

You think it's hard to live like Henry lives—socks rolled, wastebaskets emptied, lawn clipped and raked, car waxed, furniture polished, the dog in its bed and the people in theirs—not that there are either pets or people in Henry's life—clean, matched guest towels in the downstairs bathroom, glasses inspected for spots before they're lined up by size in the cabinets? It's not hard. Just ask him.

"Nothing to it," he answers. "It's the only way to live."

All you have to do is hold your breath all the time.

Malvina, sometimes, used to walk by and whack him in the stomach with the back of her hand, so that he'd go "Ooffff!"

"Attaboy, Henry," she'd say. "Let it all out."

Henry would pick up whatever it was he'd been carrying back to its proper place—the kitchen chair that had somehow ended up in the bathroom, the three plastic dishes he'd found under the wicker table on the porch, the dustmop that was lying on the backseat of the car— and go on his way without a word. Not that he wouldn't be thinking some words. He'd be thinking plenty of words, most of them pretty much the same: For example, how can you survive in the midst of such a mess? how can you see where you're going? how can you find anything?

Actually, Malvina is having a hard time finding what she's looking for. The telephone is down there under that pile of clothes somewhere, but every time she drags her hand through it she comes up with a knee sock or a bra or a blouse with one sleeve inside out. She hears a muffled mechanical voice telling her to hang up the receiver

and try her number again. Before she can find the receiver to do what
she'd been told, the voice is replaced by an awful buzzing that even
the pile of clothing does nothing to subdue. She's not tired and she
doesn't have to be at work until afternoon, so she thinks, Maybe I
should get some of this stuff picked up and put away. But pretty soon
the terrible buzzing stops, and she thinks, Nah, screw it, I'll do it tomorrow, knowing perfectly well she won't.

The reasons she won't are simply these: one, that she doesn't have
the slightest idea where she'd even start, given the incredible volume
of stuff to be picked up even in just this one room, with the records
and record jackets, separately, spread over the floor around the stereo
system and the books and dishes piled in layers on the chairs and the
makeup on the coffee table and the clothes, yes, the clothes everywhere; two, that once she started, there clearly would never be an
end to it, what with the bedroom still to go if she ever got the living
room cleaned up, and the bathroom after that, and the kitchen, and
the study, and meanwhile she'd still be living, right, changing
clothes, dirtying dishes, dust would be collecting, the wastebaskets
filling up, the soap dish thick with scum and her brush full of black
hair; and three, that if she went at it hard enough, if she kept at it
long enough, if she succeeded, that is, if she finally got the dishwasher emptied and all her pantyhose washed and put away, if she
got the army of overgrown dustballs swept out from under her bed
and the crud off the floor around the toilet bowl, if she cleaned the
ashes out of the fireplace and alphabetized the bookshelves and
moved her out-of-season clothes to the back hall closet and cleared
a path to the washer and dryer by stacking up the empty boxes and
grocery bags mildewing on the basement floor, pretty soon, well,
eventually, at any rate, she would find herself living in Henry's world,
with a place for everything and everything in its place, no sooner removed and used than cleaned and put back where it belongs,
known, set, fixed, immutable.

That's living? she thinks.

You think it's hard to live like Malvina does—kitchen garbage can
overflowing, records stuck away in the wrong jackets, mold flourish-
ing in the plastic container of ham salad, overdue library books

hidden under the newspapers piled on top of the refrigerator, the dog sleeping on the bed and shedding everywhere, the drawers of her desk full of scraps of paper with phone numbers on them—no names, just numbers—well? It's not hard. Just ask her.

"Nah," she says. "It's a snap. Nothing to it."

All you have to do is just let things happen all the time.

Henry, sometimes, used to walk by and pat her gently on her round little tummy, which always made her feel like purring.

But then he'd say, "Suck in that gut, lady."

And just like that her purr would turn into a growl.

*   *   *

People used to say that Henry and Malvina were the perfect couple. At the wedding, which, Henry being an Episcopalian and Malvina a Lutheran, was held at a friend's home and presided over by a mail-order minister of the Church of All Saints and Saviors, people said, searching carefully for just the right word even as they spoke, that Malvina and Henry had a certain, ahh, well, you know, a kind of . . . balance.

Can you believe that?

A balance of power, maybe. Like identical weights set on the opposite ends of a playground teeter-totter. Not a chance of ever coming to earth. A geopolitical stalemate. No wonder that, divorced, they live at opposite ends of the Twin Cities, Henry in a southwestern suburb of Minneapolis and Malvina in a northeastern suburb of St. Paul. The fulcrum on which they now balance as precariously as they once did on the thin peak of their marriage is the telephone. Which Malvina is going to pick up at any moment now.

Yes, she is going to find the now separated receiver and cradle under her pile of discarded clothing. She is going to reunite them temporarily and reestablish the missing dial tone. She is going to dial Henry's number and all hell is going to break loose. But before she does, let me ask you this:

Do you know either of these people?

Is there anything you find even remotely familiar in the behavior of either of these people?

Don't lie.

And now that you have answered that in the grudging affirmative—be thankful that, for the moment, you haven't been asked to identify *whose* behavior makes one of theirs seem so familiar to you— try this one:

Whose side are you on?

Because make no mistake about it: This is war, and you have already enlisted on one side or the other.

Be honest, be quick: because the phone is already ringing.

If Malvina's rampaging barbarian horde swept suddenly across your world, ransacking the starched and folded piles of laundry, pillaging the freshly mopped linoleum kitchen floor and other gods of household order, scattering everything at random across garage floors and lawns and suburban streets, would you be standing on the rooftop welcoming her ragtag guerrilla mob by littering those same streets with confetti or would you be huddling in the far corner of the basement, behind the home-canned peaches and tomatoes still stacked and labeled in orderly fashion on the row of metal shelves, plotting a tidy insurrection?

And if Henry's neat and soldierly columns of invaders came marching lock-stepped and starched-uniformed across your frontiers, sweeping the streets and trimming front-lawn hedges as they passed, repairing broken tricycles, oiling the city-hall clock, passing out new—and accurate—bus schedules, would you be sitting quietly at your desk composing a well-thought-out welcoming letter to the editor, or would you have fled to the slums, hiding out among rats and garbage, your mind filled with inchoate thoughts while you passed out badly printed revolutionary pamphlets in a wild-eyed attempt to rouse the citizens to rebellion?

Are you at the barricades yet? Little time remains. Henry, wondering who could be calling at this hour, has already switched on the bedside lamp and is staring at the phone that sits on his dresser, its angular edges precisely lined up with the sides of the dresser.

Malvina, wondering by now if perhaps she hasn't dialed a wrong number, is still trying to free a shirtsleeve tangled in the phone's coiled cord.

Before you know it, the first reports from the front are coming in.

✳   ✳   ✳

Did Henry know who was the only person in the world—discounting random wrong numbers, which have no place in his thinking—who was likely to be calling him at three o'clock in the morning? You bet. He is a smart fellow, much respected by his superiors in the lucid, hierarchical management structure of—you guessed it—American Container Corporation. He knows, as they all know, what belongs where. What could only go where. But, as is often the case, this knowledge neither solves nor saves. He still wants to know why. Why, Malvina, why?

And was Malvina, a smart cookie in her own right, who sets her own work hours and whose satisfied and very picky clients return again and again to have her plan the always surprising trips that only she could arrange for them, in the least bit of doubt about how Henry would react to a 3 A.M. phone call? Not a chance. But, as is often the case, certainty provides no solace either. She can't see why Henry has to be so upset.

"I guess," she says, given the terse hostility of his initial response, "people don't like to have their routines tampered with."

"This is no routine, Malvina," he tells her. "This is sleep. I have to get up to go to work at 6:30."

"Sleep is a routine, Henry."

"Work, Malvina, work."

"Work is the routinest routine of all. Why are you so defensive about your routines?"

"Because you are attacking me, Malvina," he says, and she can hear that he is about to hang up.

"Don't," she says very quickly.

"Give me one reason," he says.

"Because," she says, "I love you."

From Henry's end of the line, nothing but silence. And yet more
silence.

"So tell me, Henry," says Malvina after the silence has gone on for-ever, "how are you feeling about people these days?"

More silence. Another forever. Then: "On the whole, I would have to say that people tend to live up to your expectations of them."

"Why, Henry," exclaims Malvina, "that's the nicest thing I ever heard you say!"

What Henry meant, however, as you probably expected, was that if you expect the worst of people, then, indeed, they probably will live up to your expectations. When he explains this to Malvina, she no longer thinks it is the nicest thing she has ever heard him say.

"Some days, Henry," she finally says, "you almost convince me."

"Why, Malvina," he mimics, "that's about the nicest thing I've ever heard you say."

What Malvina meant, of course, was wreathed in the poison gas aura of sarcasm, as befits the battlefield. Aware of the lethal hazards of modern warfare, however, Henry was, as we have seen, safely en-sconced behind the gas mask of irony.

What we want to know is: Can anything of value—civilization, for example—survive the conditions of such a no-man's-and no-woman's—land as this?

And if so, how?

*   *   *

Did he say "civilization"? you've got to be wondering. I mean, these are just a couple of people, right? One basically quite screwed up and the other with a pretty reasonable perspective on life. Or, if you want, both of them complete assholes. Whatever. But "civilization"? You've got to be kidding. I mean, "Henry," for Christ's sake! "Malvina Knott"! Why, they're hardly even people, you know, why, they're just fantas-tic exaggerations, that's all, whattayacallits, stereotypes, what a joke, you can't tell me the fate of civilization depends on a pair of stereo-types, even if one of them has in fact got things figured out pretty straight. Surely you jest.

Wrong. I am not kidding. It is no joke. I never jest, at least not about matters of life and death like this.

Henry and Malvina used to live right down the street from me.

Also, I suppose, it's simply an inescapable fact that some people actually do live out more or less stereotypical existences. Maybe more people than we want to admit. That does not make them any the less real. Any the less people. Or the fate of civilization any the less dependent on them.

Stereotypes: Think of your uncle, The Absentminded Professor; your brother, The Playboy; your old college roommates, The Wimp, The Jock, and The Brain; your kid, The Teenager; your mother, The Mother.

Think of Henry. Think of Malvina.

Is the fact that she loves him, and has even managed to say so, even if it is at a totally inappropriate hour under less than ideal conditions, rendered any the less relevant because she — my former neighbor, I remind you — is, as you like to put it, a stereotype? Is the fact that he — also, remember, once a neighbor of mine — also loves her, even though he hasn't, at this miserable hour of the night, been able to say so, rendered any less ditto? And if so, what about yourself: The Salesperson, The Waiter, The Teacher, Bricklayer, Bartender, Student, Steelworker, Doctor, Policeman, Bus Driver, The Optimist, Pessimist, Moralist, Liberal, Gambler . . . we could go on forever trying to make sure there are no loose ends, but you know what I mean.

What are they going to do?

What are *you* going to do?

On whom does the future of civilization depend?

Whose side are you on *now*?

"Now" is Thursday morning. 6:29 A.M. Henry is sitting up in bed waiting for the one remaining lurch that will set off his electronic clock radio, informing him of the precise temperature and wind velocity awaiting him outside. Not that, given his projected trajectory from house to garage to car to enclosed parking ramp to elevator to office, he'll be subjecting himself to actual outside conditions. But it never hurts to know: Useless knowledge is still knowledge.

He is staring at the telephone receiver, which he still holds in his hand, on his lap.

This is the last thing he heard from the telephone receiver:

"Sterility, Henry: It's unnatural the way you've got everything so locked in place that there's nothing alive there; it's a world of things. Your house always looks like no one lives there. It's a good thing you don't have a dog; you'd spend half your life vacuuming it."

This is the last thing he said into the telephone receiver:

"Chaos, Malvina: That's the natural way of the world all right, everything scattered meaninglessly at random; nothing but things. You've got such a total mess in your house that there's no room left for anyone to live there. You spend half your life looking for your car keys."

Nothing emerges from the telephone receiver now. Not the buzz of the dial tone. Not the voice of a recording nagging someone to replace it. Not the screech of its displaced discomfort. Silence.

Malvina rolls over, face down on the couch, the silent receiver wedged against her jaw. No alarm clock is preparing to go off in her living room, but an early ray of sunlight through the front window illuminates the layer of dust on the small portion of coffee-table top that isn't covered with books, magazines, cups, glasses, a crumpled potato-chip bag. . . . With one eye cocked open, even face down she is granted by the angle of the sun a clearer perception of the density of dust than she has ever had before and thinks: Who needs it? Knowledge rendered useless because you don't intend to do anything with it is still knowledge.

So here they are, each in her, his, separate world. Hours, obviously, have passed, and the last things said resounded with the clear political overtones of the classic impasse. Now nothing passes through the channel of communication but silence. But note: The lines are still open. Soon things will begin to happen. Henry has to rise, dress, take himself off to that inescapable meeting with his boss, because . . . because . . . because that is what Henry has to do. And Malvina, likewise, is going to have to arise, sooner than she expects, because even now the dog is edging its great, shaggy body off her bed, stretching, slouching down the hall toward her, ready to demand that she take it for its morning walk and, well, that is what she is going to have to do. Or else.

So here they are, for the moment, still. Hostilities appear to have ceased, but negotiations do not appear to have begun. Can civilization survive under such a tenuous truce? In a moment the world is going to be making demands of them equivalent—or nearly so—to the demands they make of themselves, of each other. And then what? These are my neighbors, don't forget; I liked it when they lived just down the street from me and, let's face it, I miss them now that they've moved away. Why else would I be spending so much time and working so hard here trying to bring them back—when, as I'm sure you're dying to tell me, there's no way I can really know what's going on with them in their private worlds and late-night, early-morning hours since they moved off in different directions to those far-flung suburbs.

But I had better know, hadn't I? They're my neighbors, after all. At least I shall always think of them as my neighbors, even if it means remembering how Henry's always-polished car shamed mine and what Malvina's dog did to my lawn, even if they have fled in anger and dismay to those distant, disparate suburbs, abandoning me here on the home front. The telephone, I would like to remind you, is only one of the miracles we have devised to erase great distances. Here we are, after all. Anything can happen. So, like I say, I had better know. And so had you. Or else.

Closed Mondays

TODAY IS MEMORIAL DAY, a Monday naturally, and I am sitting on the steps of the museum in a T-shirt and jeans. A glorious spring day, the very edge of summer, the day that when I was a kid we always did take to be the real beginning of summer because it was the day when all over town, from the country clubs to the municipal parks, the swimming pools opened. Across the street hundreds of people are frolicking in the park right now, with children, dogs, Frisbees, balls, bottles, on the grass, in jeans, in shorts, without shirts. Lorna is sitting in the car.

Memorial Day: You would think that would jog your mind about history, wouldn't you? What I mean is, the museum is closed on Monday. It's always closed on Monday. That's a fact, a historical fact, the kind you could look up: at the library, in the newspaper, in the museum's own monthly schedule. Of course, it's also a fact that Memorial Day is May 30th, which is Wednesday, the day after tomorrow. A true fact. Just check the calendar. Only the government, of course, has long since decreed that all national holidays, regardless of the true date on which they fall, shall be observed on the nearest Monday. Except for Independence Day, which stays on the fourth of July, no matter what the day. Anyway, history being the sort of thing it is, it seemed to us more than likely that when a major holiday like Memorial Day fell on a Monday, then it wouldn't be a Monday anymore, exactly. History changes things, right? And besides, don't these holidays always feel like Sundays? Just look at all those people in the park, sprawled out on the grass with their families and six-packs and picnic baskets and baseball caps pulled down over their eyes and not thinking about going anywhere or doing anything at all. So it's not really like a Monday, you see, so naturally, especially with people having all this holiday free time on their hands, the museum should be open.

Which it isn't.

Lorna is wearing a white sundress, very pretty, sleeveless, just little straps over her shoulders, also very sexy in a sort of innocent-looking way, but not at all the thing for playing in the park, not even for sitting on the grass.

"Grass stains, William," she said when we were both still sitting in the car. "You think I want grass stains on my white dress? I'll never get them out. You go roll in the grass. Leave me alone."

We don't have a picnic basket, either, because we were going to have lunch in the museum restaurant. No blanket to spread out on the grass, no bottle of wine, no Frisbee, no dog. It goes without saying that they are not going to allow food and pets and fun games inside the museum. We don't have a dog, anyway. We used to have a dog, but that's history now, too. Sitting on the concrete steps of the museum and trying to squint through the glare of the sun into the front seat of the Datsun to where I can barely make out the figure sitting behind the wheel, I begin to get the feeling that Lorna and I—that is, Lorna-and-I—are also about to become history.

There has got to be a certain amount of history, after all, simply in the matter of why Lorna is sitting over there looking very classy in a white sundress and white shoes and a white band around her blond hair while I am sitting here in jeans and a T-shirt. Perfectly fresh and nearly new jeans, however, and a T-shirt that I particularly like, because it's from the first and only marathon I ever got up enough nerve to run in, just last month. It wasn't always like this. In the beginning, if I showed up in jeans to pick her up, she'd be wearing jeans too, and if I'd arrive in a suit and tie, which was never all that often, she'd be wearing a dress and heels, and it always just happened like that without our ever saying a word to each other ahead of time about what we were planning to wear. That, like I say, was in the beginning, and it might be worth looking into. There are whole books now, I hear, on what happened in just the first six seconds of the universe, which seems like a bit of overkill to me but certainly shows you how important beginnings are. They are the very guts of history, you might say, whereas the present is all too often just a sort of blank face, like the way the Datsun is sitting over there staring at me with its lights and grill and polished hood, the sun glaring off the windshield so I can hardly see there's anyone behind it.

We congratulated ourselves, when we first pulled up here, on being lucky enough to find a parking place on this side of the street right in front of the museum on a day like this. Just as we drove up a couple was throwing a pair of screaming kids into the backseat of an old Ford. We waited while they stood there on opposite sides of the car and glared at each other for a minute over the rusty roof; then finally they got in and slammed the doors and took off in a dark cloud of exhaust. May they have a long and happy history. Lorna pulled neatly into the spot they'd abandoned and turned off the key, and we sat there looking at the front of the museum and realizing that no one was going in or out. To them, I suppose, it was just another Monday.

"Feeling pretty smug, aren't you?" she said.

I knew perfectly well that what she was talking about was how I was dressed, even though she didn't specifically say it—didn't have to: I saw the way she'd looked at me when we left the house. She threw me one first-class look, what they call a "haughty look" in historical novels, which I think is the only place I have ever seen that word used. What I like about historical novels is how they take you into the guts of a period, I mean what people are really thinking and doing, what they wear and what they eat and drink and how they act with each other, while all that stuff that we were always taught was real history is just like a sort of shell around them, inside of which they are busy leading their lives. To me, that's the real history: the way people just go on leading their lives.

Well, she looked at my T-shirt with its purple logo and she looked at my jeans and she looked at my Sauconys, which look nearly as good as new from the outside, though the insides are so pounded down I can't use them for running anymore, and then she looked at the ceiling. Then she went out the front door with me trailing right behind her. There was nothing there to criticize, really, and besides, we've always been good about not telling each other how to do things. If she'd wanted to go off to the clinic some morning in her green pajamas, I suppose I wouldn't have said a thing. She'd learn whatever it was she had to learn from how the other people reacted at work and she'd learn it much better than from anything I said. And vice versa the time I bought her mother a rod and reel for Christmas. What good is history if we don't learn from it; that's why I think it's mostly mistakes.

Maybe my getting out of the car was a mistake, too, which is what I'm sitting here trying to learn.

"Hey," I said, "let me go look inside and see if there's anything going on." The doors are glass and it wasn't quite noon yet, so I thought maybe it was just that they were opening late today; if I could see anybody moving around inside, there was hope yet.

"That's dumb," she said. My hand was on the door handle already, but I'm not one to walk away when someone is talking to me.

"Beg pardon?" I said. I have this habit of getting very formal whenever someone starts coming on hostile to me. It lets them know that you know what they're up to, and at the same time you don't have to get belligerent yourself. It also gives them a second chance. They can say, "Oh, nothing," or change the subject or apologize or just walk away or whatever. I credit it with keeping me out of a lot of fights. Lorna hates it.

"I said," she said, "that that's just the dumb sort of thing I'd expect from someone who'd go to the museum in a T-shirt and jeans."

I knew she didn't say all that and she knew she didn't say all that, but at the same time we both knew that she did, because we both knew just what she had said—the simple historical fact—and that what we were getting now was interpretation, which seems to be what people always think they have to do with the simple facts. I didn't need it.

"I see," I said, though I wasn't 100 percent sure that I did. That is, I didn't see why she was making an issue about what I was wearing, especially now that we were here, and more especially since it didn't look like we were going to get in, anyway. Basically, I was just interested in the question: Was the museum going to open today or wasn't it? If my clothes were an issue, it seemed to me that was really past history by now and should have been dealt with before we started out. She knows as well as anyone that I have to wear a uniform all week— she wears one herself, the same color as her sundress—and she knows that anyone who wears a uniform to work should have a right to be as casual as he wants on the weekend. That doesn't mean be a slob. I'm no slob. She would never have got hooked up with a slob. It just means comfortable. She looks comfortable in her sundress — or did till we got here — and I'm comfortable in my T-shirt and jeans.

By that time I had my door open and was halfway out of the car, mumbling something about just wanting to check but mostly just wanting a breath of fresh air. It was beginning to feel very stuffy in there. No sooner was I out than she leaned over and grabbed the handle and slammed the door shut behind me.

"You just take your time, William," she said.

It didn't take any time, of course — I could see right off that there wasn't a soul moving in there, and of course there's a sign on the door that lists all the museum hours, Tuesday through Sunday, and then at the bottom says, "Closed Mondays" — but then I thought I'd better take a little time, anyway. Just strolling right back and casually saying, "Nope, nobody home," didn't seem like quite the right thing to do. It was an invitation to sarcasm, that was what it was. Going back with some sort of an apology would have been all right, if I could have figured out what I was supposed to apologize for. Going back and saying nothing was also a possibility, but it seemed to me that that would leave us right where we were before. Like I said, it was probably getting out of the car in the first place that was a mistake.

So I'm sitting here on the museum steps in this nice sunshine, watching shirtless young studs chasing soaring Frisbees in the park across the way and girls in shorts and halters sitting on blankets sipping diet colas and little kids and big dogs chasing each other around in circles, and wondering what I've learned. Sometimes I think my real problem is that I know too much. I know that sounds like an odd sort of thing to be a problem, and that most people would probably like to know a lot more than they do, but one of the things I know is that knowing too much can get in the way of learning. Frankly, when Lorna and I first started going out, I did think of myself as pretty dumb. In a lot of ways I probably was. I mean, I had a good job, I was earning good money — assistant chief of security for a large corporation is not bad for someone my age, just ask around — and I'd put myself through school to get there, too, because they expect you to have some education for a responsible position like that. And with good reason, too, considering the kind of people you come into contact with. But there was a lot I didn't know, too, especially about people. Probably the fact that I had to work all the time, all the way through school and everything, and mostly in solitary jobs at odd hours—cleaning toilets in parochial schools, sweeping out factories between midnight and morning, locked in a Plexiglas cage collecting money at an all-night self-serve gas station—has a lot to do with that, but I don't want to make excuses. When I met Lorna I was ready to learn. And she was ready to teach.

That was when we got the dog. Fido. I'm sorry, but that's the truth; that was its name when we got it, and even though it was still pretty young, neither of us could make the move to change it. We were still that new with each other, that neither one of us wanted to claim the right to rename it. Naming is a very important act. Like when you call someone "dumb," right? But I had to keep the dog because Lorna was living in a new apartment that didn't allow pets, so I said she should at least get to name it. And she said no, since I had to be training it and calling it all the time, at least I should have the right to decide what to call it. So in the end we just left it Fido. It was an ugly little thing, anyway. Big head, short legs, thin white fur but black blotches in odd places, like over one eye. Poor little bastard.

It probably seems like a strange thing to do, to get a dog right at the beginning of a romance, but sometime along there in those first few weeks we were going together, it came out that each of us had always wanted a dog, but for one reason or another had never had one. For me, it had been school and work, the long hours, that is; it wouldn't have been fair to get a dog and then just leave it alone all the time. And before that, my parents, who hated all pets, even goldfish or turtles, and made my sister give her lucky cricket away. For her it was always having lived in apartments that banned pets, even when she was a kid, which was probably why she'd moved into a place just like that on her own, even though she loved dogs. Pets are important: We agreed on a lot of things like that.

Besides, I think we both also felt that a dog would be one more thing to tie us together, I mean something really solid, not like the feelings, which were there, sure, but you can't get your hands on them like you can on a dog. Or maybe even a cat. At least I know I felt that way, which was why I was glad to have the job of taking care of Fido, in spite of his not being housebroken and all. He was there when Lorna wasn't around, and that was important to me. After a few weeks, when he'd learned to behave pretty well around the house, I signed us up for obedience school, being careful to schedule it on a night when Lorna was out—going to school herself, as a matter of fact—so it wouldn't interfere with our time together. She's a nurse and has to keep her training up-to-date, so every once in a while she takes an evening class at the university.

Needless to say, I wasn't prepared for what happened when I told her about the obedience course.

"You what?" she said. We were in the car then, too. I'd picked her up at the clinic and we were going out to dinner as soon as she had a chance to change. It does seem to me that an awful lot of important things happen in cars. For good or for bad, cars are certainly a part of our history, and I don't just mean mine and Lorna's. Fido's, too, for that matter. He was in the backseat.

Well, it turned out—in some people's opinion, at least—that what I was doing was not helping to make a better, happier, and more obedient pet, as the ads for the course promised, but engaging in an out-and-out power play. Namely, turning Fido into *my* dog.

"But I'm doing this for us," I protested. At least I honestly believed I was. All I'd been thinking when I signed up for the course was how we'd take him for walks together, and he'd heel and fetch and stay right with us and not run around picking fights with other dogs or pestering people the way some dogs I've seen do. But like I said, Lorna was a teacher—that's what she really wants to do, in fact: teach in a nursing program—and I was ready to learn. It was rush hour and the traffic was pretty heavy, both inside the car and out, but I felt that even in the midst of it all I was already learning something, namely, that things aren't always what they seem. A very important lesson, but, frankly, not always a very helpful one, as is often the case when we are only told what things are not. I mean, does it help for me to say that that was not a Jaguar I was driving that afternoon?

Meanwhile I was trying to keep my attention both on the freeway traffic and on what Lorna was telling me, and I wasn't having an easy time with either. Friday afternoon brings all the crazies out on the freeway, hot to get to their end-of-the-week parties, and it doesn't look good for someone in security to have black marks on his driving record. And Lorna was coming on hot and heavy about manipulation, which was not all getting through to me clearly both because she was rant-and-rave angry and because I was upset at seeing her angry like this. It was the first time that either of us had let go at the other like that. And I really was trying to understand—I mean, to explore my own motives, which she was so busy calling into question—even though I couldn't see how sweet, ugly, little Fido, who I could see in the rearview mirror was sitting up in the backseat like a perfect gentleman, could be a symbol, as she said, of my attempt to take control of our relationship.

So, to get it over with, as soon as we pulled up across the street from her apartment building, and she hopped out of the car, not having cooled down one bit, while I was trying to ask her if we were still going out to dinner and what with one thing and another not paying as much attention to things as I should have, Fido jumped out after her and on those short little legs of his was chugging across to her building, which he knew from having accompanied me to the door to pick her up so many times—well, the fact is, we did sneak him in for a few hours now and then—when the Caddy got him.

So, just like that, Fido was history. Ditto the lesson, argument, whatever it was. Something I should have learned, probably. Tears. Her fault. My fault. The driver of the Caddy was very insistent it was not his fault. Also very red-faced, like his car, and fat and drunk. Just go away and leave us alone, we asked, which suited him fine. In her apartment we both got a little drunk ourselves and never did go out to dinner. She hung on me and cried, "William, William," and, "Fido, Fido," without much seeming to distinguish between the two, and I

tried to figure out what exactly had happened, but the only thing I
could come up with was that Fido was dead.

No, that's not really all, though in my humble opinion it was more
than enough. No, if I learned anything else that evening, while I took
turns drying Lorna's tears and my own, and refilled our wineglasses,
and eventually unbuttoned our clothes, what I learned was that there
is a price to be paid for knowing too much and also that someone else
usually pays it. Yes, I learned that there is no learning without loss.
Which, I decided sometime later, was not a piece of knowledge worth
paying for with Fido's life. When you think about learning from history, you don't usually think of history as being someone, or something, you care about.

Meanwhile, I see from the museum steps that there's this pretty
young woman coming across the street toward me, dragging a pretty
little look-alike girl behind her by the hand, both of them looking very
uncomfortable. They're both barefoot and dressed in identical green
shorts and pink T-shirts with pictures of Mt. Rushmore on them,
which reminds me again that it's a national holiday rapidly going to
waste here. A Memorial Day to be remembered. Well, they're not too
thrilled, either, with what they find out from me.

"Would you believe it?" says the woman. "This whole goddamned
park and not a single public john, not even a whichamacallit,
satellite."

She was hoping, probably every bit as badly as I'd been, that the
museum was open, which of course I have to tell her it's not. The
little girl is squirming around behind her mother, squeezing her legs
together. I look around, trying to see if there are any other possibili-
ties in the neighborhood, because obviously there isn't a lot of time
left, and also wondering if Lorna is watching and, if so, what she's
making of this. Across the street in the park I can see which guy these
two belong two. He has a thick black beard and a terrific tan, and he's
sitting on an old army blanket watching them, shading his eyes with
his hand from the sun, which is pretty much right overhead now.
High noon. Also he's got the other hand on the collar of a young
Airedale that's sitting beside him on the blanket, panting like crazy.

Beyond the two of them there's that whole park full of people and, like she said, not a sign of a public toilet that I can see, even with the advantage of being up on the museum steps where I can overlook the whole place. Across the park are a couple of churches, which are a good ways off—from the kid's squirming I have to doubt if they could make it in time—and not likely to be any help anyway, it not being Sunday. On the other side of the park is a row of stores along the highway there, but not the kind that's ever open on Sundays and holidays: the Firestone Tire Center and a dry cleaner and an office-supply store and a few others like that. It looks pretty hopeless to me, and I look back to the park to where the guy's sitting, wondering isn't he going to be any help, he must be the father after all, but he's not there. He's about ten yards away picking up a stray Frisbee and tossing it back to two longhaired blond teenagers in bikinis, standing there with their hands on their hips watching him.

And the dog, which of course he is no longer holding onto, is making a wild dash across the street to the woman and the little girl. And so help me, there is a red Caddy bearing down on it.

"Oh, shit!" I say. I jump to my feet although I know there's nothing I can do.

The woman looks around and screams. I look down at her from where I'm standing a couple of steps higher up and see that, behind her, the little girl has finally let go. There is a puddle already running down the concrete steps. Then I hear the thunk and the yelp.

By the time I get to the street Lorna is already there. She is kneeling in the middle of the street with the Airedale's head leaning against her. The dog is panting even harder now, probably in shock, and bleeding from a gash on its left shoulder, but it doesn't actually look all that serious. Possibly a broken leg and definitely in need of a vet, but the car wasn't moving all that fast, what with all the kids and picnickers around, and it was probably as much a case of dog hits car as vice versa. It'll live.

I look up over it at Lorna to tell her what I think, but what I find myself saying is, "Your dress!"

The skirt of her white sundress is covered with brown dirt and red blood stains. She doesn't even look at it herself. She gives me not ex-

actly what they call in historical novels a "withering look," but something not all that far from it, either.

"William, it's just a puppy," she says. For a moment there, I think
that what I have heard her say is, "William's just a puppy," but then
I look down at the young Airedale again and realize I must have been
hearing things.

Meanwhile, a considerable crowd has gathered around us. The
woman with the little girl is standing right behind me, I see, crying,
holding her daughter on her hip so that the wet stain is now spreading to her own shorts.

"It'll be OK," I tell her. "It just needs to be taken to the vet right
away."

The tall, gray-haired woman who was driving the Caddy is trying
to lean in from behind the crowd to see what's happening. She
catches my eye.

"I never saw it," she says.

"Lady," I tell her, "you never had a chance."

There's a sudden commotion in the crowd on the opposite side,
and when I look I see that it's the black-bearded guy trying to push his
way through.

"Jesus Christ!" I hear him saying. "Now what?"

Which is what I'm thinking myself as I look at Lorna. But that's always the question, isn't it: Now what? And how much help is any of
what you think you know, any of what you've been through before,
really going to be when it comes to that? I'm not talking your practical stuff, of course—naturally all the first-aid training I got when I
started working security comes in handy at times like this—but all the
rest, all the rest, where what it comes down to finally is that all you
have got to rely on is yourself. On the best of days that can make you
feel pretty dumb. But you have got to do what you can with what
you've got—what you are—or else you risk falling back into . . . what?
Stupidity, maybe. History, I suppose. And, I am thinking as I reach
across the panting dog to brush some of the mess off Lorna's skirt, you
do not want to close yourself down like that, now, do you? But I see I
am just spreading the stains.

Found

WHEN FOUND, he was sitting in a meadow, propping himself up with his right arm and with his left hand feeling around in the high, bristly grass for his glasses, which were not there. A warm wind was twisting its fingers through his thin hair, and in the distance, warmer still, thick black smoke was making a terrible mess of the late spring sky, though without his glasses he couldn't see any of that. Nor, in his current state, would he have realized it had anything to do with him.

When the ones who found him asked his name, he only hesitated a moment before answering. And perhaps it was just their odd solicitousness, the way one bent down over him and another, kneeling in the grass in front of him, breathed out a thin, surprised whistle, and a third, beside him, reached out her hand to wipe something from his forehead, that made him hesitate.

"Professor," she said, reaching into the leather bag she'd laid by her side and taking out a tissue to wipe again at whatever it was on his forehead that so bothered her, "do you know what you're doing here?"

"Of course," he answered. "I'm looking for my glasses." He smiled, or thought he did, and peered hard into her face, looking to make sure that she understood him, but without his glasses her face remained mostly a pale blur, a vague white flower surrounded by fuzzy dark foliage.

"Can you help me find my glasses?" he added.

They said nothing, however—the only sound that came to him was the deep, prolonged, distant barking of a large dog—and made no effort to assist in his search, being reasonably certain that his glasses were nowhere to be found.

✳   ✳   ✳

As the sole survivor of the crash, he was, of course, the object of intense media attention. A professor of literature, he would have liked to tell them, in the glare of bright afternoon sunshine and their brighter camera lights outside the hospital's emergency room exit from which he was emerging, "I alone am left to tell you." Only he had nothing to tell them. Embarrassed, not just to be there but to be there in such profound ignorance, he ducked his head and squeezed his wife's hand as hard as he dared without hurting her. The light bounced off his bowed, bald head, making a pale corona of the thin fringe of hair that circled it above his ears. Turning slightly, he could see his wife squinting in the glare, the fine lines that radiated outward from her eyes filled with moisture—tears or sweat, he couldn't tell.

The hospital spokesperson, a tall woman in a dark suit, whose features, towering above him, he couldn't make out in that enormous wash of light even though his wife had brought him his extra pair of glasses, sniffed into the bouquet of microphones pushed into her face and said something he couldn't understand. From somewhere in the back of the crowd a reporter whistled loudly between his fingers and barked out a question. He felt relieved when she simply ignored this rudeness and went on with her prepared explanation: that he had no injuries beyond a few scratches and bruises, that the hospital was releasing him, that he apparently knew, or remembered, nothing of the event. Intermittent flashes burst through the whiteness of the afternoon, like supernovas exploding in the vast distances of a universe he was not really sure he was a part of. He had the vague feeling that someone had barged into his classroom in the middle of the afternoon while he was engaged in an animated discussion with his senior seminar on Twain, and had marched to the podium he never used and begun a lecture on a topic of which he was wholly ignorant. One of those postmodern theorists. The whole class was fascinated, but he himself had no idea what it was all about.

Mercifully, at last, the class seemed to be ending. A dark car drew up in front of them, and it was only when his wife had eased him into the backseat and slid in beside him, and he saw the metal screen in front of him and the uniform of the driver, that he realized it was a police car.

"Now what have I done?" he wondered aloud.

His wife patted the thick-veined hand she held and tilted her head against his shoulder.

*   *   *

When he entered his eight o'clock class the following Monday morning, a sudden hush fell over the twenty students, who were usually so busy chatting away over the Styrofoam cups of coffee and plastic yogurt containers and doughnuts and Diet Cokes that he encouraged them to bring that he had to call loudly for their attention. They were, he saw, all staring at his desk in the front of the room, where there was no space for the armload of books he'd been about to set on it. It was covered from edge to edge with a strange variety of objects: unlit candles upright in cracked china saucers; small plastic figurines, including one of a dog that bore a remarkable resemblance to his own golden retriever, Salman; a coffee mug emblazoned with the college seal; a couple of CDs with wholly unrecognizable titles; several of those small, blank-paged books his students loved to carry about with them; a scroll rolled and tied with a purple ribbon; a silver whistle attached to a long, braided lanyard; a plastic-framed newspaper clipping of a photo of himself taken outside the hospital; several pieces of fruit, a bagel, and an oversized Baby Ruth candy bar; a single red carnation, the base of its stem wrapped in foil.

He hadn't seen anything like it since a trip to Mexico many years ago, when he and his wife had been taken by friends to visit their village on Día de los Muertos, the Day of the Dead. It was an altar, a shrine. He had no idea how to respond. He was still hugging his armload of books to his chest, so he set them down on the arm of an empty desk in the front row and then, not knowing what else to do, sat down in the desk himself. After a little time had passed, he leaned forward and wrestled his handkerchief out of his back pocket and took off his glasses and breathed on them and carefully, slowly, polished them. Then he placed his glasses back on his face, stuffed the handkerchief halfway back into its pocket, and resumed staring at the laden desk before him. With his back to the class and hardly a sound to be heard from behind him, not a cough or a whisper, only the occasional slurp of someone sipping at coffee or a Coke, he had no idea what was happening.

Nor did he have any idea how much time had passed when the students began to rise and gather their belongings and slowly leave the classroom, each of them pausing to touch him on the back or shoulder as they passed.

He was still sitting there, staring blankly at the strange collection on the wide desk in front of him, when students began to file in for the next class.

*   *   *

When the police car had delivered them to their home, there had been a substantial crowd gathered on the sidewalk and lawn in front of the two-story Victorian they had so carefully restored with their own labor. The officer had ushered them quickly through the dense throng: neighbors, people they recognized but had never exchanged more than nods with over all the years they'd lived there, some with their dogs on leashes, as if they'd just been out for a stroll; strangers as well, people they'd never seen before; and, of course, the media folk with their microphones and video cameras. It was beginning to rain, softly, just as his wife dug her key out of her purse and swung the front door open, and he felt relieved, thinking that would disperse the crowd, but glancing back out as he thanked the officer and pulled the door shut, he saw that it only produced a flurry of opening umbrellas, as if they had all come prepared for such weather, though the sun had been shining in clear spring skies when his plane had made its brief departure from the ground in the early morning and shining still as he left the hospital not fifteen minutes ago. It briefly crossed his mind as he walked through the oddly empty house where no dog leapt up to greet him and into the kitchen where his wife was putting the teakettle on, that if it had suddenly started to snow all those people out there would have been pulling on down jackets and woolen hats and mittens. It was as if all the world was ready and waiting for something like this to happen.

The strange ringing he was hearing as he entered the kitchen was, he realized, the telephone. He looked at it hanging whitely on the wall with a dim sense that it was summoning him to some sort of obligation, but was happy to see his wife crossing the kitchen with a flowered dish towel in her hands, waving him away from it. She took the phone from the wall and stood there listening for a moment, then said, as smoothly as if she'd been long rehearsing these lines that he was to hear her utter into the telephone many times over the coming weekend, "Yes, he's fine, just a little shaken up as you might expect. He remembers nothing of the crash, though."

Well, he thought, easing himself onto a cane-bottomed chair at the kitchen table, unlike everyone else apparently, I wasn't anticipating something like this happening. I wasn't prepared. I wasn't paying attention. Wouldn't you know, the professor slept through the most important class in his life. He took off his glasses, laid them on the table in front of him, and rubbed his eyes. Then he smiled blurredly up at his wife, who was already repeating herself for the next caller, who had the phone ringing the instant she'd hung up from the first. She pointed toward the range, where the teakettle was just beginning to whistle, so he hooked his glasses back over his ears, pushed himself up out of his chair, and went to fill the pot.

It was going to be a long weekend and they were going to drink a lot of tea while she answered one phone call after another in nearly identical fashion and from time to time reported to him, from the television that he refused to watch, that there was still no news about the cause of the crash.

He himself felt mildly curious about that, but in a distant, disinterested sort of way. There was doubtless going to be a question about it on the final exam, but he had slept through the lecture, and now there was no way to make it up.

*   *   *

Although his other colleagues had pretty much left him alone, respecting his reputation for privacy and assuming that his immediate return to campus was a clear indication that he was, indeed, as fine as his wife had asserted when they telephoned, the dean of students caught up with him later in the week at lunch in the faculty dining room and gradually brought the conversation around to suggesting that he might find some benefit in counseling. There were various people she could recommend, off campus, needless to say. She could see that he was functioning perfectly well, of course, but deep down there had to be trauma. Deep down, she assured him, there was always trauma.

He demurred, politely. How could there be trauma on a day and in a place like this? The campus was at the height of its spring glory, tulips and crab apples and flowering shrubs blossoming everywhere; the dining room hummed with the animated conversation of colleagues at half a dozen tables around them; through the open windows they could hear the chirping and whistling of birds and the cries of students tossing Frisbees on the lawn; and the glare of sunlight streaming in turned his glasses nearly opaque, a sensation he found surprisingly pleasant. Besides, he had never found the need to consult a therapist before, and what would they be doing, anyway, exploring his childhood, sibling rivalries and parental peculiarities? What did that have to do with anything now?

"There's that memory-loss business," she reminded him.

He set the second half of his ham and swiss sandwich down, thinking, What memory loss? He remembered his siblings and his parents perfectly well, too much so, if anything. Then he realized what she was referring to and that she knew about it because, as his wife had reported to him, the media had given it considerable attention, finding it the one bit of comic relief in the greatest mass tragedy the city had ever suffered.

"Believe me," he assured the dean, "it's no loss."

But she didn't believe him. She was, after all, a trained clinical psychologist who had come to her current position after a decade of counseling students through all sorts of traumas—through broken romances and parental divorces, crippled old dogs and precious childhood possessions disposed of while they were away at school, through drug crises and suicide attempts—and she knew whereof she spoke when she spoke of repression.

"This is issue oriented," she said, assuring him that the issue was not his family of origin, not for now, anyway.

But he couldn't see what the issue was. "It's a blank," he insisted, going back to nibbling on his sandwich. "There is no issue."

"Just like the Nixon tapes?" she taunted.

"You're implying I did this deliberately?" he wanted to know.

"What do *you* think?" she replied in her best therapeutic style.

✳   ✳   ✳

Although not a regular conference goer, he'd thought the trip would be a lark, his first visit to the Deep South in the springtime, so he'd booked the earliest available morning flight in order to have a full day to himself exploring the Oxford area before the Faulknerians gathered earnestly for the evening's inaugural session. He'd invited his wife to accompany him, but as a member of the Metropolitan Transport Commission she was already scheduled to attend a long weekend planning retreat. Still, she had plenty of time to drive him to the airport before dropping off Salman, who was happily curled up on the backseat, with the friend who would be keeping him for the weekend while they were both away. At the departure area she got out of the car to give him a farewell hug and kiss—he remembered that quite clearly—before he went on to pick up a *New York Times* at the concourse newsstand and roll his carry-on bag through the security checkpoint and barely find time to take a seat in the waiting area before his flight was called.

It was like any other flight he'd ever been on, except for a certain tone of slightly excessive jollity. The several children who boarded just in front of him skipped happily down the ramp ahead of their laughing parents. He'd never seen flight attendants quite so chipper and attentive to passenger needs. They were as gracious as party hosts to a young couple who boarded at the last minute, their arms filled with long-stemmed red roses. The fat man who finally squeezed into the aisle seat next to him was whistling as he hoisted an enormous piece of luggage into the overhead rack. Even the captain, welcoming them aboard over the intercom, sounded as if he were on a holiday.

He found this all mildly amusing, if a bit odd, and, as the plane backed away from the gate, he let himself slip quietly away from it, adjusting his glasses on his nose and burrowing into the pages of his newspaper—he always looked forward to the Friday education section—while the jet rolled down the runway gathering speed for its takeoff.

And though it was, later, as obvious to him as to everyone else that something of enormity occurred shortly after, that was, in fact, all he remembered.

✻   ✻   ✻

The air-conditioning in the therapist's waiting room was on, but something faulty in the system, perhaps a vent not properly opened, was causing it to make a whistling sound in which he thought he recognized, above the bubbling of the fish tank, the melody of a popular song from his youth, from the days of dances in gyms and his first crushes on girls in tight sweaters. It's Prufrock, he thought, the mermaids singing, each to each, he could almost smell the heavy lilac perfume most of the girls he knew wore back then, and he hoped that this wasn't the sort of thing he was about to be drawn back into. What, he had to wonder, was he doing here? His wife, perhaps the only person in the world as uncurious as he was about those missing minutes, that gap in the tape of his memory, was waiting at home to hear how this session went. He could easily picture her, curled up in a corner of the living-room couch, a cup of herbal tea cooling on the low table in front of her, immersed in one of those grand nineteenth-century Russian novels. Turgenev, he recalled it was just now, whom he'd never read himself but who ranked high up on the list of authors he'd been saving to read during his retirement.

He was shivering slightly, goosebumps pricking his bare forearms. Earlier, he'd debated with himself over how to dress for this appointment, but by the time he'd come down from his shower to have coffee and toast with his wife, the early summer heat wave had decided for him, and he was wearing a polo shirt and khakis. Now, remembering how uncomfortable air-conditioning generally made him, especially in public places, movie theaters and restaurants, he wished he'd worn a long-sleeved shirt and a sport coat. He rubbed his arms to little effect, then picked up off a side table the June issue of *Field and Stream*, which seemed somehow an odd thing to find in this setting — did therapists hunt and fish? — though he did admire the golden retriever pictured on the cover standing over a pair of mallard decoys.

He sat in a hard plastic chair and idly flipped the pages for a few minutes, registering absolutely nothing. When he dropped the magazine back on the table, it occurred to the teacher in him that if the psychologist he was about to see were to begin, as he began so many of his own classes, by administering a reading quiz, he would clearly fail. Here was another gap of some minutes in the transcript of his life. Had it now become a major focus in his life to find, once again, these little snippets that had been cut out by . . . what? Distraction? Absent-mindedness? Indifference? Senility? Trauma? Choice? Could one so readily choose, deliberately, as the dean had implied, not to remember something, or wouldn't it be like that old comic routine where you told someone, Now, whatever you do, don't think about elephants?

Just then the door to the inner office opened, and he stood up to greet, or be greeted by, the tall, darkly bearded and dark-suited youngish man who marched out, shoulders thrown back and a wide, pleasant smile on his face. But when all he received was a nod as the man exited quickly through the outer door into the hallway, he realized it was not the therapist he had risen for but, no doubt, the patient who had the previous appointment. Still, he thought, that smile was promising, and the posture likewise, though who knew what had really gone on behind that closed door, muffled by the sad old melodies of the fish tank and the air-conditioning, what secret pains had been probed till they ached anew, what terrible losses had been dredged up out of ancient sea bottoms, out of the rancid, decaying muck of the past, and held, dripping, to the light.

He couldn't really explain, when he got home, how he had then suddenly found himself standing out on the hot asphalt of the parking lot beside the professional office building, his glasses fogging up from sweat and humidity, his hand on the door of his Toyota, watching the young man who'd preceded him pull out into the street in a gleaming black BMW.

✳   ✳   ✳

For several weeks immediately following the crash, he had found himself pursued rather relentlessly by media people, both local and national, seeking, sometimes even demanding, interviews. They called his home at any hour from dawn to midnight, and on occasion he found one of them standing on his doorstep when he went out to fetch the morning paper he was still refusing to read—a small task he soon asked his wife to take over, as she had already taken over managing the phone calls—or lurking there when he returned home from the college. On one occasion he caught a young man with a camera standing in the petunia bed, attempting to peer in through a living-room window. They showed up at his office as well and sometimes even his classroom, had the nerve to sit right down at his table when he was eating lunch at one of the campus-area restaurants, and would not be satisfied with his brief, clear, simple, and honest assertion that he knew nothing, remembered nothing. They had their lists of questions: What did it feel like to be thrown from a plane plunging earthward at hundreds of miles per hour? When did he first realize what was happening? What was his initial reaction? What actions did he take to save himself? He had nothing to tell them.

For the most part they seemed to him decent people who only wanted, they insisted, the "human interest angle" on this disaster that was still being investigated, but even that was a term that puzzled him, though he'd heard it all his life. Wasn't everything of human interest, from the behavior of atomic particles to the affection of a dog for its master, from the workings of the internal combustion engine to questions of international law, missing matter, and the mind-body dichotomy? What he would have asked them if he hadn't wanted to bring these increasingly painful little encounters to a speedy conclusion was, Isn't all interest human interest? But then, he supposed, he would have had to add that he didn't intend to preclude the interests of the rest of the animate world, which unfortunately he knew little about though he assumed that reading newspapers and watching TV were not among them.

Most demanding of all were the people — he couldn't bring himself to think of them as reporters — who came literally pounding on his front door from the weekly checkout-counter tabloids, holding signed contracts up for him to see through the diamond- shaped window set into its solid oak frame. The sums they offered for what they referred to as his "story" seemed to him quite amazing, but equally amazing was how nonplussed they remained when he told them that he had no story, that he presumed the whole world must know by now that he remembered nothing of what had happened, that he hadn't the slightest clue as to how or why he and he alone had survived. Never mind, they were quick to assure him, all they really wanted was the right to use his name; their own writers were quite capable of providing the story. But as nice as the money sounded, when he pictured the front page of, say, *Weekly World News*, headlined PROFESSOR SURVIVES FATAL AIR CRASH, LOSES BRAIN, right above a photo of a three-headed dog chomping down on a thrashing child with each sharp-fanged mouth, he found he had to turn it down.

Even the campus paper had come to him, in the person of a young woman he remembered from a freshman Intro to Lit course a few years back — where he recalled her spending the first few minutes of practically every class bent over the floor in front of her desk searching for a dropped contact lens — and a scraggly-bearded photographer who came whistling into his office right on her heels. Because she had called ahead to make an appointment to see him and had promised to keep it brief, because the photographer so obviously adored her and was barely able to take his eyes off of her long enough to snap half a dozen shots of the professor seated at his desk, because, he supposed, they simply were who they were, he found he was willing to accommodate them, though of course he had nothing to tell them. No problem, she explained; they mainly just wanted his picture to accompany a longer piece on the crash. He noticed that she hadn't even taken a notepad from her backpack when she set it down on the floor just inside his doorway.

When he had arrived on campus the next morning and picked up the paper from a stack in the little kiosk outside his office building, he found that his photo on the front page was next to photos of two students whom he recalled meeting at a departmental social event early in the semester. They too, the article informed him, had been on the plane, on their way to a national debate tournament in Birmingham.

My God, he had thought, carrying the paper up three flights of stairs to his office, refusing to make eye contact with anyone he passed in the halls, closing the door behind him, dropping his briefcase on the floor, and slumping down in the swivel chair at his desk, I have not only remembered nothing but I have known nothing all along, nothing at all.

✳   ✳   ✳

Salman, the big golden retriever, pushed himself up from the carpet at the foot of the couch and stretched and ambled over to lick his hand when he returned home from his aborted visit to the therapist. His wife was just finishing her novel as he entered, and he noticed as she set it down on the coffee table to rise and greet him, its bright, multicolored paper cover shining up at him like a garden in full bloom, that it wasn't Turgenev after all; it wasn't even Russian.

"Let him out, won't you?" she said. "He hasn't been outside all morning."

He walked through the house with the dog padding along at his heels and let him out the back, holding the screen door open for him. The dog paused there, shaking his head as if to clear the heat and the morning's sleep away, then went out onto the small back porch, looked around, and slowly descended the steps into the fenced yard, ignoring the loud bang of the screen door as its tight spring snapped it shut.

In the kitchen, his wife was poking around inside the refrigerator, wondering aloud if there was enough of yesterday's tuna salad left for another lunch, but he wasn't hungry. There was an emptiness in the bowl of his belly, but it didn't feel like something food could fill.

He stood in the middle of the kitchen, pushing his thumb and forefinger up under his glasses to squeeze his eyes shut. "I didn't see him," he announced abruptly.

His wife straightened up with the plastic container of tuna salad in her hands. "I didn't think it was very likely."

He didn't know what to make of her tone: judgmental or simply matter-of-fact? He didn't know what to think of his actions himself: fear or foolishness or simply a fact and facet of who he was? At commencement, roasting in their black robes under the hot sun on the campus lawn while uninspired speakers struggled to deliver inspiration, one of his colleagues had leaned over and asked, in a whisper, if he suffered now from fear of flying. It hadn't occurred to him. There was nowhere he'd been thinking of going, anyway.

Looking into the container of tuna salad his wife was holding out to him and deciding that, well, maybe he'd sit down and have a little something to eat with her after all, he realized that he was quite happy to find himself just where he was and not particularly in need of understanding how he got there. There was a lot that he didn't know or remember; maybe it was mechanical failure, as had only a week ago been reported about the crash, and maybe it was something else altogether, some sort of emotional terrorism at work, but he did know where he was now, and whatever might be missing, whatever gaps hung there like empty parentheses in the book of his life, what he had was a pure gift.

While his wife was setting plates on the table and dishing out the salad onto beds of lettuce, he opened the back door and stepped out on the porch to look for Salman, who didn't like to stay outside in such hot weather and would ordinarily have been barking at the screen by now. It was only than that he noticed that the little gate back by the garage was swinging open, probably left that way by the meter reader, who usually came in from the alley. No Salman.

When his wife called out that lunch was ready, he was still standing on the back porch whistling for the dog, who had a habit of disappearing like this for hours at a time, whenever the gate was accidentally left open, but always found his way home.

The High Hard One

THE TRUTH IS, it's just a job. That may not make it sound like much, especially when a lot of other people both inside the game and out of it seem to think otherwise, but I have come to learn not only that that is what it is, but that that is what it's truly all about. Once you get past the thin veneer of the glitz and the transient smoke of the glory, which don't mean that much to anyone who's ever looked death straight in the eye and seen it fire a vicious look back at you like a live fastball thrown at your head with every intention of putting you out of the game forever, you've got to face the fact that what it is, is a job, which is not just a way of earning a living, but a chance to do what you can do, which is the most that anyone could ask for.

And this one is a blue-collar job at that. You work it with your hands, with your body and your sweat, and there's nothing wrong with that, either. It was blue-collar bodies that built this country and blue-collar sweat that keeps it going, though I'm pleased to see that the pay's gone up considerably for this sort of laboring man at least, the one who sweats for it gripping a bat or ball, his hand in a glove, his feet in the field or running the bases, flinging his body across real dirt or artificial grass, and I'm glad they're not just paying us by the hour, either. It's not a bad life, and I never forget at the end of any game, any dog-day week or losing season, that no matter how beat I am, no matter what I did or didn't do out there, whatever the final score or standings, I have done what I can do and I'm still not dead.

So even though I'd agree that the money's too much—not just for guys like me, but for anybody—in my eyes money's not the point of it, doesn't really have anything to do with it, and therefore I don't have much patience with the people who throw my dollars up to me, whether it's the fans, the sportswriters, or people like my ex-wife, who won't even call me by my real name anymore. "Hey, Big Spender," her message on my answering machine says, "how 'bout buying your kid a new bike?"

I just bought Robin a bike last Christmas, but if she needs a new one already, OK, I'll buy her a new one, it's almost time for her birthday anyway. But I get tired of the "Big Spender" this and "Moneybags" that. Is it my fault she decided to cut and run while I was still struggling at Fort Wayne? She should have done her job, kept the faith. Thank God somebody in the organization did—there were times I was beginning to wonder myself—but it's a fact that she was never a team player, even when we were on our personal winning streak. Not on my team, anyway.

"Hey, Big Spender, see you couldn't get the ball out of the infield last night. What's the matter, moneybags holding you down?" That was her last message. It's easy to see whose bench she's sitting on.

I'm sitting on ours late in the game thinking about these daily digs she loves to leave me—she must listen to the games because she never calls when I'm home—when Goody Goodson squeezes my leg, hard, just above the knee, where he knows the swelling is, then grabs his bat and heads for the on-deck circle. Asshole. He'd rather see me on the DL than win a pennant. Looks like he may get his wish, too, because we're seven games out with less than a month to go and I figure I'll be lucky if the knee holds out another week. And if the knee goes, you can bet I won't be far behind.

Goodson strikes out on a McCaskill pitch that wanders away into another county, and like the bad sport I've become lately, I don't even toss him his glove, don't even look at him when he comes back to the bench to fetch it before heading out to right field. I've got nothing to say to him because I know that in spite of our three-game losing streak he's hoping I'll go down the same way if I come up in the ninth, which is fairly likely because we're one run down, it's our last shot, the pitcher is due up fourth, and if anyone gets on who else is Candy Ass gonna pinch-hit but me, even though he'd rather see me fall out of an airplane?

I love to hit.

By the time I was at Memphis and starting to put up some real numbers, Sandra ("Call me Sandy and I'll throw some in your eyes") got to making the case that it was nothing to be that proud of, that I was just a latecomer to a rather narrowly defined way of exhibiting male aggression. I think we were separated by then, but if separation means out of contact we've never been further from each other than McCaskill's pitches from his spit since we met. Messages on the answering machine are the least of it. I don't even bother to open all the letters I find piled up when we get back from a road trip. She uses Robin like a ventriloquist. Each time Robin and I are together I don't know who I'm listening to for the first hour. She's had notes delivered to me on the bench by personal courier. On the bench! I could say a thing or two about aggression if I wanted.

Anyway, I would never consider myself aggressive, certainly not aggressive enough for Candy Ass, who's always bitching that he wants more power out of my bat. I just happen to be a guy that got into a groove on the job one day and hasn't lost it yet. A bricklayer who's found the rhythm, if you want, a sheetrock taper who walks those stilts as if they were his own legs. In short, the best singles hitter and on-base percentage this town has ever seen. I don't *hit*, if you really want to know—even that's too aggressive a term for what I do. I lay it out there, that's what I do. I lay it out left, center, and right, down the line and up the alley, and if they don't go far enough for Candy Ass, that's too bad, they go far enough to do the job. I'm not a hitter, I'm a batter. I'd actually prefer that old-timey term *batsman*. That sounds to me more like a guy who's just up there to do his job. Mailman, garbageman, batsman. I'm a precisionist, is what I am. I could be working on a Japanese assembly line tweezering chips onto computer boards. In fact, I might *be* working in Japan before long, the way things are going here. Meanwhile, I'll do what I do best.

Fielding's another matter. Maybe we all have some side of our job that we're only adequate at. I'm no bum, and anybody can tell you I've got a good arm, but I can't say I've ever been in love with crouching at third base staring down into those loaded cannons they keep lining up at the plate. The one thing they do, though, they keep me thinking, though once I step into the on-deck circle I totally forget how often they go off in my face, how deadly they can be if you're not on your toes.

Meanwhile, I'm sliding down the bench a ways because I can see that I'm probably going to the plate here in the last of the ninth and I don't want Goodson's claws digging into my knee again just before I head up there. It's my front knee, the bad one, my left, not the one I hit off of, so it doesn't really bother me at the plate, but no one wants to step up there with pain on his mind. And I'm going.

"Go for it, Teddy-O," mumbles Sir Maxwell Candlemass, almost under his breath, after Muck walks to lead off, Washington sacrifices him to second, and he goes to third on Grundy's ground out to the right side. The "Sir" is for real, though even the newspapers are getting tired of making fun of it. He was actually knighted by the Queen herself for being the first Brit to manage a professional baseball team. A hundred smart ex-major leaguers out there, including some Black and Latino greats who've got more baseball in their little fingers than this guy'll learn if he spends the rest of his life here, and this is what we get, a guy who calls pitchers "bowlers." It's living proof of what I read in a political history book I happened to pick up in the library the other day: Imperialism is still alive and well. Only nobody wants to call it what it is.

So here I am, Theodore A. Ohmans, waiting for the spit to fly in my face.

First the conference, like it's going to make a difference. Last-place team or not, no way are they going to bring in the rookie lefty they've got warming up to face the best right-handed batter in major league baseball. They've already got a guy in there who's only given up five hits and two runs all night. And strategy? We all know I don't have any real weak spots; every manager in the league except my own has said that I'm the one guy they'd want at the plate when the game's on the line.

"Welcome back," I say to Majorsky when he finally settles in behind the plate. He just spits through his mask.

"I know where you got that," I tell him.

And here it comes. I actually see the spit flying off of it before I get a fix on the ball itself. It's a click high, a notch outside, maybe not even a strike, but it's got no movement on it and I know exactly where I can poke it and I do: on an easy loop off to the right of second and out toward right center. Muck is trotting home with the tie run as I push out of the box and I can hear that nice roar from the stands, but I'm not half a dozen steps down the line when the knee gives out on me completely and I go down in the dirt and by the time I drag myself up again and start hobbling toward first I can already see the throw coming in from the center fielder, hear the groan from the crowd, and know the game is over, I've been fuckin' thrown out on a clean single to right center.

I'm sitting on the ground still thirty feet from first base as the guys in their grays come trotting in from the field, smirking as they pass, and even Doc Schmidt, the trainer, doesn't come out to help me.

"What's the matter, Moneybags," says the message on my answering machine when I get back to my condo well after midnight. "They're not paying you enough to run to first base anymore?"

Now I'd call that aggressive.

*   *   *

When I was just a kid, ten or twelve maybe, in love with playing ball but not very good at it yet, in the earliest stages of my career, you might say, but still struggling to find my vocation, and one that nobody whatsoever was giving me any encouragement in, the only thing that interested me as much as baseball was death. Most of all, I think, I was amazed at its dependability, the one thing I could see none of us young ballplayers could be relied on for. We could hit a homer in one at bat and fall down striking out the next, to say nothing of missing games because of Saturday chores, family vacations, or parental whims. Even our coach would take to sending his college-age son in his place more and more often as the summer and our losing ways dragged on.

Death, on the other hand, was there every Saturday morning, all summer long, in the basement of Eddie Baumgarten's house when we stopped to pick him up on our way to play Knothole ball. Dangling our gloves and dragging our bats, we followed Eddie around to the side of the house, where we took turns sticking our heads down into the window well to peer through the dusty basement window of Baumgarten Brothers Funeral Home and into the gleaming, white-tiled room where every Saturday morning, dependable as the strike-outs or bad-hop grounders that were sure to come my way, a body lay on the narrow table, usually covered by a white sheet, sometimes not. Game time and the fear of Eddie's father kept us from lingering too long at this spectacle, but death, I came to learn over the many years of playing on Eddie's team, never missed a Saturday.

In some odd way I came to envy this. Death was a regular, better even than Lou Gehrig. Unlike me, death never rode the bench. Even a twelve-year-old could figure out that death always batted a thou-sand. Frightening as the idea was, it seemed to me back then that you'd rather have death on your team than playing for the other guys. Of course, I was just a kid.

What I eventually learned was that death never chose sides.

A simple and obvious fact, you might say, but one to which I at-tribute my becoming a ballplayer, my being a singles hitter rather than a slugger, my marriage, my daughter, and my divorce, to say nothing of my support of the symphony orchestra, my reading habits, my dog, my preference for cooking for myself rather than eating out, my freezer full of chocolate-peanut-butter ice cream, and my inabil-ity to sleep without the TV on.

You might say I owe my life, such as it is, to death.

*   *   *

Others, meanwhile, are calling for my head.

Three different sports columnists in this morning's papers want to know why, after last night's slapstick, I haven't been put on the DL, the operating table, waivers, or a plane to the Antarctic, not neces-sarily in that order. But hey, the way the rest of the division went last night we're still just seven out with a few weeks to play, and the sched-ule, as they've been saying from day one, is in our favor. We're not dead yet. And how're they gonna keep us alive without my bat? We just need to put our heads together and figure out a way for me to make it ninety feet from home to first. But not this morning. This morning I'm down on the living-room carpet playing with the dog, a half-pint mix between a black lab and no one knows what else. I got her from the Humane Society, the last of an unwanted litter some old farmer had said he'd shoot if they wouldn't take her. She had bright eyes, a shiny coat, and a better disposition than anyone else on my team. Robin took one look at her chunky little puppy body when I first brought her home and promptly named her Kirby.

You might question the wisdom of having a dog when you live alone and are on the road as much as a ballplayer is, but to my way of thinking, those things just make it all the more important to have a dog. Especially if you're lucky enough to have neighbors like Pat and John, who I'm always teasing that they can't wait for me to go out of town so they can have Kirby all to themselves. "Kirrr-bee!" John hollers, just like the PA guy at the Twins games announcing Puckett at the plate, whenever I take her outside for a walk. Me, I'm just glad to have her jumping all over me whether I'm coming back from the gro-cery store or picking her up after a two-week-long road trip. To say nothing of what it's like when Robin's around. Without a dog there'd be a lot of dead space here, and even I can't handle all the dead space it seems like a person has to face in his life. But there's no dead space with Kirby, a great little fielder who'll keep trotting back to me with the red ball in her mouth as many times as I'm willing to roll it across the living room and down the hallway. Toward the bedroom, where the TV is still on from last night, without which there would also be a lot of dead space around here at certain dark hours. No thanks. Here, Kirby.

Suddenly, here on the living-room carpet, I'm flopped in the dirt partway down to first base again. I can smell the grass, still wet from a pregame shower, see the humidity floating up in the glow of the lights above me, feel the sudden heat of my own sweat spilling over me. My mouth is dust dry, though, and I don't hear anything I can identify. Just a heavy rhythm, like the whole world breathing in sync while I'm lying here in the dirt, a man fallen into his own grave while the fu-neral crowd hovers over him, not weeping, not laughing—panting.

It's Kirby, hanging over me with her tongue out, breathing heavy, the red ball dropped at her feet, right in front of me, while my hands are scrabbling at the carpet, trying to pull me up, to run, where? Why? How did this happen? Just being down on the floor, I suppose. Not thinking. Not thinking can get you in a lot of trouble.

Believe me, last night wasn't the worst thing that ever happened to me. You perform night after day after night in front of thirty, forty thousand people, and you can bet you're going to end up looking like an ass from time to time. The ball you lost in the lights comes down two feet in front of you while you're covering your head with your glove. You slide headlong into second on the back end of what you're sure was a double-steal sign and find your teammate standing there staring down at your dirt-streaked face. It happens. Think of Wrong Way Corrigan or the runnning back who took the pitchout and sprinted downfield across the other team's goal line or the defenseman whacking a clearing shot off someone else's skate and into his own goal. And there's always a photographer there to catch it, as if they had advance notice it was coming, as if there was always a little voice telling them, "Hey, Popeye, aim it over there, right now, shoot!" My favorite one is me standing at the plate, bat pulled back, ready to swing (ready to foul out to third, as I recall), with a Frisbee perched on top of my batting helmet. I didn't even know it was there, in fact it couldn't have been sitting there for more than a second, must have come sailing out of the stands, hung there just long enough for the photographer to snap it, then went flying off again when I swung. In living color the next morning, with a caption noting that I was in the worst slump of my career (O for ten, big deal) and ready to try anything.

When I came to the plate first time the next night, the air around me was alive with Frisbees, sailing every which way, around the plate, over the infield, curling down from the top decks of the stands. They had to stop the game and call out the grounds crew. It seems like everyone in the stands had a Frisbee. We were away, on the West Coast, I think; they'd had a Frisbee competition before the game — dogs leaping around the outfield pulling Frisbees out of the air with their teeth — and had given free Frisbees away to the first ten thousand or whatever through the gates. It had all been planned, just another promo night for the midseason doldrums, nothing for me to take personally. I didn't. What I remember I did do was end my little slump in no uncertain fashion, four for five or something like that. The way I see it is, you look like a fool on the job one day, you just pick up your tools again the next and go back to doing what you do the best you can do it. The teacher who totally screws up one day has got to be able to look the class in the eye at their next meeting and get on with the job. Shake it off. We've got work to do.

That's what I tell Kirby when I pick up the red ball and flip it into the wicker basket where I keep magazines: "Sorry, kid, we've got work to do."

She could easily dig it out of there herself, and many mornings I come out of the shower and find her standing there with her nose half in the basket, but she never does. It's like she's waiting for me to start the game, to call out, "Play ball!" Dogs know: There are some major forces at work in our lives and you have got to build your game around them. The earlier you recognize them, the better.

*   *   *

It was midmorning, midsummer, stunningly hot already, though as a kid I never minded that and still get a certain nostalgic edge when the heat and humidity climb the ladder hand in hand. I was walking to the game, to meet Eddie Baumgarten and the guys first, of course, because the evening before I'd bent the front wheel of my bike riding home across the cow pasture. Not that we lived on a farm, we lived on a tidy little residential city street, but it was bang up against pure country, farmland picking up where backyards ended. Not the way you see cities these days, housing developments dribbling out into the countryside so you can't tell where urban ends and rural begins, and even the farmhouses looking like suburban ramblers or split-levels. No edge to it at all. I liked being right on the edge.

So picture me standing at the edge of the bridge over the little river I crossed every day on my way to school or to play ball or to make a run to the grocery store for my mother. I'm leaning over the rail. I've got my glove in my left hand, my bat in my right. I'm wearing my grimy Knothole uniform, cream-colored with red pinstripes, that I forgot to throw in the laundry basket after our last game. My cap is on backward, and I've got a wide-eyed look on my face. A Norman Rockwell classic. Only what I'm leaning over the bridge railing staring at is a group of three men dressed in ordinary clothes, work pants, denim shirts, standing over a naked woman lying on her back on the sandy riverbank down below me, arms spread-eagle, wet, tangled hair covering her face.

This is not the first naked woman I've seen. Eddie Baumgarten's basement has taken care of that.

Then one of the men looks up at me, hollers: "Hey, kid, you know anything about artificial respiration?"

I do. Ever since school let out I have been going to Red Cross life-saving classes on Wednesday afternoons. I know pressure points. I know the cross-chest carry. I know what to do for shock and snakebite. I know artificial respiration. I have been practicing all these things on my classmates for the past month and a half. In two weeks I would have taken a test and gotten a certificate and a patch to sew on my jacket.

"Turn her over!" I'm yelling as I charge off the bridge and down through thick underbrush toward the river, dragging my bat and glove, branches snapping in my face, my gym shoes sliding on the steep, gravelly bank. "Get a doctor!"

I drop my bat and glove as I hit the sandy bank. Two of the men have just finished rolling her over and I see the third heading up a narrow dirt path I missed in my headlong descent, but even as I see this I am already doing what I've been taught. I'm kneeling over her, my hands firm on each side of her rib cage, pushing down, counting the rhythm, letting up. Her skin is wet, and glancing aside at the two men standing in front of me, by her head, I can see that their shoes and their pants, up to their knees, are also wet, from which I understand that they have just pulled her from the river. I am leaning, pressing, releasing, breathing. Besides being wet she is also cold. She is much too cold for a day like this. She is so cold it is making my hands cold, though I suddenly realize that everywhere else I am sweaty, itchy, crawly.

And just like that I know with absolute certainty that she is dead.

I stop what I am doing. I lean back on my heels. I don't know what to do with my hands.

One of the men leans over and touches me on the shoulder. He says, "It's OK, kid, you're doing fine."

"No," I tell him, "no, I'm not."

The other man is clutching my baseball cap in both his hands. He says, "Keep going kid, keep going. It's working."

"No," I tell him, "no, it's not. It's not working. It won't work."

And I am standing then, backing off from her body. I don't want to be there any longer. I want my cap and my glove and my bat. I can't spot the path where the third man went up. It's all dense brush on one side and water rushing by on the other and the bridge almost directly overhead, and all I can hear is the traffic going by up there, out of sight.

✳   ✳   ✳

Later on, when I met Sandra, one of the things that attracted me was how she made light of my obsession with that incident—certainly something I had never been able to do all those years. On maybe our fourth or fifth date, approaching some sort of verbal intimacy—we'd long since, maybe too quickly, now that I think about it, arrived at the other kind—I told her the whole story of that traumatic morning, even how I'd gone on to the playground and never let on to anyone what had happened and gotten two hits for the first time in my life, including the game winner, and came home and told them only about my baseball heroics, nothing else, never anything else.

All she said was, "So?"

"A dead woman," I tried to get her to understand. "I was trying to pump life back into a dead woman. I was just a kid."

We were at the Chinese restaurant that had become the starting point for most of our dates. I couldn't hold my teacup. My hands were shaking. She didn't seem to get it. People died, she pointed out. Thanks to Baumgarten Brothers, I had not been unaware of that.

But instead of attributing her response to callousness or lack of empathy, I (in love, of course) instead bought into the notion that I'd never been able to sell myself: that what had happened wasn't, in fact, any big deal. People did die all the time. They died whether you were there or not and in spite of any would-be heroics you brought to the scene. That this particular scene had obsessed me for the better part of a decade, that I saw the whole thing unfold all over again, from my first glance over the railing of the bridge to the long silence that finally hung between me and those two equally helpless men, every single day of my life (and many nights) and from time to time could still feel that deathly wet chill in my hands, didn't mean a thing. The rest of the world—which was to say, Sandra—found it trivial, so it must be so. If there was any problem with that, it must be mine.

The better part of another decade passed before I realized otherwise.

We are such slow learners!

It would be nice for Sandra, Sandy, Sand-in-my-eyes, if she could say that she supported me through all those slow, trying years and then I dumped her when I hit the big time. Actually, I know for a fact (if what you read in the newspaper is a fact) that she has indeed said just such a thing on occasion, the occasion usually being contract time and a call from a nosy sportswriter. But it isn't true. While I was struggling through the minors, riding buses in season and driving trucks for UPS off season and wondering if the latter was what I was finally going to spend the rest of my life doing, she was back in school, getting her M.S.W. and taking her time at it, in part because of taking time out to have Robin but also in part just because that was the way she felt like doing it and so far as I can tell has felt like doing most everything else since. Which was OK with me. I had no complaints then and I've got none now. But it wasn't as if she'd been out there working her wifely fingers to the bone to pay the rent. And when it finally looked as if success might be coming, she was the one who bailed out, not me.

I saw a shot at the majors on my horizon, but I did not see that blow coming. Apparently everyone else did. It probably set me back a full year before I got my head straight again.

But it was an eye-opener.

What it told me was, There is nothing wrong with looking things straight in the eye, no matter how harsh they seem, and every day of your life if need be. It keeps you alert. Otherwise you could end up taking a high hard one upside the head.

You could end up dead.

✳   ✳   ✳

It is 10 A.M. now and I am sitting in his office with Doc Schmidt, our trainer, listening to him apologize for not coming out to my aid last night.

"I just couldn't stand to see it, kid." I'm thirty, but Doc Schmidt calls everyone "kid." "I didn't even want to look at it."

There's no one else around this early. A big place like a stadium has a special kind of silence to it when it's empty. Almost like a library. For a moment, sitting on the edge of the examining table, I swing my knee. No pain. The loudest sound is Doc Schmidt chewing his soggy, unlit cigar. It only hurts when I laugh, I'm tempted to tell him.

What I do say to him is, "Just do whatever you've got to do." We both know that the fact that there's no pain now doesn't mean it'll hold up under the least bit of strain tonight.

"Kid," he says, talking around the cigar, "I've done everything I can do. I've shot everything in my medicine cabinet into that knee of yours. I've wrapped it, iced it, heated it, braced it, taped it . . ." His eyes kind of wander away. He's not a real doctor, though the rumor is he once wanted to be, and you can see sometimes how that gets to him. Finally his eyes focus back on me, or rather on my left knee, and he goes on: "You've seen orthopedics guys in every major league city there is and some that aren't. We've got a collection of X rays big enough you could start autographing them instead of your baseball cards. Your knee is fucked, kid, big time. Whaddaya want?"

I spell it out for him very slowly: "I. Want. To. Play. Tonight. To-morrow. The day after. Et cetera."

"Jesus, Ted." He stubs his cigar out, hard, in the big ashtray shaped like Yankee Stadium in the center of his desk, even though it's unlit.

For a few minutes the library silence takes over again. On off days, especially in other cities but at home, too, while other guys are out looking for the nearest golf course or sitting around blanked out in front of a big-screen TV, I like to go to the library, the main downtown library, which is always the biggest and usually the oldest. I never check out books. If I want a book at home or in my hotel room, I buy it. At the library I just wander into the open stacks, it's almost as if I've got my eyes closed, and take down a handful of books from whichever shelf I happen to find myself standing in front of. Then I sit down for a couple of hours and read whatever it is I find in my hands. Sociology. Physics. Histories of classical civilization. Japanese literature. Dinosaurs. The only time I ever put books back and try again is if they're in a foreign language. Or on math, which is also a foreign language to me. Philosophy seems that way at times, too, but I stay with it all the same. I have a decent college education, even if it was at a big state school, even if I did major in communications, which I know many people don't consider a truly academic subject. But there is so much out there, more than I could ever have imagined back then, probably more than I can imagine even now. A lifetime seems such a short time to get even a glimpse into it all. You could do what I do at the library every single day for the rest of your life, and there would still be so much more. It's absolutely amazing. Life itself is such an amazing thing. In all seriousness, I tell myself, what would we be without it?

Doc Schmidt's eyes are grinding away at me now, I see, as if I were the cigar and this stainless steel examining table the ashtray. He has been with the club maybe twenty years, and behind his back the players call him Dr. Puppydog for the affectionate way he comes running onto the field, his big rump wagging, for even the slightest injury. But he has his tough professional side, too, or he wouldn't have been here this long, believe me. This is not a place where puppydogging it will take you very far.

When he's done glaring, he looks down at his pudgy hands folded on the desk and says, "I'm telling Sir Max you belong on the DL."

"My ass you are," I say.

"Before you get that ass in a sling, let's talk about the off-season surgery all these guys are recommending."

I stay calm, though I realize I'm swinging my legs off the edge of the examining table like a little kid. "This isn't the off season," I remind him.

"What do you think's gonna happen if you don't play out the season?" he asks. "You know what our chances are as well as anyone does. Face it, kid, we're out of it. Think about taking life easy. You can sit on your couch and watch the games on TV for the rest of September and you'll still win the batting title." He makes a little tent of his hands on the desktop, as if he's trying to pray that I'll listen to him.

"What do you think this is?" he concludes. "A matter of life or death?"

I feel myself back in the library again for maybe another minute or so, surrounded by all there is to learn, all there is to do. Then I tell him what I think. "Yeah," I tell him, "that's exactly what I think."

And because I genuinely like this man and because I genuinely do not want to go on anybody's goddamned DL and because deep in my gut I genuinely do feel that it is somehow a matter of life or death, I go on and tell him the rest of it while he gives up praying for me and lets his hands slide down flat on the desk and leans forward staring at me like I'm some sort of crazy man. I tell him that we have each of us got our job to do, but that in addition to the job that we or someone else has decided is our job—the one we get paid for, that is, our career, if you want—we have another job, a job on a higher level is how I see it, and that job is to do our job, whatever it is. And if we just do the job of doing our job, whatever it is and however we got there— "I like working with my hands," I tell him, "and so do you," I add, remembering those deep, muscle-easing massages we're always begging him for—if we all just do it, without making excuses, without begging off, do it right and do it the best we can, then yes, I think that is life, I think that is what pumps life into the whole world, I think that is exactly what keeps the world alive and well, and I think that without it what you get is death. Or something like it. I refrain from naming names.

"Anyway," I end up—I am kind of struggling with it now—"anyway, it makes a difference. It may not be exactly the difference you wanted to make at some time or other in your life, but it makes a difference."

And then I see from the way his eyes suddenly cloud over, from the way the deep blue suddenly fades to pale as if they've turned mostly inside, that something has in fact made a difference. He sits up straighter and his hands build their little steeple again for a moment and then he says, looking at his medicine cabinet, "Well, I suppose there is always one more thing we can try. And if I tape the knee a lot more heavily *and* we put a brace on it. Of course it'll be like walking on a log."

"No problem, Doc," I tell him, "I haven't got that far to go."

FREE-43

JOEY AMPERSAND spends more time in his car, a midnight blue Cadillac Seville, than most people spend in their houses, and except for its lack of a bathroom, he prefers it to his house. Often, driving around the city late at night, alone of course, he reminds himself that it even cost more than his first house did, a house that had two bathrooms. What he does have, though, is a cell phone, a CB, a CD player, a hot-wired radar detector clipped to the sun visor above him, a Global Positioning Satellite device, a laptop computer complete with modem nestled into the bucket passenger seat beside him, and, on the floor in front of that, a combination printer and fax machine. He even has a little coffeemaker that plugs into his cigarette lighter. He doesn't have to go anywhere, except to go; he has it all here, he can go anywhere. He thinks he has the best of both worlds, renting a town house and owning his car. Owning it outright: *He* owns it, not the banks, the banks don't own one damned bit of his life, not a toilet seat, not even a spare tire. He is, as his personalized license plates say, FREE. It only bothers him a little bit that the state has seen fit to tack a number, 43, onto the plate, even though that is, for the moment at least, his age. Pure coincidence, he's sure, and mostly just a sign that at least forty-two other drivers also think they're free, though surely not as free as he is.

For him that means free to roam, as he was doing tonight, cruising the city's lake and park system, from Lake of the Isles to Calhoun to Harriet and on to Nokomis and Hiawatha. Except he didn't like "cruising," a word with all the wrong connotations for what he was doing. He wasn't out to pick up anyone, wouldn't have moved his little electronic office out of the passenger side for anybody. No, he was touring, that's what he told himself he was doing. When he said the word it brought him images of times gone by, those gigantic, open

201

touring cars of the twenties that he'd only ever seen pictures of. Dusenbergs, names like that. That must have been the life. No, Joey thought, this is the life, it's one in the morning, I know my way blindfolded through these tangled streets around the lakes, but if I get lost for a bit that's OK too, I have my GPS unit and I'm not accountable to anyone, anyway. Come morning I'll flip on the computer and modem and see what they've got going for me. Until then, I'm a free man.

Once, at an even later hour, three, maybe four in the morning, driving through the Crocus Hill neighborhood, up one street and down the next, looking at the wonderful rehabs by moonlight, he'd been stopped by a pair of St. Paul cops. Suddenly his rearview mirror filled up with flashing lights, a second car angled in front of him, forcing him to the curb, and both front windows were lit up by flashlights. When he lowered the electric windows the flashlights danced around the inside of the car, and the harsh words of first the one cop and then the other rattled around the cockpit, demanding to know who he was and where the hell he thought he was going. He gave the cop on his side his driver's license but stood on his constitutional right to freedom of movement and refused to say why he was there at that hour of the night when he lived across the river or where he was going. Eventually, they let him go. He lived, as he had kept telling them, in a free country, and he was free to go where he wanted.

Unlike most of the rest of the world. Late at night he listened to public-radio rebroadcasts of *All Things Considered* and the BBC *News Hour* and Monitor Radio and heard over and over again, night after night, the same reports from South Africa and Nicaragua and Haiti and Burma, which he would never get used to calling Myanmar, and the former Yugoslav republics, or whatever they were calling them these days. Places where you weren't allowed to go anywhere, where you didn't dare go anywhere, especially after dark, places people mostly only seemed to want to go somewhere else from. Places where few people had cars anyway, even fewer cars like his, and if they did they couldn't get or afford the gas to go touring with. Where if the police, or more likely the military, stopped you on the streets, they were just as likely to shoot you or confiscate your vehicle as to ask to see your license. He didn't really understand what was happening in most of those places—certainly not to the extent that he could have explained their problems, except maybe South Africa's, to someone else—but he was fascinated by these reports coming to him from public-radio correspondents all around the world, and found himself listening to the same ones over and over again, even when he had a stack of his favorite recordings of baroque music on the CD changer in the trunk all ready to go, and he was perpetually glad that those things were happening where they were happening, somewhere else, far away, and that he was here, untouched by them and free to come and go as he pleased.

But tonight he was listening to music, not one of his discs, though, but public radio's *All Through the Night* classical music program, which was in the midst of broadcasting a Mozart symphony. He couldn't have said which one, they all sounded so much alike to him, but he loved the way the music went around and around, so he decided to follow its lead, and instead of moving onward along his lake-to-lake progression, he was driving around and around Lake Calhoun, the air-conditioning off and the front windows and sunroof wide open because it was such a mild July night and the music in its lightness filling up the inside of the car and flowing out through all those openings, when the rock came through the windshield and thumped off his chest and dropped into his lap. There was glass all over him and a gaping hole right in front of him, though most of the windshield was shattered but intact, a mosaic of small pieces clinging precariously together, sagging inward. Safety glass, he said to himself as he edged over to the curb, I could have been killed or blinded. As it was he felt a sharp pain, like sudden heartburn, where the rock had struck his breastbone, and he wondered if he'd been seriously injured.

He unbuttoned his madras sport shirt and flipped on the interior light and looked down at his chest. There was nothing more there than a scrape, just at the bottom center of his breastbone, the skin barely torn, no worse than when you banged your head on the edge of a kitchen cabinet, and when he poked at it with his forefinger, it didn't feel any worse. The pain was deeper down, far inside. Then he suddenly remembered to flick off the interior light. What if his attacker, the rock thrower, or maybe there was more than one, what if they were out there in the dark watching him, planning another attack? He powered up the windows, slid the sunroof closed, and hit the switch that threw all the door locks. He sat there feeling for the moment more secure, feeling as if now that he was just sitting there, in his own car, safely locked up, engine idling in park, time was finally beginning to slow down. He wondered if he should call the police.

It was a question he could feel he was having trouble processing. He didn't like having to explain his presence there, as he had with the St. Paul cops. The Minneapolis cops were rumored to be much tougher on the citizenry, but on the other hand this was a crime that had been committed against him and he knew he'd have to get something on the record for the insurance company anyway. 911 or not? He eventually decided that since no one seemed to be following up the attack and he was apparently in no immediate danger, this was no emergency, so finally he punched the zero and asked the operator to get him the Minneapolis police. He lifted the rock off his lap while he was waiting for the call to go through and slowly placed it on the floor under his seat. It was round and heavy, the size of both his fists together. He didn't know enough about geology to know what kind of rock it was, but he kept thinking granite. It seemed like he had a lot of time to think granite. He was proud of himself for how calm he was being, how reasonably he was handling this assault on him. No, on his car. He was having a hard time making the distinction. He was, he gradually realized, not altogether sure what he was doing sitting there in the blue-white glow of the boulevard lights holding his car phone in one hand and picking bits of glass off his pants and shirt with the other. There were sounds coming from the phone, but he couldn't make sense of them. He was staring at it, wondering who had called him, when the crowbar came through the window on the passenger's side and an arm reached in, flipped the lock, opened the door, swept the computer off the seat, and a very tall young man ducked into the car, black motorcycle boots coming down heavily on the electronics on the floor as he slid into the seat.

Jesus, thought Joey, watching all this happen in a kind of slow motion, feeling the telephone being slowly lifted from his hand, he's just a kid, half my age, probably less. But he also saw that the kid had a heavy growth of dark beard and a couple of angry-looking tattoos on his left upper arm where the ripped-off T-shirt sleeve should have been. And he was still clutching the crowbar in his hand.

"It's not the first time we seen you around here," the kid said.

Joey didn't know what to say. He searched and searched but couldn't seem to find any words. Finally he managed one: "'We'?"

"Yeah. We."

*   *   *

Joey had a female friend, Elaine Etherton, who worked nights in production at the *Star Tribune*, and when she came to visit him at the hospital she said, "I knew it was going to come to this."

"And I knew you were going to come to say that," said Joey, who had already climbed far enough out of the swamp of the anesthesia by then to have been on the phone with his car-insurance guy before Elaine arrived. It was midafternoon, and she hadn't known he was in the hospital because when she came home to go to sleep in the very early morning she always turned the ringer on the phone off and the answering machine on. When she woke she found the message he had left her just before he went into the operating room. By then he was back in his semiprivate, exchanging clichés about the Twins with the bleeding ulcer in the other bed. Duwayne Peterman, his car-insurance guy, who was also an old fraternity brother, had agreed to go take care of the car himself, drive it to the glass place, get it cleaned up. He assured Joey that it would be safely tucked away in the garage under his town house in mint condition by the time Joey got home. Joey had wanted to say, It *is* my home, but he didn't want the Big D, as they used to call him when he played linebacker for the U, to think that he'd gone off the deep end because of this, or to raise his insurance rates by bumping his car up into some new house-on-wheels category.

Elaine pulled the privacy curtain across between the two beds, dumped her purse on the wide windowsill, and sat down in the plastic chair at the foot of his bed. Joey could tell from the fact that she didn't sit down beside him on the bed and touch his face, his forehead, his hair, that her sympathies weren't altogether with him, that she was going to demand to know what happened before she'd be willing to soothe him with her concern. She was just starting to ask when the kid showed up around the edge of the white curtain. He looked exactly as he had last night: unshaven stubble on his jawbones, greasy hair, sleeveless T-shirt and jeans and black boots. No crowbar. But he was much bigger than Joey remembered, not the tall, skinny kid Joey thought he had seen slide into the front seat but big all over, broad shouldered, muscular, thick through the chest and waist and hips. He wasn't, Joey realized, a kid at all.

Elaine, meanwhile, had gotten out of the chair and backed up behind it, against the windowsill, where she was clutching her purse. From where he lay in the bed it looked to Joey as if she'd realized that once Will had entered there was no longer enough space left for her in the room.

But she made no move to leave. Instead, she said, "Who the fuck are you?"

"I'm Will, ma'am. Will Fontaine."

"And you're responsible for this, aren't you?"

Will had stopped at the foot of the bed. "I guess you could say that." His dark eyes were focused on Elaine; it was as if Joey wasn't even there. He felt like a spectator at his own funeral. Elaine couldn't hold Will's gaze, however. She turned away and glared at Joey.

"Why?" she demanded. "What'd he do to you?"

"He brought me to the hospital."

"Put you in the hospital, you mean."

"Put him in the back of his Caddy," said Will, "and drove him to the hospital."

"Jesus," said Elaine, "you people."

Will had never taken his eyes off her: "How's that, ma'am?"

Elaine wouldn't look at him. "He knows damn well what I mean," she said to Joey. Joey groaned, suddenly feeling the pain in his chest for the first time since he'd woken up.

"Hey, old man," said Will, "I just come by to see how you were doing."

"I'll be fine. I'm very grateful," said Joey, that "old man" nagging at some fuzzy back corner of his mind at the same time, but before he could say anything more Will had turned and gone. Joey was still waiting for him to say something as he left, but all he heard was the disembodied voice of the bleeding ulcer from behind the white curtain.

"I didn't know you was a member of Hell's Angels."

✳   ✳   ✳

The next day Joey's doctor brought him the bone splinter they'd removed from his chest. It was an inch and a half long, almost as thick as a pencil, sharp as a nail at the end that had punctured his lung. It looked like something left over from a bad meal in a greasy diner, pork chops maybe.

"I thought you might want to give it to Elaine. She could use it in one of those funky pieces of jewelry she likes to make."

Joey humphed and studied the white slice of bone he held between his thumb and forefinger. Close up, he thought it looked like a potsherd, something from an archaeological dig, a fragment of the past. The doctor, Neville Schottenstein, whom Joey sometimes played racquetball with, had once gone out with Elaine for a while, years ago, before he married the lanky Dane Joey had had a brief fling with right after he got out of the army. Joey didn't know if Elaine had ever slept with Neville or not, but he supposed so. Back then, everybody slept with everybody else. Now, everybody was afraid to sleep with anybody. Whenever Joey thought about this, which was rarely, he ended up wondering how much, in terms of their freedom to make their own choices, anything had changed. But it wasn't a topic he ever pursued very far. He tested the pointed end of the bone splinter with his finger. It was needle sharp. He knew that when Elaine saw it she'd tell him how lucky he was, it could have punctured his heart. Then she'd drop it into her purse and he'd probably never see it again.

Neville, who'd been sitting on the edge of the bed, got up to go. He patted Joey on the knee and said, "You're a lucky guy, you know. That little sucker could have nailed your heart just as easily as your lung."

"So?" said Joey.

"So you'd have bled to death long before your punk friend could have got you in here."

The cop who came later that afternoon also wanted to know about the "friend" who'd brought him to the emergency room. She asked Elaine to leave while she conducted her interview, sat down with her clipboard on her lap in the plastic chair at the foot of the bed that Elaine had vacated, and started by asking Joey what he had been do-ing in the park at that hour. Driving, he told her. She wanted to know where he had been going. He told her, as he had once told the St. Paul cops, that he didn't have to answer that.

"OK," she said, "then suppose you tell me about your relationship with Mr. Fontaine."

"I have no relationship with Will Fontaine," he said. "He brought me to the hospital. Maybe he saved my life. See this?" He held up the bone splinter for her to look at. "This could have pierced my heart just as easily as my lung."

"You're just a lucky guy," she said.

When Elaine came back in, after the cop had finished and left, he was still holding up the bone splinter, as if he wanted the whole world to see it.

"Jesus, Joey," she said, "what if that had gone through your heart?"

✳   ✳   ✳

One week to the day—the night, really—after what he and Elaine now refer to as the "incident," Joey is again circling Lake Calhoun on the parkway. It is another lush summer evening, the beginning of August. The car, as the Big D promised, is in mint condition. Almost. Every time Joey is convinced that there's not a sign that anything ever happened to his Cadillac, his critical eye catches the glint of a tiny glass fragment embedded in the midnight blue carpeting. He pulls over to the curb and stops, digs the piece of glass out, and drops it into the ashtray, the only use his ashtray has ever been put to. And each time he reaches over to probe the carpeting, Joey is reminded that he himself is not yet in mint condition. There's a sharp pain deep inside his chest, like something digging at him there, hard, every time he bends or stretches.

He first felt it last Friday, the day he was released from the hospital, when Elaine brought him back to the town house and, after a quick visit to the garage to check on the car, they tried to make love. It was his idea, but no matter what position they tried, every time he moved, he felt like she was stabbing him in the chest. He just couldn't stay with it. Finally she eased him over onto his back and told him to just lie still, to let her do the moving. It was one of her favorite things to do anyway, but as usual he found he couldn't just lie there, not the way she moved over him. I'm not made not to move, he wanted to tell her, but all he could get out was a harsh grunt, which for a moment he was afraid she might mistake for a sign of sexual excitement. But she rolled off of him onto her own back and said, "All right, then, but don't complain to me about being horny."

He's complained about the pain to both Neville and the surgeon, and they both say the same thing: What did he expect after that kind of accident and operation and did he want some pain killers? He's filled the prescriptions from both of them but hasn't yet taken either the Darvon or the APCs. If there's something still wrong in there, he wants to know it. He's always subscribed to the idea, which he probably got from Neville a long time ago, that pain has something important to tell you. But except for toothache, which was obviously telling him to get to the dentist as soon as possible, Joey hasn't had much experience with pain in his life. So he wants to be sure he hears and understands the message as clearly as possible. Still, he has both vials of pills in the glove compartment. Just in case the message gets too loud.

The next night and the next he's out on the parkway again, but he still hasn't seen anything of Will Fontaine or, for that matter, anyone who resembles him in any way, any of whoever "we" might have been. The weather is unchanged, windows down and sunroof open weather, it's as if it's going to be the perfect summer evening forever, and Joey decides to broaden his search a little, moving out to circle

Lake of the Isles to the north and Lake Harriet to the south. Still nothing, although he notices tonight that he's not the only one doing this. There's a rusty yellow Honda that's shown up both in front of him and behind him several times, and at several different parking spots around the lakes he keeps seeing the same dark maroon Plymouth Voyager van gleaming under a boulevard light as if it's just had a wax job. Twice a group of motorcyclists swings around and passes him as he's making the cut from Calhoun to Harriet, but he doesn't know whether it's the same bunch or not, all motorcycles look alike to him. The three cop cars he's seen, though, he thinks are all different even though they all wear the same label on their plates in big, easy-to-read letters — POLICE — and of course he knows how recognizable he is, in the big dark Cadillac with the personalized plates, to anyone else who's keeping track of the traffic around the lakes.

It's nearly midnight when he's stopped at the traffic light waiting to cross Lake Street from the Lake of the Isles loop back to Calhoun that he hears a deep voice just beside him saying, "If you're so fuckin' free, how come you're just drivin' around in circles all the time?"

Then the light changes and the car behind him honks because he's at the head of a larger pack of traffic than he thinks ought to be there at this time of night, except it is Friday, so he surges ahead. He has to make a right turn onto Lake before going left onto the Parkway, and there are cars turning on both sides of him, so he can't look around, but he glances in his rearview mirror as he starts his turn and thinks he sees Will, or someone who looks a lot like Will, standing in the intersection, right in the middle of all that moving traffic. But then he's being swept along by the traffic himself, making his move for the left turn, swinging onto the Parkway where suddenly it's single-lane traffic and everyone is just creeping along now and the air is full of loud music from the cars and the partyers on the beach, and he knows it will take a good ten or fifteen minutes to follow the One Way signs around the lake and back to the intersection.

✻   ✻   ✻

"Once is enough," Elaine tells him when they're at lunch the next day—breakfast for her—at an outdoor restaurant on the Mall not far from the high-rise where she lives. They're both wearing white shorts and yellow knit shirts and white sneakers without socks, and they're sitting in the shade of a big umbrella that says Cinzano all the way around on each of its scalloped edges. They look like an ad for a summer vacation, but Joey keeps fiddling with his straw, taking quick little sips of his iced tea. Each time a cold wash of the drink goes down it feels like it has to find its way around that spot in his chest, like it's almost about to make the pain leap out at him again, the way it did when he woke up with a start this morning and sat up suddenly in bed. Nothing ever happens, but it worries him, and he has to keep taking additional sips to see if it *will* happen.

"What are you so nervous about?" Elaine wants to know.

"I'm not nervous. I'm just drinking my iced tea."

But he knows that she knows that he never drinks anything through a straw, that he likes to pick up a cold glass of iced tea or Coke or beer and drink most of it straight down right from the glass. He's not really nervous, though, just impatient, impatient to be free from that ache in his chest, impatient for it to be night again.

As if she's reading his mind, Elaine asks, "You're not going back out there again tonight, are you?"

When he sucks at his iced tea again instead of answering, she adds, "What is it you're looking for, another trip to the hospital?"

He knows it's not fair to her to think this way, but he wishes he had as many answers as she has questions. He's tried to convince her ever since he got out of the hospital that Will was the one who rescued him, not the one who hurt him, but she keeps questioning how he can be so sure, maybe it was Will who did both, what kind of person was that anyway? Who goes around at night with a crowbar in his hands? Maybe it was his gang or whatever they were, didn't he know there were street gangs in Minneapolis just like in L.A.? Not just like L.A., he argues, but he realizes that doesn't really answer her concerns.

"I just want to know what that was all about," he tells her.

He pushes his iced tea away, then pulls it back for another sip. He's said the same thing, to her and to himself, dozens of times already since the "incident." It's true in a factual kind of way—he wouldn't lie to Elaine or even, he hopes, to himself—but he also knows there's something more involved, something he can't quite put his finger on, something beyond just the facts of what happened out there that night. Somehow he seems to have gotten the notion—this was what he woke up with a sense of sudden, absolute certainty about this morning—that the pain in his chest isn't going to go away until he finds out what the "incident" was really all about. And that only through Will Fontaine is he ever going to discover that. Sitting here across from Elaine on a sunny afternoon, he doesn't feel so absolute about it any longer; in fact, he knows it's more than a little irrational. But at the same time he's concerned that until he finds out what really happened the pain is just going to get worse and worse, pills or no pills, until . . . what? Until he can't stand it anymore?

"Isn't there anything you ever just absolutely had to find out about?"

"Yeah. What makes you tick."

Elaine has some errands she has to run and then she wants to work out. They've already had sex, rather gingerly but successfully this time, before lunch. She finishes her veggie sandwich and gets up, telling Joey that she's worried because he really does seem nervous, that he looks stressed, that she wishes he'd go home and take a nap or something.

"I think I'll go for a drive," he says.

*   *   *

Instead of going for a drive, however, Joey just sits in his car in the parking ramp where he left it when he drove downtown to meet Elaine. At a buck and a half an hour, it's cheaper than the gas for driving around, and with the breezes blowing through the open ramp he doesn't even have to turn the motor on and run the air conditioner. Not that these little expenses mean anything to Joey, but he does like to rationalize the whole process. Besides, he tells himself, if he's free to drive, he's also free not to drive. He powers the electric seat all the way back, stretches out his legs, and leans his head back. He parked on the next-to-top level of the ramp with plenty of unoccupied spaces on either side of him, but now all the slots have been taken. On his left is a mud-splattered BMW, a little puzzling since it hasn't rained in weeks, and on his right is a yellow Honda, not unlike the one he remembers having seen around the lake last night.

After a while he gets out and walks around the back of his car to get a better look at the Honda. There's a fair amount of rust around the edges of the doors and the bottoms of the panels. It has Minnesota plates, but when he peers in through the front window he sees last Sunday's *Chicago Tribune*, neatly folded, as if it's never been read, lying on the passenger seat. There's an infant seat in the back, and the rear floor is thick with crushed pop cans, candy-bar wrappers, and paper bags from fast-food restaurants.

Finally he gets back in the Cadillac, hits the memory button to reset the seat to his normal driving position, and puts his key back in the ignition. He isn't a great reader, but whether this is the same yellow Honda or not, he knows that there are a lot more coincidences in life than there are in fiction. Still, he sits there a long time. Eventually a tall man in a gray pinstriped suit and dark glasses climbs into the muddy BMW and sends it squealing down the spiral exit ramp. A few minutes later Joey pulls out and leaves, too, much more slowly.

✳   ✳   ✳

The first night he was home from the hospital, after Elaine had scrambled him some eggs and left for work, he'd gone through the phone directories for both cities. There were Fontaines galore, but only a couple of Williams and no Will. He cross-checked them with the city directories he always kept for business purposes and came away quite certain that none of the Williams was Will and that none of the other Fontaine households listed had a Will, either. Then he went down to his car and did what he had never done before and knew he shouldn't do but was going to do all the same, and not without some pain, either, since a little bending and twisting couldn't be avoided. He turned on the computer, and, working only by the light of the computer screen, which filled up the inside of the Cadillac with its otherworldly glow, he activated the modem and then, consulting a small leather-bound notebook he'd pulled out of the glove compartment, watched a directory to Minneapolis Police Department records scroll onto his screen. After a couple of false starts, he found the list of gangs, nearly twenty of them, from the expected Crips and Bloods, the ones that made the papers regularly, to the Beanballs and the Heartaches. There was a membership list for each of them, and though there were a lot of question marks posted beside names and a lot of initials rather than full names and a couple of Billys and a fair number of AKAs, there was no Fontaine, no Will, not even a W. After he left the police files, Joey accessed the public-library records to check out cardholders, then the university to look at student registrations, then even the community colleges, and finally the State Department of Revenue to check tax records, but everywhere he looked the results were the same. The Fontaines got around a good bit—they were season subscribers to the orchestra and members in good standing of the AFL Teachers Union and contributors to the United Way and former patients at several local hospitals and multiple parking-ticket offenders—but not Will.

I am a helluva detective, Joey told himself as he turned off the computer two hours later and headed wearily for bed, especially considering that I have never tried to access any of this stuff before, but I am not much for results. If it hadn't been for exhaustion and the pain that nagged at his chest with every step as he climbed up from the garage, he probably would have gone out driving yet that night. He fell asleep considering that this was the first time he'd ever actually worked out of his house. Sure, the computer was in the car, but look where the car had been all night. It felt like there was some sort of slippage going on in his life. The last image he had was of adding one small handful of sand to a huge sandpile, a sandpile as big as a house, and watching a landslide begin, but maybe he was asleep already then, dreaming of a seaside vacation his parents had taken him on one summer a long, long time ago.

*　　　　*　　　　*

He does go out driving, finally, the evening after he's had lunch with Elaine, but not around the lakes. This time he leaves the Cities altogether, and goes breezing down U.S. 61 at a smooth, easy fifty miles per, south along the Mississippi River, down through Newport and Hastings and Red Wing, past Winona, hours and hours, nearly as far as Crescent City and LaCrosse before he turns back. He thinks of it as an exercise in freedom. The country air is as mild as it's been in the city, and he drives with the AC off and the roof open, listening at first to the local jazz station and when that's out of range to the classical public-radio station and then his own music and finally, on his way back, to the late-night rebroadcast of *All Things Considered*.

It's as if they've picked a theme for the day. Aside from a few items about international politics on the half-hour news summaries, every segment seems to have something to do with the environment: decaying chemical weapons dumped after World War II endangering the Baltic, hazardous waste sites being sited on Native American lands in the Southwest, American business involvement in the destruction of South American rain forests, and of course the perennial global warming. He listens to a cranky-sounding writer from Chicago berating the environmental movement for only thinking of endangered animals and lakes dying from acid rain while suffering urbanites like himself lived in the midst of an environmental disaster area every day of their lives. He can't take a single step, the commentator whines, without feeling the crunching of broken glass underfoot.

Coming back off the Hastings bridge over the river just then, the Cadillac hits a bump and Joey hears his own collection of broken glass fragments rustling around in the ashtray. It's almost as if he can hear their sharpness, their razor-thin edges: a sound as penetrating as a cold November rain. He checks the fuzzbuster, floors the accelerator, and heads toward the lakes. Along the way he calls Elaine and leaves a message on her machine, telling her not to worry, he's had a great drive down the river, it's another lovely summer evening.

Circling Lake Calhoun, however, he realizes it isn't evening any longer. It's Saturday night, late, and though it has cooled off a little, it still has that pure midsummer feel to it. But there's hardly anyone out, one guy walking a pair of enormous dogs and a few cars moving right

through, clearly with an immediate destination in mind, not lingering along the parkway. No rock throwers. No Will Fontaines. Not
even a police car, though he can hear the faint wail of a siren far off
in the distance. Gliding around the far end of the lake, it seems to
Joey that he —or rather the Cadillac—is the only thing moving. It's a
smooth, easy motion, floating on the Cadillac's amazingly soft sus-
pension, a motion that has a timeless, this-could-go-on-forever feel to
it. A man in a car suspended in the still center of the universe, free of
every attachment to the world. A glance at the dashboard clock, provoked by this sense of timelessness, tells him why, of course: It's past
3 A.M. An innocuous fact—many a night these past years he's stayed
out driving this late and later—but somehow it gives him a jolt tonight to suddenly realize how late it is, an actual physical jolt that sits
him up straighter in his driver's seat. And when he shifts his posture
like that he feels that thing again, digging its sharp little pain into his
chest, that phantom bone splinter, that shard of glass, that knife, that
slippage.

Construction Zone

THE PARKWAY

"WE'VE GOT TWO SEASONS HERE," he'd heard ever since he was a kid growing up in the neighborhood, "winter and road repair," and never had that seemed truer than this year. No sooner had the last, dirty-white dregs of winter been flushed down the storm sewers by the spring rains than the heavy equipment started rolling in. There was ample warning—stacks of orange barricades waiting to be deployed, signs several blocks in either direction on Stillman Parkway announcing that it would be closed beginning May 10th—but it was only when he was awakened at six that Monday morning by the roar of the big trucks, by compressors chugging into the early quiet of the neighborhood and jackhammers clanging abruptly to life, that it took on a reality for him.

By seven he was standing at the end of his driveway, twin parallel strips of cracked concrete with scattered patches of grass struggling to stay alive between them, talking to his next-door neighbor, Mort Kaminsky, who was on his way to work, about the tide of dirt and noise rolling their way. Mort and his wife both parked their cars in the street in front of their house because their garage, which faced the alley like most in the neighborhood, was an ancient dilapidated thing, much too small for most cars, useful only for storing snowblowers and lawn mowers and yard equipment. His own garage, barely large enough for even his small Escort but at least well maintained, was one of the few on the block with a driveway to the street.

"It's always like this, Mr. Gall," Mort was saying. "Always has been, always will be."

"Go on, Mort," he said, "what would you know?" Mort was a young businessman, midthirties, built like an athlete, newest guy on the block, with his doctor wife and two little kids sure to be off to the suburbs in another couple of years. Over the past decade or so the neighborhood had become a sort of way station, Gall thought, a stopover for young families on their upwardly mobile journey; he hardly knew anyone on the block by name anymore.

"Just ask my dad," said Mort.

Gall, a thin man, remembered Mort's dad, glumly. He'd gone to school with Mort's dad. But Mort's dad had been dead for half a dozen years already, so what was this "ask my dad" stuff? Was it some sort of figure of speech? He didn't get figures of speech, usually. Usually, when he asked his wife to explain one to him, he didn't get the explanation either. It seemed like a lot of extra work to him, when you could just say how something was, straight out. So did what was going on along the parkway, down there at the end of the block, a perfectly serviceable street so far as he could tell, already in the process of being ripped up, a poor butchered thing with its guts being laid open even as he watched, great bloody wet globs of red clay spilling up through gashes in the dark asphalt.

"I'm gonna call my councilman," he told Mort.

"Woman, Mr. Gall," said Mort. "Council*woman*."

"You think so?"

As Mort headed off in his shiny new Jeep, Gall—wondering what you called these things now, *vehicles* was it?—strolled up the walk toward his own front porch. The lawn was looking good for so early in the season. The crocus bulbs he'd buried in it the first fall after his retirement had bloomed and been cut back already. He loved that look, the little blue flowers popping up when there were still clumps of snow in shady spots around the house; he'd admired it for years whenever he'd driven through the classy part of town nearby that was famous for its yards and gardens, and now he had it himself. The thick grass had greened up nicely and was darkening richly now, thriving on the high-nitrogen fertilizer he'd spread a week ago. The shrubs around the foundation were thickly leaved already, even the hostas at their base that had looked so burned at the end of last summer were coming up bright and strong, and the double petunias he'd planted in the window boxes around the porch over the weekend were beginning to open their first pink buds.

But down at the end of the block, just three houses away, two guys in ragged gray coveralls were shutting things down. Almost as soon as Mort's red Jeep had paused at the stop sign and skittered across the intersection, they had begun setting up a string of orange barricades, ugly things, like overgrown sawhorses, across his street, West Worthington Avenue, and cutting off his access to Stillman. Stillman, named for an early settler best known for his paranoid fear of the peaceable Indian tribes who fished and hunted in the region, ran north-south; West Worthington ran east-west, straight out from the center of the city but ending only a block and a half farther west, where a deep, overgrown cut slashed diagonally across the neighborhood, leaving him now with only little Agmont Street, narrow and deeply potholed, for egress.

Fucked, he told himself, wondering, at the same time, just when he'd started using language like that. Margaret would be appalled.

The cut had been the center of controversy for the past couple of years, and one evening the winter before last he'd actually gone to a community meeting sponsored by the city council, where there was considerable heated discussion concerning the future of what he was amused to hear them calling the Elementary Canal. He suspected that he alone among the small crowd there was historian enough to remember that it had indeed once been a canal, built in the late nineteenth century to barge goods into the center of the city, which, because of Stillman's never-ending fear of Indian marauders sneaking up on his encampment by canoe, had not initially been located directly on the river. Originally known as Alemakers Canal because of the many barges that used it to supply grain to the local breweries, from the very beginning the newspapers, noting how it fed raw materials into the great industrial maw of the burgeoning city, referred to it as the Alimentary Canal, and eventually, as it fell into disuse in the first decades of the twentieth century, it came to be known as the Gut Cut.

Dried out now, choked with brush and weeds and the detritus of long-abandoned hobo camps, it had become a nearly impenetrable thicket where Gall had often taken a dog he once owned, a little black-and-white mutt, to scare up rabbits. But that was years ago, when he used to like to go for an evening walk after he came home from work. The dog had disappeared one summer—run away, been stolen, hit by a car on some distant street, who knew?—and Gall, who found himself somehow oddly relieved, had never gotten another one or walked in the Cut again. Now only kids—kids from other neighborhoods, he suspected—used it, mostly for late-night beer parties, smoke from their campfires sometimes visible on warm evenings from his front porch, and no one knew its real name anymore, though it amused Gall to think how, in an odd way, the beer-drinking kids had returned it to its original use.

But concern had grown. Several times each summer the fire department was forced to hack its way through the thicket to extinguish brushfires. Neighbors called it a nuisance, feared it was attracting a drug-using, criminal element, and wanted it turned into a park. A consortium of developers was proposing building either a strip mall or an enclosed town-house community. The school board was showing signs of interest. One council member had vigorously promoted the idea of turning it into a limited-access road connecting with the major interstate highway that ran through the city, but no one understood who it would serve or what its other end would be connected to. Studies had been done, factions formed, for a year now a court-ordered moratorium had been in effect. Gall was convinced that, like himself, hemmed in by age and construction, it was going nowhere.

THE ROAD

On Memorial Day, in midmorning, Gall's wife, Margaret, whose asthma had never been worse, threw her dust rag into the kitchen sink and announced that she was going to live with her sister in San Francisco until this mess was finished.

"It never stops," she said, and Gall, who had just come inside for a drink of water, knew she was talking not about her cough but about the dust, which seemed to follow her around the house like some malevolent child, smudging tabletops, dressers, cabinets with its dirty fingers as soon as she was finished wiping them clean. They kept the doors and windows closed, but even so the kitchen counter was perpetually gritty, clothes fresh from the dryer were already dusty, their throats and noses dry and stuffy. He himself had been working outside for the past two days, loosening the garden soil choked and compacted with cement dust, moving the sprinkler around to wash the pore-clogging grit from the drooping leaves of grass and shrubs and flowers. His own throat was bone dry and scratchy.

The only good thing he could think of was how quiet it had been for going on two days, a Sunday and now a holiday Monday. The rest of the time it was endless noise and dirt. The crews began work at six in the morning, and it had gotten so he was always awake now even before they started, lying in bed waiting for the first explosive roar of the big diesel shovels, the muffled rumble of the backhoes grinding into action, knowing the next things he was going to hear were Margaret's harsh, hacking cough and her daily outburst of anger. And now that the days had gotten longer they worked into the fading light, till seven or sometimes eight, so that Gall and his wife, finally succumbing to the roar of heavy machinery ripping up the fabric of their day hour after hour, tearing the quiet of the neighborhood to shreds, pulverizing their peace of mind and shrieking relentlessly on into the soft spring evenings, had abandoned all attempts at dinner-table conversation. And Saturdays—they worked Saturdays as well!—Gall thinking that no doubt this was because they had bonus incentives to complete the project on schedule. But all they were ever doing, he saw on his daily stroll down to the corner at Stillman, was tearing up, ripping open the street as far as he could see in both directions, smashing curbstones and sidewalks, excavating buried sewer and water pipes covered with red clay and rust, dredging ever deeper, leaving great, gaping, water-logged gulches in the middle of the street and mountains of thick red mud at every corner.

So of course he agreed that it was the right thing for her to do, this temporary move to the West Coast, but when she urged him to come with her—"You don't need this any more than I do, Marvin"—he balked. He refilled his glass from the kitchen tap, swirled the water around in it, dumped it out—they had long since gotten in the habit of rinsing off everything in the kitchen, every dish, glass, cup, pot, utensil, before they used it—and filled it again for a long drink.

"Can't," he said, sliding his empty glass back down onto the counter, feeling, hearing, the grit crunching beneath it. "Can't leave the house, Margaret, not with all this going on. Someone's got to be here."

And Gall was that someone. Self-nominated, a volunteer, not a martyr, but maybe, to his way of thinking, a guardian of sorts, a holder-down-of-the-fort, a watcher-out for the barbarians at the gates, the captain of a sinking ship, bound to his duty, alone on the bridge as she foundered in heavy, storm-swept seas, relieved that passengers and crew were safely away.

Two or three times a week he got a postcard from Margaret, safe on her distant, sunny shore. The messages were brief, cheery, uninformative; the cards showed pictures of blue skies, blue waters, craggy headlands, great golden bridges. On Saturdays at midmorning—early still where she was—she called, chatted with him while she sat sipping coffee on the high balcony of her sister's hillside condo, exclaiming over the white sails on the bay. Sometimes, though, the noise of the construction equipment, ripping up the asphalt on Spense Road now, the east-west street just north of their house, was so loud he could barely hear her. He kept thinking he should tell her to call on Sundays instead, but he had so come to relish the Sunday quiet in the neighborhood that he found he didn't even want to talk to anyone then.

THE STREET

Standing on his front porch one Sunday morning, he saw the Kaminskys next door at work packing the Jeep. He hadn't had his own car out of the garage for weeks now, except to pull it out in the driveway now and then to hose off the dust. He'd taken to walking to the grocery store, up Worthington, over Agmont, then just a block farther west on Spense, where at least the sidewalks were still intact even if the street was mostly chewed up, not really a problem, especially on a pleasant summer afternoon, except for the constant cloud of dust in the air. He was looking at his drooping, window-box petunias, which were dying in spite of his daily efforts to keep them watered and clean, when Mort came out of the house with a pair of sleeping bags under each arm, a pair of kids at his heels.

"Making an escape," Gall said, strolling over to where Mort was stuffing the bags into the back of the Jeep, begging his kids for a little patience. He meant to tell Mort that the councilwoman had never even bothered to return his call.

"Oh, hey, Mr, Gall, how're you doing? No, we've had this camping trip planned since last winter."

"Good timing all the same, I'd say."

"Well, yeah, that took some effort, Ginny and I matching up our vacation time. I see Mrs. G's off on vacation now, too."

"What I meant," said Gall, sweeping his arm out toward the mess on the corner, the barricades, the great bloody trench where the Stillman Parkway traffic had used to run, the ten-foot-high mound of drying red mud, "was all this."

Mort squeezed the last bag into place, slammed the back hatch tight on it, looked up and said, "Hey, it's no big deal, just a job that had to be done sooner or later, might as well get it over with now." But Gall barely heard him. Turning back from his gesture of disgust he'd suddenly noticed, down at the far end of the block, the intersection with Agmont Street, stacked up against the dying old elm in front of the big corner house where Doosie Golfman's widow, Elise, still lived all by herself, a dozen or more orange barricades like those that blocked off his own end of the street.

Go, he wanted to say to Mort. Get out of here. Make a break for it while you still can. But while he was standing there thinking about it, the four Kaminskys were piling cheerily into the Jeep, rolling down the windows to wave good-bye to him, wheeling away down the street, around the corner at Agmont, past the stacked barricades, out of sight.

Monday morning there were no cars on the street. Gall, up and about even earlier than usual — he could see the road crew just starting to arrive on the job — was reading one of the signs taped to trees and lampposts along the street advising of its closing, when the newspaper carrier, a short, balding, middle-aged man Gall only knew by his first name, Walt, came trudging down the sidewalk with a bundle of papers in his arms.

"Morning, Mr. Gall," he said, too cheerily to Gall's way of thinking. "Got some bad news for you, I'm afraid."

"Nothing but bad news around here," Gall groused.

Walt handed him his paper and said, "Well, if no news is good news then maybe I got some good news for you, because what I gotta tell you is, after this, no more news. Can't get through. Can't do it all on foot. Gotta suspend home delivery."

"Well," Gall consoled both himself and Walt, "I guess I'll have to get my paper from the box up at Stillman and Spense."

"'Fraid not," said Walt, moving on down the street. "They took that away when the sidewalk got ripped up. Diner's closed, too." He waved, then added, "Must be nice, not having all that traffic noise around here."

Well, thought Gall, heading back inside, paper in hand, to make his morning coffee, I never did eat there anyway. And folks always complained that the diner brought the wrong sort of people into the neighborhood. Not that he saw a lot of his neighbors these days; there were times lately when, if it weren't for a few lights he noticed on in the evenings, he might have thought that he was the only one still living on the block. It made him wonder if perhaps *he* had somehow become the wrong sort of people. He stopped for a moment on the porch, noticing that the barricades were up now at the far end of the street, hearing the heavy engines roaring into action out of sight over on Spense. There were already dirt stains, vague gray smudges, on his clean white shirt and clean khakis, fresh out of the laundry last night.

He had taken to doing several loads of wash a day. He couldn't stand climbing into gritty sheets at night, wearing the same dusty shirt

and pants a second time, even looking at the smudged towels. The
second load was on its rinse cycle when Gall, upstairs in the kitchen,
heard a terrible grinding sound, then an agonizing metallic shriek as
the machine shut down. He hurried down to the basement, though
he knew it was no use; the constant struggle with the hard, granular
dirt that Gall had to wipe from the bottom of the washer's tub after
every load had finally gotten into the motor, burned out the bearings,
and what were the chances of getting a repair truck into the neighborhood now? Standing in his damp basement, pulling dripping, tangled sheets out of the still full tub, Gall could feel the whole house
shaking around him under the pounding of the heavy construction
equipment. In the morning light slanting in through the window
wells he could see a fine gray powder sliding down inside the cinder-
block foundation walls. He heard the doorbell chime upstairs.

By the time he got up there Johnson, the half-senile old mailman
who regularly left mail in the wrong boxes, as if it didn't matter who
got what, was already halfway down the block, and the mail, as usual,
was half in the box, half on the porch floor though at least, today, all
addressed for him, aside from the large white piece marked "Postal
Customer." He sat down on the wicker porch chair and studied
Margaret's postcard, unable to figure out what all that green stuff in
the picture was until he turned it over and read that she'd been to the
arboretum. He put aside what looked to be a couple of bills and
opened the folded notice from the Postal Service. It informed him
that delivery was being suspended due to lack of access; his mail
would be held at the post office designated below, to be picked up at
his convenience; the post office designated below, Gall knew without
looking, was a good two miles away. He let the notice fall to the floor
and opened the quarterly statement from his garbage collection service, Dirty Dan's, which apologized for the fact that his weekly
garbage pickup was being suspended until further notice because the
alley behind his house, where he always set out the cans, was being
closed off at both ends. Piss Alley indeed, he thought, because that
was what he'd heard the neighborhood kids call it though it didn't
have any official city designation. Dirty Dan didn't suggest what he
might, at his convenience, do with his garbage. What looked to be a

bill from the water department was yet another notice, advising him that road construction in his neighborhood would require that water service be shut off for certain yet-to-be-determined periods, perhaps as much as a day at a time. When the phone rang he knew at once that it wouldn't be his councilwoman calling back, though he'd left several messages by now, but the phone company itself, or the electric utility, or the gas . . . By the end of the day he was right on all counts.

THE AVENUE

It had been a month or more—who knew?—maybe two, since Gall had received a postcard from Margaret, almost as long since they'd spoken. Two miles to the P.O.! He wasn't about to walk that, especially with the sidewalks ripped up, the intersections impassable mountains of mud, heavy equipment roaring away far down below what had once been street level, gouging, pumping, dredging, shifting, tamping, hauling, God help you if you tumbled down into that. Late in the evenings—already it was getting dark earlier, but they worked on under floodlights mounted on flatbeds the tractors hauled in—or on Sundays, when they fell silent, the post office was of course closed. Were the postcards piling up there, he wondered, or had she long since quit sending them? And the telephone service was so intermittent Margaret had given up calling out of frustration. Even when she could get through, half the time they were cut off in mid-conversation; the rest was static or other people talking right over them; Gall couldn't believe the sorts of things people said to each other over the phone these days, and Margaret didn't want to hear them.

Neither did he want to tell her about the state of the house, his clothes, himself. When water was available he took a quick shower, rinsed out a few pairs of socks, some underwear, in the bathroom sink, hung them over the shower curtain to dry, put them on stiff and gritty. He'd given up watering outside; the grass was patchy brown, the shrubbery wilted, the petunias dead. He'd tried dusting a few times a week, but the stuff just shuffled itself up into the thick air of the house, hung miserably there through the hot afternoon, then re-settled on furniture, countertops, windowsills, even himself—his thin hair felt permanently thickened with . . . something. It wasn't pleasant. The two garbage cans he kept beside the garage had filled, and the alley was slowly becoming clogged with plastic bags, mostly his; he couldn't understand why it wasn't the same for his neighbors, how they were dealing with this, where they'd gone, how long their summer vacations could last. In the late summer heat the alley had begun to stink, to truly earn its name, Gall thought, but in the house his nose was always so clogged with dust he couldn't smell a thing. He assumed it was late summer from the heat. With the electricity on one day, off the next, the clocks screwy, the TV zapped by power surges, no paper delivery, he had no firm sense of what month it was, what day, what time of day. Sunday was the day the ruckus in the street paused for a while—the pounding and screeching and rumbling, the horrible shrill beeping of the backup warnings—and Monday, or morning, or dawn, before dawn even some days now, was when it started up again.

When he thought of Margaret he had a hard time calling an image of her face or the sound of her voice to mind. Would he recognize her voice on the phone if she were to call again, be able to pick her out from the tangle of speakers on the crossed lines? He scrounged around in his desk drawers one morning, the ratty wooden desk that was the one thing he'd salvaged from his office when he retired, till he found all the postcards she'd sent him, but the messages were like empty vessels, dried out, dusty, containing nothing of her, and the pictures on the reverse sides, all of which he recalled with great clarity—the shiny black seals, the red-gold bridge, the stark island prison—seemed far more vivid and alive than any Margaret he could summon up. How could this be: that they'd lived together for forty-seven years and now clumps of trees he'd never actually laid eyes on in person—eucalyptus, redwood, acacia—seemed more real than she did? It was enough to make a fellow doubt his own reality.

Especially with no one around to confirm it. The Kaminskys had never returned. His councilwoman never returned his calls. He saw no one on the block, though he often stood on his open porch or out on the sidewalk for an hour or more at a time, tolerating the worst of the heat and noise just for a glimpse of some neighbor he didn't even know by name. But their doors and windows stayed shut, and he could only assume they were gone or, like him, cowering inside most of the day. Still, you'd think they'd come out for a breath of air after dark, when things quieted down, when they'd eaten supper and could relax a bit. Gall's own meals were quick and frugal. He had a pantry full of food he'd stocked up on when he could still make the walk to the grocery easily—canned goods, soups, noodles, dried beans, toastables and microwavables—but no appetite. Everything tasted of dirt, even the soup. Sometimes he left his dinner uneaten on the kitchen table and walked down to the corner where the workmen were still at it under the violent blue glare of the floodlights, hoping that one of them would look up at him from down in the trench where they were wrangling huge concrete pipes into place and acknowledge his presence, the fact that there was still someone up there on the avenue. But all he ever saw were the ribbed orange tops of hard hats.

Was it September—October?—the morning Gall awoke in his living room, later than he'd slept in months, from a horrendous dream of earthquakes, thinking suddenly of Margaret—and how long had it been since he'd thought of her at all?—perched with her fragile china coffee cup on the high, overhanging balcony of her sister's condo on a steep hillside overlooking that distant, precipitous shore? Weeks ago he'd given up sleeping in his bed upstairs, doing nightly battle with gritty sheets and dust-filled pajamas, and taken to sleeping on the couch, rarely even bothering to get out of his clothes; what was the point, they were soiled as soon as he got up, anyway. Sitting on the edge of the couch, running his fingers through his thin hair, over his crusty scalp, feeling about with his feet for the old pair of sandals he'd kicked off last night, he couldn't shake the dream, the sudden, nightmarish shifting of the earth and the roar it set up, the thunder of tumbling cement and crashing of twisted metal, rock slides, mud slides, the great plates of the earth grinding angrily against each other. Minutes passed, the whole world still tumbling down about his head, before he realized that it wasn't the Pacific coast crumbling predictably into the sea but his own West Worthington Avenue.

By the time Gall got to the porch the street looked like the parking lot for an earthmoving equipment company. Enormous, bright orange dump trucks, as shiny as if they had just come from the factory, lined the opposite side, and at each end of the street a gigantic machine was slowly chewing up the asphalt while a front loader trundled along behind it, shoveling up the thick hunks of gray-black tar clotted with dripping masses of red clay and avalanching them into the back of a dump truck waiting with its heavy engine rumbling. The air was thick with dust and truck exhaust and diesel fumes and the beep-beep-beep of the next empty truck backing into position with a grinding of gears, and then with the thump of metal tread on concrete. Gall, standing motionless on his front porch, looked up. It was a bulldozer grunting right down the sidewalk on his side of the street from the corner at Agmont, flipping aside the big square paving blocks as if they were cardboard so that they landed upside down on the lawns, its one set of treads half off the walk and tearing into the burned grass as it came onto the stretch in front of Gall's house. It paused for a moment where the walk crossed Gall's driveway, as if that were an odd configuration, something worth considering. Gall, wrapping himself in his thin, dry arms, watched as the operator leaned his hard-hatted head out, looked down, and then, starting the dozer up again, straightened in his seat, glanced toward the house, caught Gall's eye momentarily as the heavy machine groaned forward now, ripping up sod and cement, and tossed Gall a quick salute.

How the Dead Live is ALVIN GREENBERG's fourth collection of short stories. A previous collection, *Delta q*, won the Associated Writing Programs' Short Fiction Prize, and his work has twice been included in the annual *Best American Short Stories*. He has received multiple fellowships from the National Endowment of the Arts, the Minnesota State Arts Board, the Bush Foundation, and The Loft, as well as the *Chelsea* Poetry Award and the *Nimrod* Pablo Neruda Prize. Greenberg is a novelist (*Going Nowhere, The Invention of the West*), essayist, poet, (most recently *Why We Live with Animals* and *Heavy Wings*), and librettist (including *Horsphal* and *Apollonia's Circus*, with composer Eric Stokes) and his work has appeared widely in literary magazines. Born in Cincinnati and educated at the Universities of Cincinnati and Washington, he has taught at Macalester College in Saint Paul since 1965. He and his wife, poet Janet Holmes, share their time between the Twin Cities and the North Shore of Lake Superior.

How the Dead Live is set is Electra, designed in 1935 by William Addison Dwiggins. Electra is one of the few mid–twentieth-century text typefaces not based on historical models. Rather, Dwiggins desired to make a contemporary typeface, "a line of letters so full of energy that it can't wait to get to the end of the measure." Electra was an immediate success, and remains today in constant use as a text face.

This book was designed by Will Powers, set in type by Stanton Publication Services, Inc., and manufactured by Maple-Vail Book Manufacturing on acid-free paper.